ERMIAS

Also by **WALTENEGUS DARGIE**
The Eunuch and the King's Daughter
The Reason for Life

ERMIAS
WALTENEGUS DARGIE

A Novel

LAMSI PUBLISHING

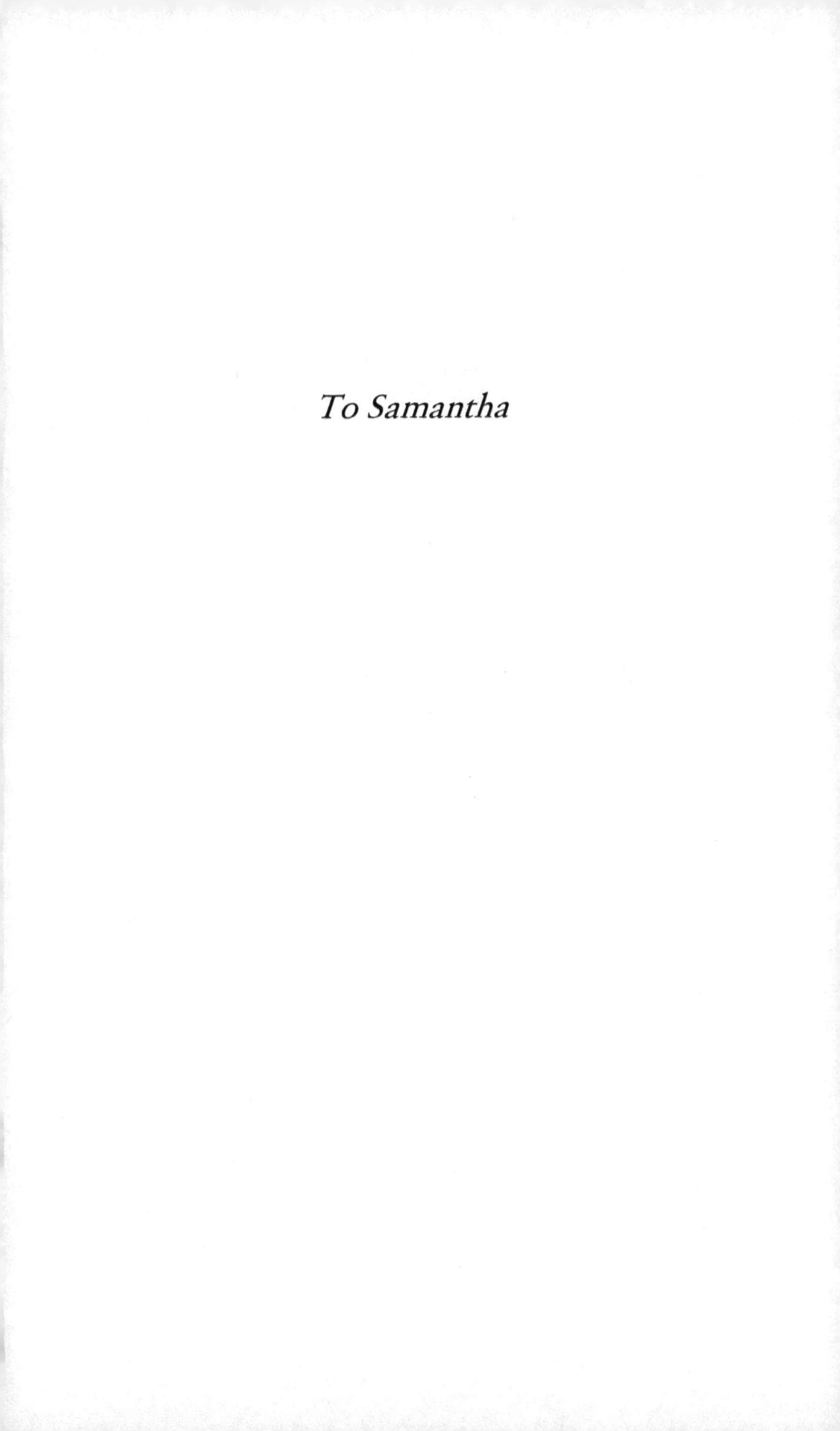

To Samantha

Part I
Gottingen

Chapter 1

Aster was twenty years old and a second year economics student when she gave birth to Ermias. He had been conceived in a hotel room in Nairobi at the same time as she had been competing in middle distance running representing her country—the one and only time she competed internationally. The father, who was twelve years older than her, was heading the accompanying medical team.
The couple had known each other for three weeks when Ermias was conceived. The paternal grandmother was persuaded that Aster became pregnant deliberately in order to *trap* her son, but this was doubtful, for the pregnancy was both humiliating to her and disruptive to her study, which she esteemed and put above everything else. But Aster was

determined to keep the child and there was no pressure from the father to pursue any alternative course of action.

Two weeks after the exam season was over, the child came into the world, on the eighth of July, so that Aster did not need to interrupt her study. She gave birth on the outskirts of Addis, in the paternal grandmother's spacious house. The child was nursed by his mother for the first three months of his life, afterwards she would take care of him only at weekends and during holidays and semester breaks, since she had taken a dormitory at the university, refusing to marry before she had graduated.

She did not marry two years later when she graduated with distinction. Instead, she accepted a job as a teaching assistant in a small college in Nazareth, a city located 120 km south of Addis. A bitter quarrel ensued between the grandmother and the mother, because the former insisted on adopting the child and refused to let him move to Nazareth with his mother. The mother won the battle nonetheless and Ermias moved with his mother to Nazareth. The father had seldom seen his child when he was living with his grandmother, but now he saw him even less often, because he, along with four of his friends, had just opened a medical centre in Addis. Besides, his voluntary occupation at the National Athletic Federation frequently brought him outside of the country.

The couple managed to marry six months after Aster had moved to Nazareth, on the condition that the grandmother dropped her quest to adopt the child. By then the mother was expecting news of a scholarship to Delft University in the Netherlands. After the wedding, she resigned from her college post and moved back to Addis, where the couple rented a house not very far from the grandmother's house and the three of them lived as a family, the mother now fully devoting her time to her child. The nine months leading up to her departure to Delft was the longest period in which the couple lived together during the first ten years of their child's life. Then at the end of September, when Ermias was three years old, his mother moved to Delft and he moved back in with his grandmother.

The grandmother's house stood on a 1500 square metre plot of land on the outskirts of Addis, the compound being surrounded on all sides by a high brick wall. The main house had separate living and dining rooms and five bedrooms. Two of her maids, a guard, and a gardener lived outside of the house in a row of service rooms. At the back and the sides of the house, she grew different types of fruit trees including orange, lemon, banana, mango, avocado, and peach, and kept a modest garden where she planted aromatic grasses and vegetables.

She was twenty-five years old and her son, Dawit, five, when the communists murdered her husband in broad daylight in front of his office. She never remarried but enjoyed a relatively happy and peaceful life, always surrounded by many servants and a host of fearful and admiring neighbours. Ermias too had a happy life with her, roaming around in the orchard and learning how to plant and climb trees. He stayed indoors only when the weather was bad, during which time, however, he would go inside his grandfather's study room, remove tons of books from the shelf and pile them up on the ground and study the pictures for hours. These were pictures of ancient emperors and empresses, kings and queens, respected diplomats, bishops, and gallant warriors.

The following summer, shortly before his fourth birthday, his mother came to Addis for the summer break. Addis was as usual cold, rainy, and muddy. Moreover, the mother was exhausted from her study abroad and from missing and constantly worrying about her child. So, the family spent much of the time at home, sleeping long hours in the morning and cuddling in warm bed, listening to the interminable rain.

When the mother returned to Delft by the end of September, Ermias experienced the first real pains of separation. He was overcome by sadness and was unable to sleep for many days thereafter. Then his grandmother decided to send him to preschool, even though he already had a private tutor who came twice a week to prepare him for school.

But December brought him his first real Christmas surprise, which was a trip to Delft with his father. They stayed abroad for three weeks, mostly travelling across the Netherlands and to Germany, and returned home with the hope that the mother would join them in Addis in less than six months and that there would be no more separation.

But in July she wrote a letter telling her husband that she had accepted a coveted, full-time PhD position at the University of Gottingen. She begged him to support her. Dawit took a long time to think about his wife's request, but finally agreed to support her, knowing how much education meant to her. The grandmother, on the other hand, was furious. She once again begged her daughter-in-law to forfeit the child and carry on with her life. The mother was equally furious and in less than two weeks she was back in Addis.

But the grandmother refused to admit her into her house and denied her access to her son. A rough custodianship battle had been raging for three months when Ermias accidentally heard from a maid that his "wretched" mother was in Addis, distraught and depressed. The bad news distressed the child greatly. He became overtly sullen and withdrawn in the subsequent days, so that the grandmother was obliged to soften her stance and to allow the mother to visit him.

Eventually the mother won the battle once again and this time she was determined to keep her son with her at any cost. Her husband, who had kept himself out of the battle, now wished to show his commitment to his marriage by moving to Germany with his wife and son, but he also saw a great opportunity to advance his medical centre by acquiring medical instruments from Europe.

Now that he knew and understood the significance of moving to Europe with his parents for an extended period of time, Ermias was deeply ambivalent. He was ecstatic, on the one hand, about the prospect of being with his mother and his happiness was reinforced by the knowledge that his father too was coming with them. On the other hand, however, it pained him to leave his grandmother to whom he was deeply attached. Mother and son travelled to Germany in January the following year and the father followed three months later.

Chapter 2

Ermias was excited and restless during the flight to Frankfurt, so that he was unable to sleep. Then he fell asleep, but two hours later the plane arrived at Frankfurt Airport and his mother woke him up from his heavy sleep and ordered him to walk by himself alongside her, because her hands were full. They moved through a long windowless corridor and stood behind a long, zig-zagged line comprising a large number of visitors. Four policemen at the other end were carefully checking travelling documents. As time went by, Ermias was unable to keep his eyes open and his knees were unable to support him. Once or twice he almost fell dangerously backward. Finally, his mother took him in her arms and pushed the hand luggage with her legs.

Meanwhile, the queue crawled forward slowly. Then, mother and son and a few other visitors were requested to step aside, and after a long wait, an old lady with a uniform approached them.

"May I have your passport, please?"

Aster gave her her passport.

"Is the young man your son?"

"Yes."

"What is the purpose of your coming to Germany?"

"I'll be pursuing a PhD."

"Where?"

"At the University of Gottingen."

"Are you travelling alone with the boy or is your husband travelling with you?"

"No, my husband is not travelling with us."

"Do you carry with you a written consent from your husband that you're permitted to travel alone with your son?"

Aster had carried no such document. Upon hearing her replies, the woman brought them to a small and dark room and left them there alone, only to return with a tall, heavily built man who further interrogated the mother. Finally, the two seemed satisfied with the answers they got, so they let mother and son enter into Germany.

Outside, they were received by a friendly-looking white couple with their small, timid girl.

"Who are these people?" Ermias asked his mother looking at the little girl curiously.

"This is Rhoda, and these are her parents, Martha and Frank."

"Where do you know them?"

"Frank was my supervisor at Delft. He's now working at the University of Gottingen. I'll be working with him."

Ermias extended his hand to Rhoda.

"Nice to meet you."

She did not understand what he said, but shook his hand. The five of them drove in a big car to Gottingen. As soon as the car left the airport, Ermias fell into a deep sleep. Two hours later, he was awakened by a sudden gust of cold wind rushing into the car as his mother tried to carry him out of the car. It was a sunny winter morning and the town was covered by a vast, abundant canopy of bright snow. The sight left a lasting impression on the child, for he had never seen snow before.

The modest two-room apartment was located in Nikolausberg, an elevated northeastern borough of the small and beautiful university town. Even though he was very tired, Ermias kept staring through the window at the abundance of clean snow long after the friendly couple and their daughter had been gone, but gradually he was overcome by fatigue and was taken to bed.

In the evening, the same people came and took Aster and Ermias to their home, which was not very far away. On the way, Rhoda taught Ermias how to make snowballs which they then proceeded to throw at each other. Then they all gathered in the small kitchen and had supper. After supper, Rhoda took Ermias to her small but comfortable room upstairs and showed him her toys and picture books and the two played together throughout the evening, even though they hardly understood each other.

In the following days he learned that the family was collectively called Holm. The two families saw each other about twice a week, alternating between their respective homes to have supper together.

Towards the end of January Ermias was sent to a kindergarten for four hours every day, for the nearby kindergartens could offer only half-day supervision. Martha, who was a full-time mother, offered to collect Rhoda and Ermias from the kindergarten after lunch and to take care of them until Aster had finished work. Dawit joined his family in March as planned and the family was complete and happy for the time being. This would be the first time in many years that Aster had enjoyed a relatively easy life, free from the persistent worry of aligning her academic plans with the needs of the family. Now the family was together, her research position at the University of Gottingen was a relatively stable and well-paid job, the research team was young and welcoming, and she was enjoying her work exceedingly.

Dawit was a cheerful and generous father, but when it came to occupying a child, he was utterly useless. Whenever Ermias was left in his care, the two rarely stayed at home, because the father would not know what to do with his son. Instead, he would take the child to places where he would not bother him with too many questions or activities.

Often the two of them would drive by train to strange and remote locations where Dawit would meet and bargain with strange, earnest looking people who would sell him cheap second-hand medical instruments or who would ship for him such instruments to Addis. On those occasions Ermias would wait for his father, as it were, endlessly, inside cold, lonely, and crowded (with supplies) rooms whilst his father closed a deal. The father would return to his son several times, albeit briefly, with a guilty and mischievous smile in order to beg for a little more patience. By the time he had finished his business it would be dark and Ermias would be in tears. But his father always made up for it afterwards by taking his son to one of the big toy shops nearby where Ermias was allowed to choose a toy.

On Saturday and Sundays, however, Dawit stayed in Gottingen. The ambience at the Holms' when the Ethiopians were with them was variable. In the absence of Dawit, the adults typically talked quietly and seemed to be of the same mind. In his presence, however, they all talked louder and seemed to disagree with one another most of the time. At the same time, however, they laughed a lot. The loudest of all was Dawit and the merriest was Martha.

Towards the end of summer that year, however, Dawit felt idle and bored and one could see that he missed Addis and his medical centre. Besides, he was anxious about the business he had left in the care of his colleagues. For the first time since they had moved to Germany, Ermias began to detect an atmosphere of tension whenever the family sat together for a meal. Sometimes even, long after he was put to bed, he heard his parents arguing vehemently. On those occasions, the mother would be the angrier and the louder. Finally, Dawit returned to Addis at the end of September and Aster was very upset for many days thereafter. So was Ermias.

Chapter 3

The departure of his father gradually brought Ermias closer to the Holms, particularly, to Martha and Rhoda. In Rhoda, whose father was also frequently absent from home, he found a companion, a playmate, and a reliable confidante. On weekdays, Martha would collect the children from kindergarten in the afternoon, but once or twice a week, she would pick them up before lunch and cook for them their favourite food. She always smelt nice and felt warm and reassuring.

Aster and Ermias celebrated their first Christmas in Germany with the Holms. They all went to church in the evening and when they came back, Martha played the piano and the others sang Christmas songs. After dinner, Aster, wearing a traditional dress, began an elaborate Ethiopian coffee ceremony.

There was no snow as the children had hoped, but when they looked out of the window, as far as the eyes could see, left and right, all the windows of the neighbourhood houses and buildings were decorated with beautiful, glowing, long-tailed, star-shaped lamps. The streets were wide and deserted, and the bare trees dark, unmoving, and mysterious. The evening was indeed silent; at once frightful and enchanting.

But as far as Ermias was concerned, his mother was the evening's most beautiful sight. Her fabulous traditional white dress perfectly contrasted with her overflowing long black hair and the gold cross necklace which graced the open neckline of her garment. She looked unusually happy; a modest but palpable smile played on her face, and her eyes sparkled the entire evening.

Ermias himself was experiencing happiness and sadness simultaneously. He always missed his grandmother and his dad, but on that day he missed them both very much. Celebrating a holiday with his grandmother was a serious and clamorous business. She would brew Ethiopian beer, bake a huge loaf of traditional bread, slaughter a big cockerel and a lamb and cook a variety of traditional dishes. For the next three or four evenings, her house would be flooded with a stream of guests, who ate and drank and made loud and cheerful chattering noise. His dad too would be in his best mood. It was during the holidays that Ermias would most definitely be seeing him.

But his mother seldom enjoyed holidays in Addis. For some reason, she felt rather lonely on such occasions and out of place. Her mother-in-law and she rarely understood one another, Aster maintaining that the grandmother was a dictator, and the grandmother was equally persuaded that her daughter-in-law was haughty and callous. Aster hardly visited her own parents in the country and they never came to Addis to visit their daughter.

On the first day of Christmas, Aster and Ermias drove with the Holms to Paderborn to visit Martha's parents. There they met Martha's two brothers and their wives along with their children. Martha was the youngest child in the family. Her parents owned a bakery and a big house on a hill overlooking the ancient city with many springs and the Pader River.

Shortly after they arrived, *Oma* took all the children to the kitchen and showed them how to bake different types of *Brötschen* and biscuits. Most of the children already knew how to bake and could help each other. So, *Oma* spent much of the time teaching Ermias. Soon the kitchen became noisy and messy and the tables, the floor, and the children smudged with flour and chocolate. But the scene was delightful and everybody was cheerful and happy.

In the afternoon, the men took the children to *Schloss Neuhaus* whilst the women stayed at home. It was a cold afternoon but the children played hide and seek in the garden and afterwards were treated to hot chocolate and a piece of cake at the *Schloss* café. In the evening *Opa* took them to a small room full of toys and a complex model railway system with lots of mechanical and electrical passenger and cargo trains, and played with them for a long time. It was one of the most exciting days Ermias had experienced in Germany.

Mother and son stayed three days in Paderborn, and, despite repeated invitation by the Holms to celebrate the New Year with them, Aster was intent on departing the following morning by a fast train for Amsterdam to spend the New Year with some old friends. Ermias was very upset.

"Why can't we stay with the Holms for the New Year and visit your friends some other time?" he questioned his mother mournfully multiple times.

"I want you to meet my friends. You'll also have a chance to see Amsterdam once again."

"But I don't want to see Amsterdam! I want us to stay in Gottingen with Frank and Martha, please!"

Aster was determined to leave.

"But why?"

"We've been a great burden already to the Holms. They need some space for themselves and I want you to understand."

Ermias could not understand, particularly, as the Holms themselves were insisting that they should stay. The Holms brought them to Hannover from where they took a direct train to Amsterdam. The train was crammed with passengers and it took them a long time to find a place to sit. The journey seemed endless and exhausting and Ermias missed the Paderborn children very much and felt lonely. His mother tried to cheer him up but he refused to talk to her. Finally, she too became quiet and the two of them sat side by side in silence, looking out of the window at the receding bare trees and the grey, remote horizon, Ermias thinking about his grandmother, his dad, Rhoda, and Martha.

At the train station in Amsterdam Aster's friend and her husband received them warmly and took them by tram to their two-room apartment which was the tiniest, shabbiest, untidiest, and dirtiest place Ermias had ever been to. The tight bathroom was as dirty as the living room and crammed with toiletries. Besides, there was human hair everywhere on the floor.

They stayed in this place for four days, sleeping on an old, grating couch whilst the couple slept on a mattress, on the floor in the adjacent room. The cold and windy weather kept them inside most of the time, but in the evening the husband went out alone to meet with his friends whereas the women preferred to stay inside. Despite the prosaicness of the room and the gloomy weather outside, Ermias saw that his mother felt comfortable there and he was glad of it.

Chapter 4

A week after New Year, his mother announced that he would be going to elementary school in the summer. His mother maintained that reading and writing German was similar to reading and writing Amharic, so Ermias should have no difficulty learning German at school. The undesirable aspect of this development was that he now had to stay longer in kindergarten and would see the Holms less frequently in the evening, for his mother would come early from work to practise different exercises with him in order to prepare him for the summer.

Dawit returned to Gottingen unexpectedly at the beginning of February and life began to be lively once again. Dawit was full of energy and radiated such freshness and cheerfulness that Ermias immediately got caught up in his exciting optimism and became energetic and noisy. His mother too was happy and seemed to have forgiven her husband for having deserted them in a foreign country during an uncongenial season. From the change in her countenance and the agility of her movement and the merriness of her voice, it was apparent that she had received a much needed boost of energy following his arrival.

One morning, Dawit declared that the family needed a holiday and that they should go to Austria for skiing. No sooner had he arrived than he had persuaded Martha to join them, despite the fact that the Holms were already planning to take a long trip to Thailand in the summer for which they were saving money. But he could not persuade Frank, who already had a pile of work on his table. Dawit organised everything for his family within a week and in the middle of February they set off by train to Alpbach for a one-week holiday.

Neither of Ermias' parents had ever skied nor had they ever been to a ski resort. Indeed, Dawit was not really a sporty type, even though he spent plenty of time with some of the finest athletes in the world.

"Promise me you'll be very careful, and you'll pay attention to what your instructor will tell you," Aster exhorted Ermias on the way to the resort. He was going to join a group of children of his own age for a ski course.

He promised.

On his first arrival in Gottingen snow had made a strong impression on him. Now in Alpbach, the sight of snow, combined with the majesty and brightness of the mountains, the countless valleys and dells illuminated by the brilliant sunshine, the cloudless blue sky, and the freshness of the air, brought him into an inexpressible emotional ecstasy. In the later phases of his life Ermias would cling to this and similar memories and to his unreserved responsiveness to nature in order to ward off a consuming loneliness in Europe and the helplessness it would beget.

The ski course began early the following day. By nature, the boy was perceptive and agile and eager to learn new things, so that after a few hours of instruction, he was immensely enjoying skiing. When he met his parents late in the afternoon, the two had already exchanged dispositions. His mother, like himself, had responded to the sights and the ski experience instantly and she, too, after a few hours of instruction, was able to ski on her own, enjoying every descent exceedingly. His clumsy father, on the other hand, had fallen a number of times, was aching everywhere, feeling terribly cold and could not wait to get back to the hotel. Nevertheless, he took everything bravely and good-naturedly and resolved to return to the battlefield the next day, because his primary aim, which was seeing his son and wife being happy, was being fulfilled. Furthermore, once in the hotel, the warm, cosy room and the hot shower and sauna reinvigorated them, so that much of the setback and frustration of the day could be forgotten and the new day could be greeted with renewed strength and curiosity.

Chapter 5

This time Dawit stayed with his family until the end of October. As usual, he was travelling by train and by bus extensively, now buying and shipping off, in addition to medical instruments, different types of electrical machines from Germany and the Netherlands. His business seemed to give him immense pleasure. When he was at home, he would have little rest, now being busy telephoning and being telephoned. Yet he took time to teach his son mathematics and English.
As planned, the Holms flew to Thailand at the end of June intending to return in time to celebrate Ermias' school enrolment a month later. Martha was already six months pregnant. A week after their departure, Ermias and his parents flew to Addis to visit his grandmother.

The grandmother did not come to the airport to receive them. She disliked coming to the airport, because it broke her heart to see people going away. The day was just breaking when they arrived and Addis was, as usual, wet, muddy, and misty and its buildings and streets appeared to have aged a hundred years. But the smell and sight of the city awoke in the boy a sweet and tender affection. His eyes were so hungry that he studied everything with acute curiosity—the poorly dressed women migrating on foot to a nearby church, the shabbily dressed girls selling items at the edge of the muddy streets, the colourless lampposts, the broken up, muddy pavements, the cafeterias and supermarkets along the streets just opening and preparing to receive their early morning guests, the blue mini-van taxis which were crammed full with passengers who were being irresponsibly driven around at a murderous speed, all gave rise to a warm, yet painful sensation within him.

When they arrived at his grandmother's house, they found her nervously waiting for them in front of the main gate. The taxi had barely stopped when the boy jumped out of it and rushed to meet her. She could not contain her tears as she embraced and kissed him.

"You have already become a fine, handsome boy, my dear!" declared she, with her majestic but languid voice, keeping the boy at arm's length for a moment and objectively regarding him.

"You too have grown older!" shouted Ermias meaning to pay her compliment.

She was a small and staunch woman but now she appeared smaller and older. Her long, silky hair, flowing freely on her shoulders, was visibly grey.

"So what did you expect?" she exploded with laughter and beaming with joy, embraced him tightly.

Her house was already full of people in that early hour and everybody embraced and kissed the boy as well as his parents, but the grandmother, with her usual commanding tone, chased them out, so that the "poor people" could rest. Indeed, they were all tired, but did not rest immediately, for the grandmother herself insisted that the adults should shower before having breakfast together. The whole process lasted more than three hours during which time Ermias, seated upon her lap, was giving a fully fledged account of his adventure in Germany.

None of them slept. After breakfast, mother and son gave the grandmother the gifts they had brought for her, whilst the father was receiving and making countless phone calls. Then the grandmother took them to the backyard and showed them her new project—poultry, consisting of more than two dozen chickens and turkeys. Then they visited the orchard whose trees were covered with green and voluptuous leaves, standing erect with splendour. The mango, orange, and avocado trees were already full of ripe fruits whereas the coffee trees were blossoming. She had kept the orchard impeccably tidy.

In the afternoon the house filled up with curious children, some of whom were neighbours, others relatives, with whom Ermias played and to whom he related his German adventures. In the evening, his father's colleagues and friends brought their families with them for dinner and the atmosphere was like that of an Ethiopian New Year or Easter, people eating and drinking and arguing and laughing noisily.

Presently the sweet fragrance of incense mixed with the smell of roasting coffee beans filled the living room. Now the father was talking gleefully most of the time, telling silly anecdotes which chiefly involved some of the country's greatest athletes, laughing heartily all the while.

The next day at breakfast, the father announced that he would be driving mother and son somewhere, for he had a surprise for them. This simple hint was enough to excite the boy's curiosity, so that he nagged his dad to tell him what it was, but his father refused to budge. The mother, who also disliked surprises, looked at him anxiously, but he smiled at her and gave her a hearty kiss on her cheek.

After breakfast, Dawit drove, as it were, endlessly towards the eastern outskirts of the city along muddy and broken asphalt streets, occasionally manoeuvring his way with difficulty through herds of sheep and donkeys, and arrived at a wide and elevated open field where there was a construction site. The mother, suspecting what it was that her husband was about to reveal, stared at the sight in front of her in disbelief, not daring to utter a word or to remove herself from the car.

"Welcome to the future Rehoboth Medical Centre!" Dawit declared ebulliently, getting out of the car. "Come on, come on! We don't have much time, there's a lot to see."

He came on the other side and opened the door for his wife to alight. Ermias was already standing on the site which was about the size of a football field or a little bigger. There was an unfinished building in front of them, rising up from the ground. At a distance of about fifteen metres from either side of the main building, they could see the foundations of two additional buildings. The one in the middle could be seen in full view when viewed from the main gate, whereas the others were only visible from a sideways perspective. The middle already had a ground floor and two additional floors.

"This one will have three storeys when it's completed," Dawit explained, pointing at the building in the middle. "All clinical activities will take place here. There will also be a cafeteria. This one," he continued with his description, pointing at the emerging building at the right side, "will have two storeys and will be an advanced laboratory. The other building will be mainly a pharmacy but it'll have a library and some private rooms for the staff. It, too, will have two storeys. At the front and the back of the buildings, I'm planning to plant lots of trees and magnificent lawns and to build a big fish pond in front."

"Where did you get the money to undertake such a huge project?" his wife asked him still in disbelief and with anxiety.

"One third of the money is ours, one third comes from investors, and one third is a loan."

"How are you going to repay the loan?"

"We shall manage."

"Are you involved in corruption, Dawit?"

"Admittedly I'm always a little corrupt," he chuckled good-naturedly. "But this one is an honest investment. I'm working hard and I'm immensely enjoying what I'm doing. So do my colleagues, some of them, at any rate. By the time you finish your study the main building should be completed. We began building the others in order to keep the ground; otherwise, the city administration has threatened to confiscate it. But they can be built slowly, there's no hurry."

"Darling!" exclaimed his wife still anxiously. "I'm not sure I have your energy. Are you sure this is what we want to do?"

"Of course, I'm sure. What else can I do with all my energy and resourcefulness?"

"You, perhaps, but what about me?"

"What do you mean? You don't have to do anything here. You can do whatever is pleasing to you, which is why I'm doing everything I can to make us independent."

"But this means I've to be in Addis."

"Where else do you want to be?"

"Perhaps, elsewhere, New York, Geneva, Berlin, Paris, London, anywhere."

She knew that this subject was painful to her husband. It was conspicuous in his eyes and from the way he turned his face away from her.

"Ermias," she addressed her boy, "can you go forward and take a look at the buildings? I wish to talk with your dad in private."

"You stay right where you are, young man. This is a family business and he's every right to take part," interfered his father. The boy too had no intention of leaving.

"We mustn't burden the child with things he doesn't understand. He's too young for this stuff."

"Children understand more than you think."

"Forget it! I won't be talking."

"Come on, what's wrong with you? You know that I'll never leave Addis. Without Addis I'm but a fish out of its water. You already knew this before."

"Yes, I know," Aster consented. "I just don't want to be hemmed in, that is all."

"I'm not and will never be building a fence around you. As a matter of fact, I'm doing exactly the opposite. You'll be free to do whatever you please and go to countries you always wanted to see. But we shall make Addis our base and our home."

"I don't belong to Addis. I've never felt at home here."

"The truth is that you've never belonged to any place, you've never felt at home anywhere."

"That's right," consented his wife sadly.

"But now you belong to us, we're your home. You belong here. We shall have lots of kids, build a house bigger than my mom's and help them grow there."

At this point Aster burst into tears and, putting her arms around her husband's neck, began to weep.

"You're such a good man. I don't deserve you," she uttered incoherently between her sobs.

"You are a good girl. No one deserves having anyone, really. But we can accept each other as one accepts a precious gift."

Eventually Aster pulled herself together and wiped her tears and they carried on with their visit. She took her husband's hand in one hand and her boy's in the other and did not release them even once until they finally returned to their car.

Chapter 6

The four weeks they stayed in Addis went swiftly by and the family was once again preparing for a long journey, Ermias being at once excited and anxious. In Gottingen, there would be Martha and Rhoda, and the new baby coming. In Addis, well, here he had everything he dearly loved, not least of which was his grandmother's spacious compound in which to roam about.

Back in Gottingen, they found the city in its most beautiful splendour, its surrounding hills and forests proudly exhibiting their leafy, spreading trees. The day was dry and brilliant and the streets were calm and half deserted, for it was Sunday. They were picked up from the train station by the faithful Holms who had sacrificed a church service for their sake. The Ethiopians were excited to see Martha's visibly big tummy and eagerly asked her how she was doing. Meanwhile, Rhoda and

Ermias started sharing their experiences, interrupting and shouting at each other.

On the day of his school enrolment, Ermias did not fully understand what the occasion meant for him, but his parents looked very nervous and excited. Indeed, once or twice, he saw his mother furtively fighting off tears. She gave him frequent hugs that morning, telling him how proud she was of him. Then, they all dressed impeccably well and went to the Holms to have breakfast with them. There they met Martha's entire clan who had gathered to celebrate with the Ethiopians.

After breakfast they all had a picture taken together and went on foot to one of the university lecture halls where the enrolment ceremony was to take place. Gradually, Ermias began to comprehend what the day actually was all about. The lecture hall was swarming with children, parents, and grandparents, the adults repeatedly shooting photos from different angles. The centre stage was splendidly decorated for all to see, whilst in the background teachers and their pupils were busy with different activities, talking to each other in whispers. At that time, he realised to a certain extent that school was meant to be a serious business and he was a bit afraid.

After the ceremony, Dawit and Frank removed the book shelves, the TV, and the sofa set from the living room and replaced them with long tables and chairs, so that the room could accommodate the guests and their children. Aster and two Ethiopian students had spent the previous evening cooking a variety of Ethiopian food which they now served. Ermias was overjoyed, for there was lots of noise and laughter in the room. Only his grandmother was missing, which made him a little sad.

Two days after Martha had given birth to her daughter, Frank and Dawit took Ermias to Neu-Mariahilf to see her. She was sitting on a couch in a little room, just finishing breastfeeding the baby. She encouraged Ermias to come forward and sit beside her. His father helped him sit properly on the couch, so as to cradle the tiny baby in his arms. Then Frank took the baby from Martha and carefully placed it on the boy's lap and helped him to hold it with both his arms. The baby's eyes were wide open, but they did not seem to look at any particular object or person. Ermias looked at the tiny being with fascination and tenderness and held its fragile fingers whilst his dad took photos. It must have been at that instant that the seed of ineffable compassion for the child implanted itself in him, enduring to the present day.

The baby was named Cornelia but she would be rarely called by this name in the family. Her father, either foretelling her childhood disposition by some fatherly psychic instinct or unconsciously wishing her to complement his unyielding orderliness, gave her the name Bordélique[a] before she turned one. In less than six years, she would fulfil his prophecy by filling the floor of her little room with countless Lego bricks, Playmobil figures, and puzzle pieces as well as palaces of all seasons, castles, and castle walls.

From the time Bordélique started to crawl, the three children played together. If Rhoda and Ermias were playing or watching TV sitting next to each other, Bordélique would never be persuaded to be seated elsewhere or to play something else. Instead, she would insert herself between the two of them and try to take part. More often than not, they both accepted her interference with delight and turned her into their dearest living toy.

During the next three years and nine months that the Ethiopians lived in Gottingen, life was, as usual, full of exciting changes. Dawit would go back to Addis in October and return at the beginning of February. Aster and Ermias would celebrate Christmas as usual with the Holms and Martha's extended family. In February they would take a one-week ski holiday and immediately thereafter Dawit would return to Addis. As soon as school was over for the summer, Aster and Ermias would fly to Addis and stay there for six weeks.

In the summer before Bordélique turned two, the Holms flew with Aster and Ermias to Addis for the first time and stayed at the grandmother's house for a whole month. Dawit hired a proper mason and an electrician to teach them how to make buildings and setup electrical installations, which kept them very busy much of the time. By the end of the training, the children were able to build two mini buildings of their own, each possessing many rooms, hallways, and balconies, complete with lighting.

The first hiccup with the Holms occurred that same summer, shortly after they returned to Gottingen. One evening during the week the Holms invited Dawit to have tea with them and whilst they were having tea, Frank, after beating around the bush for a while, asked Dawit whether he could convince Aster to allow them to adopt Ermias as their son. They seemed to have already convinced themselves that Dawit would not object to their proposal.

"We shall always be friends, but the adoption will bring us even closer. We thought this is also the best for the children. They'll grow up together."

Dawit was so stunned by the request that he could not bring himself to say anything. He remained undecided for a few seconds and then stood up and left the room, mumbling, "Goodnight, folks," on his way out. On the way home, he was resolved not to speak about it with his wife, but when he saw her face to face, he could not conceal his astonishment and confusion.

The following day they invited the Holms to their place and informed them that they would not give their son up for adoption. In the subsequent days and months their relationship with the Holms remained intact. Aster, nonetheless, for some reason, made Martha responsible for the misunderstanding and never fully forgave her.

Six months before Aster completed her PhD at the University of Gottingen, Frank was appointed Professor of Sustainable Economics at the University of Heidelberg. For the first year, he rented an apartment in Heidelberg and stayed there during the week, but they all were aware that it was only a matter of time before the whole family moved entirely to Heidelberg.

The Ethiopians' departure, too, was on the horizon, for Aster was working full steam ahead towards the completion of her thesis. Following the defence of her thesis, she renewed her contract at the university for six months in order to publish her research results and for Ermias to finish the school year he had already started. Towards the end, the sight of the two families earnestly preparing to move apart to two different cities in two different continents was both sad and stressful.

Addis

Chapter 1

Towards the completion of his mother's study, Ermias was persuaded that she was no ordinary person. He had known for some time that she was admired by many, including the Holms, not only for her striking beauty, but also because she was intelligent. There were many occasions on which the boy could see how special his mother was. Her supervisor used to invite his group to his house once a month, to eat pizza and socialise. There were the Christmas parties and the long walks in the surrounding forests in autumn and spring every year, besides. On a number of these occasions, when he was permitted to accompany his mom, he had noticed the eagerness of her colleagues to engage her in conversation. She herself spoke little but listened with interest and with a friendly and encouraging smile.

Then one day, when Ermias was in the third grade, as he, Rhoda and Martha were coming home from an evening walk, Martha told the children that one of the research papers Aster had published with Frank and her supervising professor had been nominated for an important award. In the evening of the same day his mother herself confirmed the news and announced that Ermias would accompany her to Geneva. From that moment on his mom's academic success would take her to different places around the world.

After she returned to Addis, Aster joined the Addis Ababa University as an Assistant Professor, but within a year she resigned from her position and joined the United Nations Economic Commission for Africa. The salary at the university had been "non-existent", she complained, and there was no academic freedom whatsoever. Loyal, hand-picked, and carefully placed government agents and spies monitored and interfered with all aspects of academic activities within the university.

By comparison, the Economic Commission paid her a handsome salary and enabled her to travel far and wide. There too it was impossible to make a genuine and worthwhile contribution, nevertheless, owing to the fact that most of the employees were admitted into the organisation not on merit but because of their political and social attachments. For Aster, her professional life chiefly consisted of interminable and inconsequential meetings to which she was averse.

In spite of everything, she was content with her life in Addis. Her husband understood and appreciated the sacrifice she had made in deciding to return to Addis and tried his best to provide the space and time she needed to privately cultivate her academic interest. The family rented a big house in Kotebe and employed two full-time maids to assist them in their domestic life.

As for Ermias, the first two years in Addis proved to be challenging. Firstly, the drive from home to school and back was tedious and stressful. Not only were the streets of Addis, both morning and evening, always rammed up with all types of lawful traffic, including domestic animals, but there was also literally no traffic regulation in place. This was rather a great paradox considering how religious Ethiopians were! For if one were to accept the assertion that God has created the universe, one would also be obliged to accept that God loves order. The complete disregard of rules and the existence of a state of perpetual disorder on the streets of Addis contradicted these assertions.

The tragic consequence of living in perpetual disorder was that no one benefitted from it. The drivers spent billions of extra, stressful hours on the streets every year, aimlessly burning countless gallons of precious fuel and releasing tons of unclean gases into the atmosphere. Children, the elderly, and pregnant women unreservedly inhaled these poisonous gases every single second without having the slightest clue about their long-term effect on their physical, mental, and emotional health. The government bureaucracy too suffered from colossal inefficiency because it could not rely on its own transportation infrastructure.

In the beginning, Ermias' parents had tried to alternate commuting with Ermias from home to school by car but both found it difficult to adhere to a regular schedule. Finally, they hired a contract taxi for him, but this meant that the time he spent with his parents was significantly shorter now. During the week he had enough to occupy him since the school provided, as long as parents were able to pay for it, after-school care comprising of different activities, including swimming and horse riding. Besides football, his parents put him in for swimming twice a week.

In Gottingen, even when Dawit had been absent most of the time and his mom had been working full time, Ermias had had a relaxed time. Typically, mother and son would eat breakfast and walk together to his school from where his mother would either ride by bicycle or walk to her office. In the afternoon, she would pick him up from school almost predictably at around five o'clock and they would spend the rest of the evening together, often in the company of the Holms. Besides, the distance from his school to any of the people he cared about was never longer than a fifteen-minute ride by bicycle.

Now, even the evenings had become unpredictable and solitary and he was left in the care of the two maids. Only on Sundays did the family spend together, staying at home in the morning and going out together in the afternoon.

Another aspect of life in Addis to which Ermias had difficulty adjusting was school life, which was marked by elevated snobbery and competition. Even though snobbery and rivalry are the vices of almost every human society, in Addis their manifestation lacked subtlety and sensitivity and, in some respects, it was difficult to distinguish them from racism. In Gottingen, for instance, there were children in his school whose parents were exceptionally famous, rich, or well educated. But these children more or less led a normal life, going to school by themselves on foot or by bicycle. The mother of two of these children, for example, had been a leading dramatist in the city and used to appear alongside prominent politicians on the national television. The children themselves had been to many places around the world with their parents and had certainly mixed with the children of many prominent people. There was no doubt that the children were aware of their mother's social standing. At school, however, there was no marked difference in the way either their peers or their teachers treated them. They too treated everyone as their equal. One was not overly eager to become friends with them simply because they were children of famous people.

In Addis, the social status of the parents played a vital role in the choice of friends amongst the children. The treatment of children by their teachers was likewise noticeably influenced by the social spectrum of their parents.

Exceptions to this were foreign children, particularly those who were white. For some inexplicable reason, some of the Ethiopian children, particularly, those whose parents were prominent politicians and army officers, regarded white children as their superior and made every effort to be friends with them. Interestingly, only the colour of their skin seemed to affect their "desirability". Neither their country of origin nor their character played any role in this friendship selection process. Sadly, some of the white children got carried away by the overtures of their peers and behaved in a way that was pathetically hypocritical.

Fuelled by snobbery, there was an active and visible spirit of competition amongst the local children all the time. Whereas the prevailing force behind the spirit of competition in Gottingen had been the fear of being left behind by other children, the prevailing force amongst the elites of Addis was the obsession to be better than all the others. Children competed to show off who had the best clothes, shoes, school bags, mobile devices, and all sort of material possessions, and were eager to boast about the accomplishments of their parents, the prominent guests their parents had received at home or in their office, the expensive gifts one had been given, the places one had visited recently, and all of that.

Chapter 2

In the middle of his first summer break in Addis his maternal grandfather, whom Ermias had never seen, died at the age of fifty-six. Dawit did not know how to break the news to his wife, uncertain as he was as to how she would react. But in the end, he told her after they had eaten dinner together. His wife was shocked upon hearing the news and visibly shaken. Sitting in front of her husband, she blankly stared at him for some time. Then she stood up, excused herself and went to her bedroom and locked herself in. The next day, Dawit was intending to go about his business as usual, but his mother called to tell him that he should drive Aster to her family for the funeral and stay there with her for a couple of days.

For Aster, the news came at an inconvenient time, for she was preparing to travel to Vienna in less than a week to attend a conference there and visit the Holms for a week afterwards.

When she heard of the proposal her mother-in-law had made, she at first refused to let her husband drive her, but Dawit easily persuaded her. After reflecting for some time, he also suggested taking Ermias with them, saying that it was time for the boy to get to know his mother's family. This suggestion troubled Aster very much. She did not instantly oppose the suggestion, but neither could she make up her mind.

In the afternoon, having decided to prepare for the trip undisturbed, the parents sent Ermias by taxi to his grandmother's. When he returned home that evening, the luggage was already packed and he learned that his parents had been shopping. As to his going with them, they had agreed affirmatively, but he still could see in his mother's face a mixture of uncertainty and anxiety.

That evening, when she came to his room to say good night, she sat down at the edge of the bed and took his hands in hers, and looking at him with palpable concern, she asked him to promise her something.

"You'll stay with us all the time. You will not eat or drink in my absence. Promise me."

Ermias promised. Aster sighed deeply and released his hands. He saw that there were tears in her eyes, so he gave her a hug, not knowing what else to do.

They set off the next day very early in the morning to avoid the morning traffic madness in Addis and its immediate surroundings. His maternal grandmother lived some 380 km away from Addis, in a small town called Ancharo in north-eastern Ethiopia. For lack of sleep and knowledge of what the trip actually contained for them, mother and son felt dismal and grumpy, but the father was in a good mood and gave them big hugs alternately.

"Cheer up! We will be staying there only for three days. Besides, it's good to go to the countryside every once in a while. The change will do us good."

The roads were relatively free and the family left Addis without much trouble. Ermias struggled to stay awake but as soon as they left Addis, he fell asleep for about two hours and woke up feeling hungry. His parents were driving in silence and he could see his mother sitting in the front passenger seat, bending her head a little to the right and gazing blankly through the window next to her. He too turned his eyes to the side windows from time to time and looked outside.

Gradually, the diversity of the emerging and retreating scenes on both sides of the road captured his attention and distracted him from the sombre mood inside the car. Before his father pulled the car up in front of a newly-built hotel for breakfast around nine o'clock in a small, shabby town, they had passed through incredible terrain containing ranges of barren as well as grassy mountains, fascinating ravines and gorges, farmlands, and expansive, wild meadows stretching left and right as far as the eyes could see. And yet, the mother remarked that they had covered only a little more than half of the entire journey.

After breakfast, they set off once again and drove uphill for a long time, passing by caravans of camels in numerous locations, and arrived shortly before noon in Kombolcha, a busy, rusty city spreading over a relatively flat surface at an elevation of approximately 2000 metres above sea level and surrounded on almost every side by majestic and rugged mountains. The parents said that from there to Ancharo was a mere 13 km drive, but they had to drive up to a mountaintop, and the road was rough. Besides which they were tired and hungry and wished to have lunch and take a rest in Kombolcha.

While they were having lunch, father and son tried to cheer the mother up, but she talked and ate very little. Ermias could see that the journey was onerous and unpleasant to her. After lunch the three of them went out hand in hand to take a short walk along the main road. Still fascinated by the surrounding landscape, Ermias gazed at the solid and majestic mountains with reverence.

"After elementary school, I moved to Kombolcha, because there was no high school in Ancharo," his mother told him presently.

"Did you move with your parents?"

"No, by myself."

"Where did you stay then?"

"I had an aunt, my mother's sister, with whom I stayed for two years, but we disagreed and quarrelled a lot. Then I left her and moved to another relative of ours for six months, but there too it was difficult for me to stay. Then my father rented a room for me and I stayed there for two and a half years alone. It was a difficult time."

"Why did you not stay with your parents?"

"There was no transportation at the time and it was difficult and dangerous to travel on foot back and forth every day."

"Why did your parents not move to Kombolcha with you or elsewhere where you could go to school?"

"My dad had his farm in Ancharo."

"Were your family poor?"

"They were certainly not rich, but we had enough."

"Were your parents supportive of you?"

"My father was supportive. My mother wasn't."

"Why didn't your mother support you?"

"She wanted me to marry a rich farmer or a merchant."

"Why did you disagree with your aunt a lot?"

"That's something you wouldn't understand. My aunt, like my mother, was selfish and quarrelsome."

"Why did you two quarrel?"

"Why, why, why, Ermias! Endless questions for which there are no simple answers."

Then Dawit said it was time they set off. They drove back on the same busy road for about three or four kilometres, then, leaving Kombolcha to their right, followed a rough, eroded dirt road leading up to the rugged, wild mountains. Ancharo stood beyond these mountains at an elevation of approximately 3000 metres above sea level. The remaining seven kilometres or so took them nearly 30 minutes.

Years later Ermias read in a history book that the German missionary Johann Ludwig Krapf had referred to the town as the principal marketplace in the 1840s. At the time Ermias and his parents visited Ancharo, however, he vividly recalled his father's reaction of disbelief when they first saw the shanty mud houses standing on both sides of the main road. To begin with, it would have been erroneous to regard the place as a town. A village would have been a more fitting description for it, for it had no hotel, no restaurant, no electricity, no basic sanitation, and no proper water facilities. Secondly, had it not been for the rusty, corrugated aluminium sheets which had been very poorly installed upon the roofs of the dilapidated houses, one would have been tempted to think that time had frozen there for thousands of years.

A few hundred metres before the famous marketplace, Dawit turned to the left and carried on through a rougher and a more dangerous road for about five minutes and pulled the car up in front of a big white tent where there were several mourners wailing loudly. When the mourners noticed the arrival of the family members from Addis, their wailing became louder and noisier. Then there was a huge commotion of people coming out to greet them and Ermias was suddenly surrounded by strange and distraught people who hugged and kissed him on his cheek. Feeling uncomfortable, he clung to his father. Fortunately, there came an elegantly dressed old lady who skilfully disentangled Ermias and his father from the mourners and led them to the back of a moderately big house next to the tent. The mother, surrounded by the people who came out to greet them, entered into the big house through the front door, putting her hand on her head and weeping loudly.

Meanwhile, the old lady brought father and son to a small room full of children, about the same age as Ermias, even though a few of them were conspicuously bigger, and left Ermias there. The children apparently belonged to relatives who had come to the funeral. All of them seemed to know each other and who Ermias was and started to whisper and giggle, looking at him in a shy but friendly manner. Some even called him 'the German'. One of these children, a boy approximately two years older than Ermias, came to him.

"You are Ermias, the son of Aster, right?"

"That is right."

"Oh, hear his accent, he can't speak Amharic properly!"

The children giggled gaily.

"I'm your cousin; my name is Ishmael."

"But you are a Muslim," Ermias observed naively, for he knew that the name was a Muslim name.

"In this town Christians and Muslims intermarry and coexist peacefully. This has been the tradition for more than a thousand years."

The boy looked fragile and pale, yet had a cheerful face with a pair of merry, brilliant, small, and restless eyes. His voice, too, was cheerful. The boys shook hands.

"That one in the middle with long hair is my younger sister Zahara. The third from her to the left, she, too, is my second younger sister, her name is Amina. I've another sister but she's with my mother."

Both girls were remarkably beautiful. Zahara waved her hand shyly to Ermias, guessing her brother was talking about her. Ermias waved back very pleased to know that he had so many beautiful cousins whose existence he had never known before.

"Would you like to go out?" asked Ishmael in the meantime.

"Right now, where?"

"Just outside, and yes, right now, why not? Come," said he cheerfully and, pulling his cousin's hand, led the way to the door.

Ermias followed him reluctantly, remembering the promise he had made to his mother. But he also remembered that his mother had not objected when he was taken away from her in the first place. Moreover, he could not see the difference between being with Ishmael in a room without his parents and being with him outside without his parents.

"I mustn't eat anything," he reminded himself.

Ishmael took Ermias out through the back door in front of which there was a cornfield surrounded by tall, slender, and leafy eucalyptus trees. Behind the cornfield stood a modest mountain covered with wild conifer trees and herbs. The sight was impressive.

"So, how was Germany?" Ishmael asked, scrutinising Ermias with his small inquisitive eyes.

Ermias gave the usual answer such questions deserved.

"Did they have beautiful girls there?"

"Plenty."

"Did you have a girlfriend?"

"No."

"Why not?"

"I don't know."

"How old are you?"

"I just turned twelve."

"It's a pity that you haven't got a girlfriend. Do you have a girlfriend in Addis?"

"No. Do you have a girlfriend?"

"Unfortunately, no. It's not easy to have a girlfriend here. They are all virgins and they are not allowed to have boyfriends or any relationship with a man before they get married."

Ermias kept quiet.

"What else did you do in Germany? Did you have many adventures?"

"I went to school and played football and I went to the Alps to ski," responded Ermias proudly.

"But these are not adventures. I mean real adventures, like having sex with a German girl?"

This subject was not new to Ermias. Almost every second boy of his or Ishmael's age in Addis wished to know what Ermias had been doing with German girls in Gottingen. Without much deliberation he answered him in the negative. Ishmael looked disappointed.

"Have you ever had sex with a woman?" Ishmael wanted to know.

"Are you out of your mind? No. I'm only twelve."

"I was eleven when I first had sex," boasted Ishmael.

Ermias found himself at once being in awe of Ishmael, being jealous, and feeling uneasy with Ishmael's confession.

"But how can that be? You yourself just said it's impossible to have sex with the girls here," he confronted his cousin after a brief moment of thinking.

"Oh, no, not with the girls, but there are alternatives. For example, you can have sex with a married woman."

Ermias could not believe what he had just heard.

"Do you want to have some adventures here? I can organise."

"No, thank you," he replied, deliberating at speed as to whether he should leave his cousin there and hurry back to the house.

"Come on, don't be a chicken! I can show you how to have exciting adventures," said Ishmael presently.

"No, thank you."

Now Ermias turned to the door and was ready to walk back to the house, but Ishmael pulled him gently from behind.

"All right," he said timidly, "we can talk of something else, do you ride horses?"

"I haven't tried riding yet, but I want to," Ermias replied sensing from his cousin's voice that he did not wish to upset him.

Ishmael's eyes became brilliant instantly and excitedly he shouted, "Oh, that is lovely. Awesome! I can teach you how to ride horses. Do you know our grandmother has five horses?"

Ermias did not know.

"So what do you think, do you want to learn how to ride horses or not?"

"But where are the horses? Does she still keep them?"

"Most certainly! They are out in the field but will come back in the evening. You just need to ask your grandmother. She'll allow you to ride, no doubt."

"I'm not sure about that. I haven't met my grandmother yet."

At that time his mother and a thin, short, old lady came out through the backdoor, walking side by side.

"This must be my grandson!" said the woman approaching Ermias.

Her voice appeared slightly shaky, perhaps from too much crying. Unlike all the other strangers he had met so far, she did not rush to embrace or hug him. She stood in front of him instead and regarded him with her small, red, and watery eyes.

She was certainly not very old but did not seem to have had a good life. Her skin was fair and pale and she had shaved her hair completely, as a part of her mourning ritual, and put a white traditional shawl on her back.

"Say hello to your grandmother," his mom ordered him gently. He stretched his hands to shake.

"Hello."

She shook his hand calmly and without lifting her eyes off him, released the hand.

"You already had lunch in Kombolcha, I heard."

Ermias nodded.

"Good that you two have already met," said she, now turning to Ishmael.

"He loves to ride horses!" announced Ishmael.

"No, you love to ride horses and want to use him as an excuse," his grandmother corrected him with a stern look.

"Ask him!"

"We shan't talk about horses today," she spoke firmly. Then turning her face towards Ermias she added, "If you want to ride horses, you shall wait until the funeral is over, which is tomorrow."

"Is it true you have five horses?"

"That is true. We had seven horses but sold two of them to pay the hospital and funeral bills for your grandfather. Why don't you show him around? But don't take him too far."

"Are you sure?" intervened his mother hesitantly.

"Nothing will happen to him," the grandmother said dismissively, and without waiting any further reaction from her daughter, turned back and walked into the house.

"You'll be very careful, Ishmael, right?" the mother turned her attention to Ishmael.

"Don't worry!" he replied cheerfully.

Ermias wanted to stay with his mother, but could not muster the courage to express his wish. Ishmael was already moving forward towards the cornfield and his mother followed his grandmother. So he followed Ishmael.

But very soon, he was glad that he had come along. The boys crossed the cornfield and ascended the mountain up to a certain height, taking a narrow and dirty footpath, all the time Ishmael talking about horses. Ermias grasped very quickly how much horses meant to his cousin.

He also learnt that Ishmael was the firstborn of his mother's youngest sister whose husband was a supplier of animal skins to a tannery in Kombolcha. Ishmael and his father bought skins of sheep, goats, and cattle, both dried and wet, from the surrounding villages and towns and transported them on the backs of horses, donkeys, and mules to Kombolcha to sell them to the factory. They themselves did not own any animals for transportation, but rented them from Ancharo. When his father was in a good mood ("often he wasn't") he would rent horses from grandmother for himself and Ishmael, otherwise, the two would travel on foot, covering more than 80 km a week.

When the boys came within close proximity of the mountainside, they took a rest, for Ermias was very tired. They could see in front of them the entire village the houses of which were poorly scattered on both sides of the dirt road. About three kilometres to their left and behind the village there were vast meadows and the farms of the villagers and beyond these another chain of mountains.

"You see that meadow yonder? It's called Gerbi. It's the best place to ride horses. I'll teach you there."

"But you are just a boy yourself, how can you teach me how to ride? Isn't it dangerous?"

"It's dangerous. I'll teach you, nonetheless. All you need to do is persuade our grandmother to give us horses for a few days. She'll give you, no doubt, because you are a guest today. If you weren't a guest, that'd be a different story."

At this instant, Ishmael spotted a cactus below, not very far from where they were sitting, full of ripe fruits. But the slope leading to the tree was steep to descend.

"Do you like cactus fruits?" he asked Ermias, ready to pick some.

"I haven't tried before, but can't you see it's dangerous to go there?"

"Ah, you are a spoilt city boy!"

Saying this, he descended with remarkable suppleness, plucked some fruits from the tree with his bare hands and put them on the ground, cut green leaves from a nearby eggplant, wrapped the fruits with the leaves, and with the same suppleness returned to Ermias. Then he carefully rubbed the fruits on the ground to remove their thorns and using a small pocket knife, extracted the contents.

"Here, taste it!"

Ermias took a bite. The fruit was juicy and delicious.

"You like it, don't you? Here, try some more."

Ermias tried willingly. Seeing that his cousin liked it, Ishmael descended once again and collected some more fruits. They both ate and talked for a while. Then Ishmael got up and extended Ermias his hand.

"Come on, we can ascend the mountain a little."

But Ermias was not motivated to ascend further, for he had no energy left and wanted to get some sleep.

"I wish to go back; my parents will be worried."

"What for? There can be no danger in Ancharo unless you fall down from a cliff and break your neck."

"That is very possible to happen here. We'd better go back now."

Ishmael yielded and the boys descended the mountain. They arrived just in time, because Aster was about to send someone to search for them.

Chapter 3

That evening Ermias was introduced to his mother's family members amongst whom were his mother's two sisters and a brother. The brother, Théwodros, or as the entire family called him, Teddy, was the youngest child in the family and he was twenty-three years old. He lived in Kombolcha but worked on a cross-country bus as an assistant. He was not married yet. Ermias' oldest aunt, Sarah, was two years younger than his mother and had been married for eight years, but she had become a widow when her husband died in a car accident three years earlier. She now lived in Kombolcha alone and owned a small restaurant. Like his grandmother, she too had small, red, and watery eyes and flushed cheeks. Aminat, his youngest aunt (her birth name was Hannah but she had it changed to Aminat when she married a Muslim), lived in Ancharo with her husband and four children. She was twenty-five years old.

Aminat had once been the most beautiful in the family, but now she looked frail and ill and much older than Aster, who now resembled none of her family members. Aminat was timid and painfully shy and always busy. She kept herself moving throughout the evening, deliberately avoiding her oldest sister and her family. Her husband, Yasin, who was taciturn and stern-looking, was twenty-three years older than she.

The entire family, including the children of Aminat, looked mortified in the presence of the doctor husband from Addis, as they liked to call Dawit secretly, who on his part tried his best to converse with them. They also appeared to be uneasy with Aster who did not try to converse with anyone save her brother. At dinner, the grandmother talked to Yasin much of the time and never looked once at her oldest daughter. After dinner, the children were sent to bed whilst the adults discussed funeral details.

All the children, thirteen of them altogether, were brought to an empty room on the floor of which were placed seven sponge mattresses side by side and on the mattresses, clean sheets and pillows. Each mattress was assigned to two children. Two young women brought warm water and wooden bowls to wash the children's feet. There were lots of giggles and laughter as the women washed their feet. Ermias was assigned to sleep with Ishmael, who talked to him ceaselessly in a whisper in the dark, but Ermias was frightfully tired, so he eventually closed his eyes and slipped into a heavy sleep.

The next day, around eight o'clock, the entire village gathered in front of the white tent, encircling the coffin like a swarm of bees bereft of its queen, and cried and wailed loudly and bitterly, the women beating their chests. Then the strongest men amongst them carried and placed the coffin on the back of a pickup truck, which then drove slowly to the nearby church for the burial of the dead. Aster and Dawit were already inside the truck with the grandmother but the rest accompanied the truck on foot. The children were not allowed to follow the mourners.

Following the mourners' departure, they put the children back in the small room where they had breakfast and talked with each other quietly. About two hours later the mourners returned and the children and members of the family brought water for the people to wash their hands. Then the guests were admitted into the tent and placed on the floor on straw and cotton mattresses in a row to serve lunch. After lunch, a significant number of people left only to return in the evening with food and drinks. The widow and the extended family also sat inside the white tent the entire time, receiving guests and accepting condolences.

The guests inside the tent were broadly divided into three groups: the women, both young and old, the elderly men, and the young men. The women and the elderly men chatted in low voices in their respective groups, but the young men played a variety of games. Ermias too sat inside the tent this time next to his parents, but was very bored. After what seemed a very long time, his grandmother noticed his boredom and asked Teddy to go out with him.

"Why don't you teach him how to ride a horse?"

Teddy was willing to take up this assignment.

"Come with me," he said, standing up immediately and cheerfully and went out. Ermias looked at his mother, who nodded in agreement.

When Ermias and Teddy went outside, it was already getting late. Ishmael, knowing by some miracle what they were up to, joined them, coming from nowhere. Teddy lit a cigarette and asked Ishmael whether Tesfaye had already arrived, to which Ishmael answered in the negative. Tesfaye was the young man who tended the grandmother's cattle and horses.

"Then we should go and find him," Teddy suggested and led the way.

The three walked out through the front gate towards the dirt road, but before they had reached the junction, they turned right and followed a muddy footpath leading to the mountain which the boys had climbed yesterday. They followed the footpath for about fifteen minutes and arrived at a small meadow at the foot of the mountain where they saw the herd and the horses grazing. This was the place from where some villagers collected their cattle Tesfaye had tended for them during the day for a price. After Teddy had greeted Tesfaye, he carefully approached one of the horses, unwound a rope from around its neck, and led it back to the grandmother's house. Ishmael and Ermias followed him, Ishmael ceaselessly and excitedly giving Ermias tips on how to gallop a horse as quickly as possible. Once at home, Théwodros and Ishmael harnessed the horse quickly and they all returned to the same meadow.

At the meadow, Théwodros gave Ermias a short introduction about horses, how sensitive and intuitive they were, and all that, but by this time Ermias too was excited like Ishmael and was impatient to ride the horse.

"Riding a horse is all about balancing," the lecture went on, partly because it delighted Teddy to put the boys in suspense. "You should maintain balance all the time by adjusting your rhythm with the movement of the horse. Handle the reins with both your hands but never use them to balance. Guide the horse by turning your eyes towards your intended direction and by the movement of your body. Never manoeuvre the reins to direct the horse."

Finally, Teddy put Ermias on the horse, handed him the reins, and guided the horse for him. That day, Teddy did not release the horse even once, but the experience was enough to excite Ermias' interest.

In the evening Ermias begged his parents to stay in Ancharo for a week or two but his mother was set to leave Ancharo with him in three days. Ermias was very upset and tried his best to persuade his father to stay a little longer, but neither could he stay, since he had to bring his wife to Addis for her to catch her plane to Frankfurt in time. Théwodros interfered at this point and asked the parents to leave the boy behind for a week or two.

"I myself will send him by plane from Kombolcha," he promised.

Sarah and the grandmother also supported him. The father finally relented, but the mother was adamant.

The next day in the afternoon Aster decided to show her husband and son her old school, the only place she said was interesting in the village. The grandmother was opposed to the idea, because this would be against tradition, which required that the bereaved should stay at home for seven days. Aster, however, was not interested in observing tradition and her husband was on her side.

The three of them went out accompanied by Théwodros and followed the dirt road up to the junction and turned right and walked for ten minutes on the main dirt road. Then they turned left and went downhill for fifteen minutes, following an eroded and neglected footpath leading to a small compound surrounded by eucalyptus trees. This was the school compound. It was covered with wild and outgrown *poaceae* grass and there was nobody inside, as school was closed for the summer break. They saw two old and squalid buildings, the windows of which were broken and stained with pitch black dirt. Each building had three or four dusty classrooms full of shabby and broken desks and dusty, broken floors.

"This was where I went to school, nothing has changed," said Aster mournfully.

She accused the government for deliberately neglecting the school as well as the entire region because the people were fiercely opposed to its ethnic-based politics. It was hard to imagine how parents could send their children to this place every day and expect them to return unharmed. Even though this was the best place to see in the entire village, there was really nothing to see, so the quartet left the compound in the opposite direction. On their way out, Aster indicated Gerbi and Asrej, the meadows and fields behind the school.

"I used to ride horses over there," she observed with a gesture.

Ermias asked her to tell him more about her childhood.

"I don't have many good childhood memories. I remember working hard to support my parents. During school breaks, I went to the fields with my father and assisted him or tended the cattle instead of staying at home and helping my mother. I rarely agreed with her. She was always shamefully selfish and tyrannical."

"Aster used to love riding horses. She was notorious for her wildness," interjected Théwodros.

"I loved the open fields. They made me feel free. There was no mountain or valley where I had not ridden horses."

"But you never mentioned that you could ride a horse," Ermias said reproachfully.

"Your mom rarely mentions her talents," remarked his dad.

"I was unhappy here. Everything oppressed me. Instead of growing, everything shrinks. Even the size of the population shrinks every year."

They found a huge acacia tree behind the school overlooking the green meadows and the mountains beyond them and sat there until it was dark. The weather was cloudy and a gentle cool wind was moving the trees and the clouds. Except for the poor buildings standing behind them, Ermias was not able to feel the confinement his mother talked about, but he did not want to bother her with too many overwhelming questions. Instead, he snuggled his head into her chest and she embraced him.

Chapter 4

On the second day after the funeral, around ten o'clock in the morning, a priest and two elderly men came to disclose the deceased's will to the family. The adults gathered in a small room and closed the door behind them, but Aster refused to join them, declaring that she wished to have no part in the will. Still her siblings insisted that she and her husband should sit down together with the rest as witnesses but she rejected the request and left the house altogether. But Dawit joined them as a show of courtesy. The children were ordered to stay inside their room and play quietly.

Aster must have anticipated what was coming, for in less than twenty minutes the congregation inside the small room became disharmonious and loud. There were repeated immoderate reproaches, condemnations, and curses to be heard, the bitterest amongst them being Théwodros and Sarah, followed by the grandmother. The children could hear the priest repeatedly beseeching the family to honour the dead and to calm down but none of them paid attention to him. Finally, Dawit left the room and came to Ermias and suggested taking a walk. Ishmael joined them without asking permission, but Dawit did not mind. They left the house through the back door and passed through the cornfield and the eucalyptus trees and went up to the mountain. Even though it was already hot outside, all of them were glad to have left the house and the people behind them and come out in the open. They walked uphill in silence, but after some time Ermias asked his father what the quarrel was about.

"Inheritance. But you shouldn't bother yourself about this."

"Teddy is furious because grandma is partial to Sarah, even though she's wasted lots of money on men," interjected Ishmael and then he added, "Without the support of my grandma that woman would never be able to support herself."

"Leave these things to the adults," Dawit told Ishmael curtly.

Then they walked in silence once again.

"Shouldn't we look for Mom?" Ermias broke the silence at long last.

"The question is, where should we look for her? I don't know this place."

"She used to visit an old lady by the market. We can go there and check," suggested Ishmael.

"How do you know?"

"She once took me there with her."

Dawit hesitated and finally decided against it.

"Let's give her some space. She'll come back on her own."

They wandered along the mountainside, Dawit closely examining several herbs and explaining to the boys their medical significance. Then they heard Théwodros shouting their names from afar and decided to head in the direction from which his voice appeared to be coming.

When they met him, he apologised to Dawit for his quarrel with his mother and Sarah. Then he informed them that it was time for lunch and that the others were waiting for them. But Aster was not there when they arrived. They waited for her return in vain. Finally, Dawit suggested eating without her and all agreed. Later that day Ishmael told Ermias that his grandfather had omitted both Théwodros and Sarah from his will and had equally divided his share between Aminat and Aster, which made the three of them furious.

Aster came late in the evening that day, but Ermias spent the afternoon learning horse riding. His grandmother, to the wild ecstasy of Ishmael, sent Ishmael and a lad from the neighbourhood to Tesfaye to fetch a horse. Ishmael returned back galloping on his grandmother's sturdiest horse, bareback and without reins. He had not been bluffing, after all, when he had reported about his riding skills. After the horse had been made ready, Théwodros took Ermias to the same place where he had practised the previous day and taught him how to ride. This time, Dawit came along and watched his son the whole time.

The following day, the guests from Addis got up early in the morning. The white tent was half empty now, having been occupied the previous night mainly by the family, neighbours, and a few shepherds. Around eight o'clock they had breakfast with the rest of the family members and then, the parents loaded their luggage into their car and started to say goodbye. Ermias was miserable and his eyes were full of tears.

"Let him stay here for a few days," his father begged his mother gently. Whereupon she looked at him fixedly and then at her son with the same fixed gaze. Théwodros and Ishmael were standing behind Ermias.

"Very well," she said at last, after releasing a deep sigh. "I put him in your care," she addressed Théwodros.

"I'll take care of him," he reassured her with a smile and patting the boy's shoulders. They discussed the details of his flight and then the parents hugged Ermias, and after another round of farewells, drove off.

Shortly thereafter, the boys and Théwodros, too, set off for horse riding. Tesfaye had already left with the cattle and the horses before sunrise, but which direction he had taken to pasture, they did not know.

"There can only be three options," maintained Ishmael. "Gerbi, Asrej, or Gedam Sefer. It's more likely Gedam Sefer where he tended yesterday."

Gedam Sefer was another mountainous village beyond the modest mountain the boys had climbed yesterday and the day before. Apparently, there was no fixed place for Tesfaye to tend the cattle. The three of them walked along the mountainside for twenty minutes or so, passed by a seasonal river, a small waterfall, a valley with clusters of eucalyptus trees, and climbed another modest mountain, upon which stood Gedam Sefer. There they asked different women, who were coming to fetch water from a nearby stream, whether they had seen Tesfaye. None of them had seen him. Then they wandered around in the bushy ravines beyond the village, taking the direction towards Kombolcha and picking and eating wild berries and cactus fruits. Around eleven o'clock, they decided to return and search for Tesfaye in Gerbi, but then they met a small lad who had seen Tesfaye in a nearby valley a short while ago. They followed his lead and, indeed, they saw the herd scattered upon a gentle slope, grazing peacefully. Tesfaye was just finishing his lunch when they arrived. After exchanging greetings with him, Théwodros announced that they were taking two horses for a ride. Tesfaye did not object. Then Théwodros sent off Tesfaye and Ishmael to bring two horses.

"Bring Grachit with you as well," he shouted after them. Grachit was a grey mare, the only mare the grandmother owned. The two came back with three horses as ordered. Théwodros took the mare from Tesfaye and led her away into a bush. Ermias was about to follow him, but Théwodros told him to stay.

"I'll be back in a moment," he said and disappeared behind the bush.

"Do you know where he's taking her?" Ishmael asked Ermias excitedly.

"How should I know?"

"Do you want to know?"

"What for?"

"Come along, I'll show you."

He beckoned Ermias to follow him and walked cautiously towards the other side of the bush. Then he put his fingers on his lips to warn his cousin that he should make no noise.

"This was your idea!" Tesfaye warned Ishmael just audibly. Ishmael did not heed him. Ermias followed Ishmael, his heart suddenly beating fast. When the boys approached the bush, Ishmael spread his body flat on the ground and beckoned Ermias to do the same, which he did. Then they crawled carefully forward until they had a partial view of Théwodros. He was positioning the mare to have sex with her.

"This was one of the alternatives I was talking about the other day, do you remember?" Ishmael whispered. Ermias did not respond to this observation; instead, he watched Théwodros with both fascination and great anxiety. His heart was pounding wildly.

"If you wish, you can try, but not now, when Théwodros is away."

"No thanks!" Ermias replied with a coarse and thick voice.

They watched their uncle in silence, but retreated just in time before he finished. There was an awkward silence when he rejoined them without the mare, but he did not seem to notice or care.

"We've two options," Théwodros explained to Ermias presently. "Either we take the horses with us, harness them, and bring them back to the meadow where you exercised yesterday, which is time consuming, or, you learn to ride bareback."

"Whatever you choose," Ermias replied avoiding his eyes.

"Then I choose the second option, not only to save time, but it's also easier for the horse. I'll teach you how you can balance and coordinate."

He skilfully made a bridle with a rope, bridled one of the horses with it, and led the horse to an elevated position for Ermias to mount. Afterwards, he taught him how to sit erect, signal to the horse with his legs and heels, and control the horse with his legs and the bridle. After about two hours of practice, Théwodros too mounted the other horse unsaddled and let Ermias ride on his own, side by side with him. Since the surface was neither wide nor flat, they climbed and descended hills and rode through dry valleys and returned to Tesfaye and Ishmael after about an hour, with the boy's thighs and back hurting.

They stayed the remaining portion of the day with Tesfaye and returned with him in the evening. At home, Ishmael and Ermias helped Tesfaye with cutting fresh corn stalks to feed the cattle and horses and after dinner, the three of them went to the backyard and stood in front of the cornfield, Théwodros smoking, and the boys listening to his adventures, many of which consisted of seducing and having sex with female passengers whom he had met on cross-country buses. Ishmael listened with admiration and awe, as one who would listen to a warrior or a chieftain relating fascinating war stories. A full moon was shining on the cloudless sky and countless stars were gleaming above them. Nowhere had Ermias ever seen before so many brilliant stars.

Suddenly they saw Yasin rushing out of the house through the back door. He was furious with anger and paced here and there like a trapped and wounded tiger, without noticing the presence of the boys and Théwodros. Presently, Aminat came out timidly and tried to calm him down, repeatedly extending her arms to embrace him. Heedlessly, he shouted at her incoherently. She begged him to calm down and to lower his voice, but he pushed her away with all his might, whereupon she flew backward and fell down, bumping her head hard against the ground. He rushed at her with the same fury and started beating her blindly and mercilessly. Théwodros rushed to help her and pulled him from behind but the man was too strong for Théwodros. Ermias froze on the spot, not knowing what to do or where to go. Other people from the house rushed to Théwodros' aid and between them laboriously managed to separate the husband and wife. Some of them carried the unconscious wife into the house whilst Yasin, accompanied by some men, left the vicinity.

"I hate my father!" muttered Ishmael under his breath, long after the commotion was over.

The boys were standing alone. Théwodros never returned to them.

"Is he always violent?" Ermias asked him.

"Always," he whispered.

"To you too?"

"To me too. To all of us, even to the girls."

"Why is he so violent?"

"He is jealous, especially when there's a social event like this. He can't abide young people around my mother."

"Is she unfaithful to him?"

"The other way round."

"Why doesn't your mother leave him then?"
"Where to?"
"I don't know."
"She has no one to go to, she has nothing. She has nowhere to escape."
That night Ermias could not sleep for a long time. Laying down on his back and staring in the darkness, he thought of Aminat, and of the grey mare. He grasped slowly why his mother was averse to this place and showed great reluctance to let him stay behind. He now missed his parents frightfully and felt very lonely.

Chapter 5

The next day at breakfast Ishmael told Ermias that his mother had sustained multiple fractures to her skull and cheek bones and had been taken to a medical centre in Kombolcha on a horseback. Ishmael and his sisters were ordered to return to their home that same day.

"I'll be going to Kombolcha with my father to deliver the skins. Will see you tomorrow, *in sha Allah*," he said and departed dejectedly.

After breakfast the tent was dismantled and the mourners moved the cotton mattresses into the living room. Only a handful of people were left along with the widow. Around ten o'clock Théwodros and Ermias left for horse riding.

"Don't exhaust the horses!" the grandmother shouted behind them.

Ermias was immensely relieved when they left the house. They walked in silence towards Gedam Sefer, as Tesfaye had already informed Théwodros where he was tending that day.

"You shouldn't let the fight between Aminat and Yasin bother you," Théwodros told Ermias at long last, sulking and fixing his eyes on the footpath ahead of him.

"What fight? She didn't fight him, he assaulted her. He's a coward!" Ermias reacted heatedly.

"He doesn't see it that way. He said she provoked him to anger."

"How can you say that? Isn't she your own sister?"

Théwodros cursed and spat sideways on the ground before he spoke.

"I don't care. It's always been like this. She chose this life; no one forced her to marry him."

"Still you should have compassion for her and defend her. He was a coward and a brute!"

"What do you know about marriage and adult relationships? Perhaps she wanted to be beaten."

Ermias groaned with pain.

"But you are a boy," Théwodros looked down at his nephew contemptuously and spat once again on the ground. "You don't understand female psychology."

Ermias could not believe what his uncle was saying, but he shut his mouth. Both tried to forget the unpleasant topic and to talk about a more cheerful subject, but they could not sustain the conversation, so they walked much of the remaining distance in silence. As soon as they arrived, Théwodros took the mare to the bush.

"What is the matter with you?" Tesfaye asked Ermias when they were alone and Ermias related the incident of the previous night.

"Oh, the dirty salty dog!" Tesfaye cursed disgustedly when Ermias was finished. "He does that every other month."

"Even her own brother doesn't have compassion for her and the poor woman looked very fragile," Ermias lamented in a low voice.

"I know. They are all beasts. Their father was different, however."

"And my grandmother?"

"She is a witch; you should be careful with her."

"What do you mean?"

"She foresees things by the power of the devil. She is famous in the village. Everybody is afraid of her."

"Why should I be afraid of her?"

"Her own family is afraid of her, that is why."

The two kept silence for a while, and then Tesfaye spoke.

"The saddest thing is that Aminat was the most beautiful and the most intelligent girl in town. Perhaps in the entire region, too. But one day Yasin kidnapped her as she was coming home from school and raped her. She was fourteen years old. The next day he sent elders to your grandfather and grandmother to ask them to marry him their daughter and they consented instantly. Once a woman is raped no one will marry her nor will she have the respect of anyone, you know, even if it was not her fault. So they consented. The beast has already two elderly wives and keeps multiple mistresses in the surrounding villages and in Kombolcha, not secretly, mind you. In broad daylight. Everybody knows. Some even approve of it."

Ermias fixed his eyes on Tesfaye without actually looking at him and absorbed the words without trying to comprehend them. He had neither the interest in continuing the conversation nor the desire to express his lack of interest.

"Are you alright?" Tesfaye asked him worried.

He did not reply. As he continued staring blankly at Tesfaye, he felt himself surrounded by some invisible but perceivably oppressive shadow. Then he heard Théwodros calling and stood up. They mounted the horses and moved at leisure towards Ancharo, ascending and descending hills and mountains. Once they had reached the foot of the last mountain, they let the horses canter all the way down to Gerbi where Théwodros taught his nephew how to gallop for the remainder of the day.

Chapter 6

Théwodros went out to buy cigarettes shortly before dinner was served that evening, but never returned. No one went out to search for him, nor was anyone particularly concerned about his disappearance. Indeed, Ermias never saw him again as long as he was in Ancharo. Three days later his grandmother informed Ermias that Théwodros was on his way to Bahir Dar assisting on a cross-country bus and that she herself would bring him to Kombolcha to take his flight to Addis.

In the following days all the mourners, including Sarah, returned to their own homes and affairs and Ermias was left alone with his grandmother and her twelve-year-old maid. More precisely speaking, Ermias was left alone with the maid, for his grandmother went to church very early in the morning every day, returned around seven o'clock for breakfast and left the house once again and returned in the evening properly intoxicated. She tried to conceal her condition from the boy, but he could easily tell she was drunk. Every time she left, she locked all her valuables and food items in a big wooden box and took the key with her, leaving enough food for him and the maid. In the evening she simply said goodnight and retired to her room early. Ermias slept in the living room, on the floor on a cotton mattress. All the fresh sponge mattresses and the clean sheets had been taken away.

For three long and uneventful days Ermias felt lonely and bored and wandered aimlessly around the village, in the mountains and in the wild valleys. On the fourth day Tesfaye, apparently feeling sorry for the boy, invited him to come along with him. Ermias accepted his invitation gladly and tended the herd with him in the valley beyond Gedam Sefer, where he was allowed to ride one of the horses by himself.

Tesfaye was an orphan and lived with a distant relative of his, an old, frail woman who could not take care of herself. He had never been to school nor left Ancharo once. Neither was he the most religious person in town. He was perhaps the least privileged human being in that mirthless village, and yet, Ermias had never once seen or heard him doing or saying anything inappropriate or indecent. In his contract there had been an agreement that the grandmother should provide him with lunch, which she did, but the food they put in his box was the humblest food one could imagine and it was inadequate for one person. But he had learned, he told Ermias, to take care of himself by gathering wild fruits and berries from the field. In summer, when the fields were rich with crops, most farmers were gracious to him and gave him freshly cut maize, peas, beans, sorghum, and the like, some of which he roasted and some of which he ate raw. He always went about with a decorated stick, which served him not only for tending the herd, but also for protection.

"Without a stick to protect yourself, you are lost," he explained to Ermias. "It's a sign of manhood to take a stick with you when you are old enough to travel around by yourself. If some people think of you as a weakling or a coward, they could do nasty things to you. Here everything is settled with brutality."

"What types of nasty things do you mean?" Ermias asked him curiously.

"You don't want to know. Many bad things happen in this area."

"I've been everywhere by myself and so far nothing happened to me," the boy observed naively.

Tesfaye gave him a look intended to convey the superiority of his wisdom.

"That is true, many people travel around alone and nothing happens to them most of the time. Besides, you belong to a family from which one cannot escape easily. But I wouldn't take anything for granted, if I were you. Terrible things happen to some people. But I am not saying all people are bad."

Chapter 7

Two days before his departure for Addis, whilst he was having breakfast, his grandmother announced that they were going to Kombolcha the following day.

"Your aunt is eager to see you in Kombolcha and show you around. Besides, there isn't much to see here. Then she'll bring you to the airport."

He heard the news with a great sense of relief, for he was already counting the hours of his departure, but he was careful not to show his emotion lest he offended his grandmother.

"You must be strong, because we'll be going on foot. But don't worry; we'll be descending mountains all the time, which is not that difficult for a strong boy like you. Your mother was boasting the other day that you have been doing lots of sports in Germany and Addis," she added with a faintly perceptible mockery in her voice.

"I play football and swim twice a week," he told his grandmother naively.

"There you are! So there's no reason why I should worry. We've got to get up very early, however."

Ermias had already travelled on foot as far as Gedam Sefer and beyond, so he was not worried in the least. Besides which he was so excited to leave that place that he was ready to forego any comfort.

The next day his grandmother woke him up early in the morning as she had promised, so that they could start the journey before it was too hot. She cooked breakfast herself for them, scrambled eggs, and gave her grandson a glass of fresh milk from the cow she herself had milked that morning. Then before it was seven o'clock they set off, the grandmother carrying his small suitcase. She was in an unusually cheerful mood and her light and carefree gait reminded Ermias of his own mother.

"Sarah is my favourite daughter, I'll admit it," she confessed on the way, with a carefree voice. "We've a lot in common. She is proud and self-sufficient but at the same time kind and understanding. She supports me, her brother, and her sister. 'Take this, buy yourself a kilo of coffee,' she tells me and gives me money every time I go to see her. She buys clothes, shoes, perfumes, and creams for her sister and her children. The two sisters love each other very much. Sarah never meddles in other people's affairs, respects small and big people equally, and yes, she enjoys life, which is alright, as long as she doesn't neglect her duties. Now, you may not like to hear this, but she's the direct opposite of your mother. Your mother doesn't enjoy life; she's too rigid."

"My mom is clever and self-sufficient," Ermias defended his mom passionately.

"Your mom," the old woman hesitated and then spoke reservedly, "is proud and looks down on poor and uneducated people."

"That is not true!"

"I understand if you wish to defend your mother. I'd have done the same. But one might as well call things by their proper name."

Wishing to change the subject, Ermias asked her why Aunt Sarah did not have children.

"The poor child, God blocked her womb, how can she help it?"

Upon hearing the response of his grandmother he felt sorry for Sarah.

"Is she unhappy because she doesn't have children?"

"Anyone in her position would be a little unhappy, but I believe that it was for a reason. God didn't want her to have children with that shameless husband of hers. He was promiscuous, secretly kept another wife full of children in Shoa. But now he's got his hand!"

"Is it true that Yasin, too, has multiple wives?"

"That is true. His religion permits him to have multiple wives, but the other was a Christian, or pretended to be one. I never liked him."

"Mom said you wished her to marry a rich farmer or a merchant."

"So what if I wished it? I consulted a wise man for her and his predictions were accurate. One of them now owns a construction company in Kombolcha and is a millionaire. But she turned it down. God is merciful; he hasn't paid her according to her contempt."

After this the two of them walked in silence, for Ermias was hurt and sulking because his grandmother had spoken ill of his mother. When they arrived at Aunt Sarah's, her place was already busy with people eating and drinking, most of them were cross-country bus and truck drivers who were on their way to Dessie, Addis, Woldea, and Mekele, for her small restaurant was on the main road. She received her mother and nephew warmly and placed them at a corner table and ordered food and drinks for them. Then she busied herself with taking orders from the other guests and with giving instructions to her assistants.

"You see how hard she works?" remarked his grandmother with a satisfied voice.

Ermias was tired and thirsty and about to feel hungry. Fortunately, their order arrived quickly and both grandmother and grandson ate with appetite. But Sarah did not have time to chat with them. After the meal his grandmother excused herself and stood up, ready to rush to the market before it was too late.

"I'll be back in less than an hour. After the lunchtime is over, she'll perhaps have some time for you. If she's too busy and unable to come to you, don't worry, you'll be staying the night with her and tomorrow is another day."

Ermias did not mind her going. He was fascinated by the hustle and bustle inside the restaurant and along the main road outside. There were many people buying and selling items and beggars of all sorts who repeatedly tried to enter into the restaurant but who were repeatedly refused entrance.

His grandmother did not return in one, two, or even three hours. Then Sarah noticed him and encouraged him to go out and look around.

"Go to the market. It isn't very far from here. It's the biggest market in the region. Buy yourself fruits, here, take this."

She gave him some money but also warned him to be careful with crossing the main road.

"The drivers are really reckless. We see people get killed almost every week. Most of the trucks belong to people of great influence, so if you get killed, no one will hold them accountable."

Ermias went out and followed the directions she had given him and arrived at the marketplace. Sarah was right; the market was swarming with people and a myriad of domestic animals, including hundreds of horses and donkeys which were standing tightly side by side, tied up to metal posts at the boundary of the market. He saw also different people entering the market carrying frightful loads on their heads or shoulders. He entered the market and wandered from stand to stand, fascinated by the variety and quantity of items which were displayed for sale. When he returned to the restaurant after having spent a long time in the market, his grandmother was still not back from her errand. Then Sarah ordered a second round of food and drinks for him, but she was still too busy to take care of him. Late in the afternoon his grandmother finally returned, her cheeks flushed and her small watery eyes pure red.

"I'm sorry, it took me longer than I thought, but now I'm done. I already sent my purchase to Ancharo on a horseback. I just came to say goodbye."
She was properly intoxicated and struggled to talk coherently. She briefly hugged her grandson but felt embarrassed for some reason and shook his hand. Then she went inside to say goodbye to Sarah. The restaurant was nearly empty by now. Then Ermias heard Sarah and his grandmother arguing heatedly and loudly. After a short but intense dispute his grandmother emerged with brisk steps and ordered Ermias to get up.
"It turns out that your aunt doesn't need you here tonight. She said she has no free place."
"But my luggage?"
"Oh, never mind about your luggage, you can leave it here! You can pick it up tomorrow on your way to the airport. Come on, we must hurry, otherwise, it'll be dark and dangerous to travel."
She left the restaurant with similarly brisk steps and Ermias followed after her, his heart sinking with disappointment and anxiety. The woman was so furious that she moved energetically forward, so that Ermias was unable to keep up with her. She only slowed down at the location where a footpath to Ancharo branched off from the main road.
"Of course she didn't want you tonight because she wants to sleep with a lover, it's obvious. She is a harlot, you know, makes money by sleeping with truck drivers. She thinks that she's clever and that I'm stupid, but she isn't smart and I'm not

stupid. She is a harlot; that is what she is! One may as well call things by their proper name."

The boy did not know what to say, so he kept walking next to her quietly.

"She claims she's barren, but I don't believe a word of it. She keeps away from children because she wants to fuck around."

She spoke as a matter of fact and went on with her obscene tirade.

"It's no good to have too much appetite. It makes one selfish and heartless. All of my children are products of degenerated semen. They are all good for nothing."

But she could not go on for long because she had to begin ascending a mountain and was short of breath. It was a steep and tiresome ascent. Ermias considered himself lucky for having eaten something shortly before they set off. Still, he felt thirsty and exhausted and was sweating all over and fighting off tears of frustration. But, he bit his lip and climbed the mountains patiently for more than two hours.

Fortunately, there were short level planes in between and they also passed by a stream of fresh water from which he could drink and cool his head down. But his grandmother was so consumed with rage that she refused to take rest or drink and seemed not to have felt the demands of the mountain. She kept walking with light and fast steps as if the alcohol she had consumed had had no effect whatsoever on her.

As soon as they were through with climbing, and had reached the top of the mountain, she continued her monologue from the point where she had left off, as if only ten seconds had passed since she had completed her last sentence.

"If she gives money, I also give milk, fresh butter, and yogurt. Every now and then I send her honey and eggs. If she does something for her sister, I repay her in kind. Her sister also serves her like a slave whenever she has the opportunity..."
It was already dark when they arrived. She sent Ermias off directly to bed without supper or washing his feet because he had to get up early the next day to go back to Kombolcha to catch his flight on time.
"I'm sorry," she told him, "I cannot come with you tomorrow. I'm an old woman, my heart is weak and my spirit is broken. I'll find someone to take you to the airport. Don't lose heart; I shall harness a horse for you."

He could not guess how long he had slept, but he was awoken by a dull, unceasing noise. At first he had difficulty determining what it was, where it was coming from, and where he was. He opened his eyes with difficulty and pricked his ears. The noise persisted and gradually he realised where he was and that the distressing noise was coming from his grandmother's bedroom. It was a mixture of multiple sounds, including a moan and a gasp. He was suddenly alert and jumped from his mattress, thinking she was in grave danger, and rushed to her bedroom, finding his way in the pitch darkness. He was about to forcefully open the door and to scream for help when he suddenly heard the panting of another person and he stood still. His grandmother was not alone and the moan was not a signal of distress. He was unable to move, but at the same time was frightened to simply stand there. Forcing himself back to the mattress on tiptoe, he sat on the mattress and listened and waited until the oppressive noise, which continued for a long time, had come to an end. Then there were outbursts of gasps and hard coughs. And then there was silence.

He struggled in vain to fall asleep. He was desperate for daybreak, but it seemed morning would never come. Then he got up and found his way in the dark to the kitchen. He drank water from a clay pot and returned to the mattress and lay down again on his back, trying to think about everything he considered good and lovely, but he could not think about anything in particular. When he got up in the morning, his head was in agony, his temples were throbbing, his eyes were burning, his back was hurting, and he felt stiff everywhere. But he pushed aside all his pains, impatient to leave. His grandmother herself harnessed a horse for him and a hired boy from the neighbourhood came to lead the horse and to bring it back to Ancharo. After a quick breakfast, the two lads left hurriedly.

When they arrived at Sarah's, they found her anxiously waiting for them. She asked Ermias if he was hungry but he said he was not. Then she ordered one of her female assistants to take care of the hired boy and the two of them left for the airport by a taxi.

Getting on a plane was something Ermias always looked forward to, but that day in particular he was suffering from impatience and anxiety, lest anything should go wrong and prevent his boarding the plane. But things went smoothly and he finally took his seat.

"Dear God," he prayed in silence and in all earnestness, "make this plane fly as quickly as possible!"

Chapter 8

He told his parents everything he had experienced and seen,
except Théwodros' sexual encounters with the grey mare. He
could not bring himself to talk about it.

"Thank God everything is now over and you're back safe!" his
mother said with great relief and a palpable sense of guilt.

He never visited Ancharo again. Gradually his memory of the
people became dim, but not the horses and the beautiful
valleys and meadows and the wild mountains surrounding the
village. Indeed, in subsequent years, whenever he had missed
home or a loved one, he had often dreamt of Ancharo, and
almost always his dreams had been good. The following day,
he was overcome with acute nostalgia and a desire to visit that
village once again. Some of his dreams made such strong
impression on him that he had difficulty accepting that they
were only dreams long after he was awake.

But having witnessed Yasin's violence and having heard
Tesfaye speak about nasty things having happened to

defenceless people, there was a matter about which he desperately wished to ask his mother but did not know how to begin. He procrastinated for some days but it bothered him so much that one evening, when there was no one in the house except for the two of them, he entered into her study and stood before her, still uncertain. However, she understood immediately that something was bothering her son.

"Spit it out, what is bothering you?" she encouraged him, closing the book she was reading and giving him her full attention.

"Can I ask you something?"

"Certainly."

"When you were a girl in Ancharo, was anyone nasty to you?"

"My mother was."

"Besides her?"

"No one. In fact, just the opposite. Everybody was kind to me."

"Weren't the men nasty to you?"

"What's bothering you?"

"You know, Yasin raped Aminat."

"I see," said his mother with understanding. "Come to me."

Ermias went to her.

"What happens to so many girls in Ancharo and indeed, throughout the entire country, is deplorable. But nothing of the kind happened to me."

"Isn't it because Daddy raped you in Nairobi that you married him?"

Aster released a long loud groan.

"Do you think your dad is capable of doing such a horrible thing? Darling, I've never met a more considerate and compassionate person than your dad."

"In that case, why was I conceived accidentally?"

"You were not an accident. You were a great gift. Besides, your dad and I loved each other and were impatient as the wind."

At that instant some invisible heavy burden was removed from his chest and he wept silently out of joy.

"Why are you crying?"

"I couldn't help it, but I thought daddy was nasty to you."

"Not all men are like Yasin. Some of them may behave like an ass occasionally, but many of them are not that cruel."

"How did you and Daddy fall in love?"

Aster pushed back her chair a little, sat on it comfortably, and offered her son a chair to sit next to her.

"I was the first to fall in love. Your grandmother was partially right when she said that I trapped him. Your dad didn't know I existed when I first set my eyes on him. He and some people from the Athletics Federation came to my campus when I was a freshman student to recruit athletes. They gave a tedious introduction and invited us to come and talk to them during the break. He was very handsome, well-dressed, and always smiling. I liked his smile most, it was a sincere smile. During the break, I went to them and gave them my name and address. After the event, they left and I didn't hear from them for the next two or three weeks, but I was thinking of your dad all the time. Occasionally, I saw him on TV giving interviews about the fitness, readiness, or recovery of certain athletes. Then one day came a call from Athletics Federation and I was invited to compete for a pre-selection. I passed the test and began to train regularly, but I never saw your dad until two weeks before the competition in Nairobi. The rest you know."

"No, I don't. Please go on."

Aster sighed and continued.

"Your dad wasn't directly involved with the daily routine of checking up the health and fitness of the athletes, but the doctors reported to him, which was why we didn't encounter each other sooner. But one evening, there was a banquet in honour of the retirement of a certain athlete to which we both were invited. By some miracle, he came one hour late and arrived in the middle of an important speech. He did not wish to disturb the speech, so he searched for a seat in an obscure corner. Lo and behold, there I was! I was so shy I couldn't talk to him in the beginning, but he was more experienced with women," Aster chuckled shyly and carried on with her story.

"He asked me about my studies and university life, particularly, about the food in the canteen. Slowly, I overcame my shyness and we talked for a long time. It was a beautiful evening. Finally, he drove me to my university and we exchanged addresses. The next day in the morning, when I was studying in the library, a lady came to me and told me that there was a phone call for me. I was completely surprised and taken aback but followed her to take the call. It was your dad. Apparently, the villain had spies and accomplices everywhere. He asked me how well I had slept and whether I would eat dinner with him that day. I wanted to, but wishing to exercise modesty I declined the offer instead hinting at having some spare time the following weekend. Six days later we had dinner together and from that day on we saw each other almost every other day but secretly, so that the people at the Athletics Federation wouldn't make a fuss."

"But they knew eventually, right?" Ermias asked her mischievously. She understood what he was alluding to and laughed merrily.

"Yes, but that was all right. Your dad was the darling of everyone, so they let him get away with it."

"Do you still love him?"

"You and your dad are the best things I have."

The boy gave his mother a big hug.

"Your dad fills in so many holes in my life," she added, suddenly tears rolling down her cheeks. "He is a great gift."

It pleased him to hear her say that, for he too loved his father.

Chapter 9

That same year the family flew to Germany to celebrate Christmas with the Holms. In less than eighteen months the girls had grown up considerably. Bordélique was as usual stealing everybody's heart with her charm and ebullient laughter. Only the parents looked tired, thoughtful, and older. Frank had as usual been travelling extensively and the burden of building a new research team at Bergheimer Strasse 58 had already left a visible impression upon his face. Martha, too, had been carrying her portion of the weight of care, raising two beautiful and healthy children who had demands of their own. Rhoda had swimming lessons twice a week and a piano lesson once a week whereas Bordélique had a violin lesson and a swimming lesson once a week. The girls had different schedules and their mother had to chauffeur them most of the time. Martha had hired a home help who came once a week to clean the five-room apartment at the Panoramastrasse.

Ermias and his parents arrived in Heidelberg four days before Christmas and everybody was happy to see each other once again. Martha had delayed shopping thus far, so that she could buy what everybody wished for Christmas. The very next day, which was Saturday, Dawit and Frank took the children to swimming whilst Aster and Martha went shopping. By this time Rhoda was able to communicate with Aster and Dawit in commendable English, a language for which she had made extra effort for that very purpose.

On Sunday morning, Rhoda and Ermias drove with Frank to Bammental to collect the Christmas tree he had ordered two weeks ago and in the afternoon the children were allowed to decorate it. It was great to be with the Holms once again and to see everybody happy.

On Christmas Eve they all went to an international church and afterwards Martha and Aster went home whilst the rest drove to Luisenpark in Mannheim and took a walk there in the cold. The children were eager to get back and unpack their gifts, but the fathers deliberately delayed them, so that the ladies at home had enough time to display their gifts. When they finally got home, the gifts were piled up under the tree and the tree was brilliantly lit with many red, slim Christmas candles. Then Martha, Rhoda, and Bordélique played their instruments and the rest sang Christmas carols, to the frustration of the players, with bad intonation and out of tune. Then they ate *fondue* and at last came the *Bescherung*!

The next day, Frank's international students joined them for afternoon tea and dinner. After dinner, the children played under the Christmas tree whilst the adults talked around the table, drinking wine and *Apfelschorle*. The following day they all drove to Paderborn in two cars, Dawit driving the car he had rented at Frankfurt airport upon their arrival. They stayed in Paderborn for two days, and then drove with the Holms directly to Alpbach for a one-week ski holiday.

It was in Alpbach that Frank and Martha shared the news that Rhoda had problems at school. In the presence of the children they had made light of it, simply stating that Rhoda had no problem understanding the subjects, but when she wrote tests, she was always nervous and kept making mistakes which she would not otherwise do. But later that day, whilst Martha and Dawit were skiing with the children and Frank and Aster were resting, Frank shared with Aster their fear that Rhoda might not survive Gymnasium and that she might be demoted to Realschule. Frank also told Aster that Rhoda was still wetting her bed. She had been taken to a psychologist who recommended an intelligence test, which Rhoda took, but the results could not indicate the existence of any impairment: analytic, comprehension, memory, or perception.

Frank was bitter when he talked about the German school system being harsh and exacting. He told Aster that these two attributes had not changed appreciably since Albert Einstein attended elementary school more than a century ago. According to Frank, children were confronted with existential anxiety at quite an early stage and their education was driven quintessentially by fear of failure instead of curiosity or the desire to discover their world.

Frank was not the first or only person Aster knew who expressed frustration with the German school system. Almost all of her boy's teachers in Gottingen, the parents of his school friends, and her previous colleagues at the University of Gottingen shared similar views, and yet none of them seemed to be able to do anything about it. It was as if the monstrous system had its own life and its own inviolable will. Fearful of psychologically crushing their children and being themselves psychologically crushed in the process, many parents agreed to send their children to vocational schools where they would be trained to take up jobs later in life which did not require a university degree or scientific competence.

In the evening, Aster shared with her husband what she had discussed with Frank.

"That may possibly be the case," he said of the school system. "But I think Frank himself takes life seriously. Children are quick to perceive and internalise the insecurity of their parents."

"How can you say that? Frank isn't being insecure. He is the smartest person I've ever met."

"Insecurity has little to do with potential."

"Rather?"

"It has rather much to do with perception—with the way we perceive the demands of life and our own readiness to meet them."

"Hmm."

She reflected briefly.

"Your statement is not entirely incompatible with the essence of Frank's own observation. For he too complained that the education system in Germany is fear-driven. Do you think Frank is insecure?"

"I don't know. Perhaps."

"Martha, on the other hand, appears to be laid back."

"You never tell which parent has more influence on the children's self-perception and why."

"What can we do to help Rhoda?"

"Perhaps the problem will go away on its own if the parents don't take it too seriously."

"I have a proposal, but I'm not sure whether it's a clever one."

"What is it?"

"Suppose they move to Addis for a year or so?"

"Are you crazy? How can they possibly do that?"

"Frank can stay in Germany and mind his business undisturbed. Besides, he's plenty of opportunity to come to Addis. Poor Martha can get some rest and assistance and the children will enjoy being with us and help each other."

Dawit found his wife's idea interesting.

"My fear is that Martha may view my proposal as a subtle criticism of their parenthood."

"Your idea is not bad at all," he encouraged her looking out of the window but still looking uncertain. "They can rent rooms from my mom and borrow a car from us."

Nevertheless, Aster's proposal was not communicated to the Holms and the Ethiopians returned to Addis.

Part III
Dresden

Chapter 1

Shortly after he had celebrated his sixteenth birthday, Ermias moved with his mother, who had managed to secure a transfer to the UN headquarters, to New York to finish high school at the German International School in White Plains. His parents had not been of the same mind about the decision to move to New York, his father wanting him to first finish high school in Addis before he moved abroad and his mother insisting that attendance at a US high school for the final two years of his secondary education would prove critical in securing not only admission into one of the best universities in the US but also a full scholarship.

His teachers in Addis had been uncertain about his academic potential, as his grades fluctuated between very good and satisfactory. His mother was persuaded that his devotion to reading "aimless" novels was responsible for his mediocre performance and hoped that moving to New York would enlarge his horizons and enable him to understand the great sacrifice a successful life required. His father, who also enjoyed reading "aimless" novels and encouraged his son to read books, disagreed with his wife. In a way, this was a reflection of the fundamental difference between the two, as far as the future of their son was concerned. His father's primary wish was to see that Ermias was happy in life, whilst his mother's wish was that the boy would fully develop his potential, without which, she maintained, it was meaningless to talk about happiness.

Apart from their differences on the philosophy of happiness and fulfilment, his father was also concerned about the tuition fees at the International School which would amount to nearly forty thousand dollars; needless to say the move to New York would once again separate the family at least for two years.

Ermias himself was torn when he was informed of the decision. On the one hand, after struggling to settle in Addis for nearly two years, he was beginning to make friends and to enjoy the privilege of being the son of one of the most successful young couples in the city. On the other hand, he was also yearning for change and eager to discover new places and to meet new people. He had always imagined New York to be one of those beautiful, shining, and golden cities with lots of possibilities. As the certainty of his relocation solidified and the time of his departure approached, however, the splendour of New York and the fact that he would have to begin establishing his social life all over again frightened him a little. Indeed, during the last two weeks prior to their departure, he even grew physically sick, suffering from diarrhoea and a mild circadian rhythm sleep disorder.

Mother and son flew to New York a week after he had celebrated his birthday and spent an entire week inside their newly rented house without going anywhere. The preparation for the journey, the many farewell dinners, and the journey itself were tedious and emotionally exhausting for both of them. Nonetheless, they rented a car and embarked on a fortnight's tour on the second week to visit some of the east and south-east coast cities. This had been his mother's long-time dream, but during her frequent business trips to the US in the past, she had travelled either alone or with people she hardly knew so that she preferred to stay inside her hotel room most of the time. The weather was unbearably hot and the drive tedious, but he could not remember seeing his mother happier. She said she felt young, carefree, and safe, and having Ermias by her side all the time was one of her greatest joys. Ermias, too, was happy and nonchalant and felt that his dream, as far as discovering new places was concerned, was being fulfilled right in front of his eyes, without the need to apply much effort on his part.

Chapter 2

School started in the first week of September and in the coming weeks and months Ermias discovered that the difference between his present school and the German school he had left behind was not really that great. Even the city was in many respects similar to Addis: expensive, culturally diverse, and busy, and one had to spend a long time to get from A to B. But, of course, New York was also uniquely different in many respects.

Either because of his exposure to the wider world, as his mother thought, or because of him being a stranger in a big and indifferent city, or because of his maturity of age, the desire to work hard at school emerged naturally and he was even willing to put aside the "aimless" books for a while. The reward of assiduousness was almost immediate and measureable, as his performance steadily improved from the very outset and continued to do so throughout the school year.

That year he also met Nellie at a social event jointly organised by the German Embassy in Washington and the UN. She went to the same school as Ermias and her father, who was originally from Switzerland and a neurologist consulting the UN on autism and cognitive disabilities, had travelled extensively around the world, like his own mother. The two talked about school life in general and the different places they had visited. Then Nellie asked him about his parents and what they did and he told her that he was living with his mother in White Plains and that his mother was working for the UN.

"And your father?"

"He lives in Addis Ababa, where I came from. He is a doctor and owns a Health Centre there."

"Are your parents separated or divorced?"

"No, no! My mom and I moved to New York just recently, so that I can go to the International School."

"What does your mother do?"

"She's an economist."

At that very moment his mother joined them briefly and Ermias introduced Nellie to his mother.

"Your mother is very young and beautiful!" Nellie remarked after his mother was gone.

"Yes, she's young. She had me when she was twenty."

"Really?"

Ermias told her the story.

"My mother works for IBM Research in Yorktown and I have an older brother. He also goes to the International School. He's two years older than me."

"How old are you?"

"I'm sixteen."

"Are you alone here?"

"No, I'm with my dad. My mom and my brother are not here."
That evening the two exchanged telephone numbers and in the
following days Ermias often saw Nellie at school but they did
not have the chance to talk. But then one day during a break he
saw her sitting alone in a corner and he went over to her.

"Hey, how are you doing?" she greeted him forcing a smile.

"Is something wrong?"

"Oh, I just decided to sit by myself to sort out some stuff in my
brain."

"You look upset, what's the matter?"

"Is that obvious?"

"Do you want to talk about it?"

"Oh, it's just some personal stuff. Don't worry, I'll be fine."

"Trouble at school?"

"Not really."

"Then at home?"

"Where did you learn to be so thoughtful?"

"What do you mean?"

"You've this air about you, um, how can I put it, you're so
mature."

"Are you teasing me?"

"No, I'm serious. I've been watching you for some time, you
know? You seem to be older than your age."

"Should I take this as a compliment?"

"Now don't be an ass! Yes, I meant it as a compliment."

"I don't like looking mature, though. When I'm in my country
I'm sanguine and enjoy laughing and making others laugh, like

my father. But I find it difficult to be funny here, particularly, when I speak English."

"But your English is excellent."

"Maybe it's not so much the language as the whole setting. When I'm amongst my own people, I find my default setting being sanguine. When I'm amongst other people, I find myself being sober, I don't know why."

"What's your father like?"

In that instant Ermias felt his eyes becoming moist with warm tears.

"Is something the matter?" Nellie asked him anxiously, thinking that she had hit on a sensitive nerve.

"Funny, this had never happened to me before. Excuse me."

"Nonsense. You must be missing your dad very much."

"My dad is very funny and kind-hearted. He has this special quality of making everybody feel at home."

"Lucky you."

"How about your father?"

"I can't say much about him. We hardly see him, you know. He travels a lot and when he's in New York, he's always busy with work."

"But the other day you told me that you travel with him occasionally."

"Yeah, but that doesn't count for much. Even when we travel together we hardly ever do anything together. Daddy is always busy and Mommy is very difficult to be with."

"That's sad."

"It is."

"Is this why you were upset?"

"Partly," Nellie replied tilting her head towards the right. "I may tell you some other time, when we know each other better."

The next day Nellie introduced Ermias to her brother, Paul while they were having lunch in the school lounge, but her brother appeared to be disinterested and reserved. He was a person of few words and the only subject that seemed to interest him was the human anatomy, about which Ermias knew little. Then as soon as he was done with his lunch Paul excused himself and left.

"Don't be offended, he's always like that. His aloofness has nothing to do with you," Nellie reassured Ermias when they were alone. "He needs some time to warm up. But once he's accustomed to know you, he'll open up."

"That's fine with me."

From that day on Ermias and Nellie ate lunch together about once a week, mostly alone but sometimes accompanied by Paul or other schoolmates, but their relationship did not develop into anything other than a close acquaintance. The breakthrough came the following year, two weeks before the Easter break.

"Hey, how good are you in Physics?" Nellie asked Ermias when they were having lunch. Paul was with them.

"Physics is my favourite subject!" he replied.

"Do you have time to study together? I'd be grateful. I had a private tutor, but she had to leave the country because her visa couldn't be extended. It'll take some time until my parents have found a replacement."

"Sure, why not."

"I'll discuss this with my mom and let you know. Unfortunately, I'll not be coming to your place. It has to be at our place."

The following day Nellie told Ermias that her mother was willing to arrange a room at her research centre twice a week, but only until she had found a new tutor. Ermias too discussed the matter with his mother and got her approval.

On the first day, Paul dropped them at the research centre and Nellie's mother received them at the entrance. She was in her early fifties or late forties, elegant-looking but austere, and introduced herself formally with her Christian and last name and brought the young people to a modest conference room. On the way she did not bother Ermias with the usual questions with which parents would inundate friends of their children upon their first acquaintance.

"Here you can study undisturbed. My office is the one in front. I'll go and fetch tea."

"I'll be honest with you," Nellie began as soon as they were alone. "My Mom disapproves of me bringing boys to our house. Not that I have a reputation of bringing boys to our house, mind you. Daddy is cool about it, but Mommy isn't. So here we are! I'm a little embarrassed about the whole situation."

"Don't worry, I'm fine with this. My mom also liked the idea," Ermias reassured Nellie.

Nellie's mother returned with a thermos flask, two mugs and a plastic box full of biscuits, and then left. The two sat down to study but Nellie's mother kept on coming every fifteen minutes or so to see "how they were faring".

In one of the sessions, Nellie and Ermias started talking once again about their parents and Nellie told him that her parents sometimes quarrel vehemently.

"The things they quarrel about are really silly but all the same they quarrel."

"How do they find the time if your father travels a lot?"

"It doesn't matter; they always find the time to quarrel! My brother says it's Daddy's fault, but he's being unfair."

"Why does he blame your father?"

"He thinks that Mommy is being touchy because she carries much of the burden of the family."

"Is that true?"

Nellie did not answer this question.

"Human relationships suck a lot," she said instead and sighed.

"Even my brother can be insufferable sometimes."

"Hey, can we go to the movies one of these days? It'll cheer you up."

This had been on his mind for some time but until now he had not been able to harness the courage to ask her.

"I'd love to, but I don't think my mother will allow it."

His heart sank with disappointment.

"Let me know if you can make it."

Chapter 3

Nellie's mother found a tutor, and the after-school study was interrupted one month before the end of the school year, but Nellie managed to get her mother's permission to go one Saturday afternoon to a movie with Ermias. They met in White Plains and took the train to Grand Central.

"My mother insisted that I should treat you, as an expression of my gratitude," Nellie told him on the way.

"Gratitude?"

"For the time we spent together studying."

"Is this our last meeting?"

"What do you mean?"

"You made it sound like this is 'Goodbye'!"

"Are you going to let me buy the tickets or not?"

"If you insist. Why are you so irritated?"

"I'm sorry; I'm a little upset with my mom today."
From Grand Central the young people walked to Times Square and Nellie paid for the tickets and the popcorn and the drinks. In the middle of the movie Ermias searched for her hand and took it. Nellie startled a little, turned to him briefly and turned back to the screen without attempting to take her hand back. But he could feel that she was self-conscious about it. This was also his first time holding a girl's hand and he also felt slightly awkward about it. He waited for her to press his hand or send some sign of encouragement, but Nellie did not attempt to do so. After a while, still wondering if she appreciated his gesture, he gently released her hand.

"What am I doing?" he asked himself disconcertedly.

He liked Nellie but he was not in love with her. Moreover, he had taken her hand instinctively, without having any expectation. When they came out of the movie theatre, they exchanged a few words about the movie, which had happened to be a comedy, but both felt self-conscious and embarrassed at what had happened between them. Then he proposed to go to a nearby café, which Nellie accepted.

"It's been a great day, thank you for taking me out," Nellie offered on the way, her eyes giving the impression that she wanted to make up for something.

"I think it was you who took me out—I should thank you. I'm sorry if I upset you earlier."

"Nonsense. You haven't upset me. I had a good time. Stop apologising for everything."

They talked about school life and common friends but nothing specific. Then it was time to return to Grand Central.

"I must tell you once again that I wasn't upset when you took my hand. You were sweet, but I don't see a future in it. My mother will never allow it. I'm very sorry."

"Why should your mother decide everything for you?"

"She's sacrificed a lot for me. I don't want to displease her."

"Isn't that what mothers are supposed to do? What's so different about your mom? Does she have the right to take your happiness away in return?"

"There are many things which you don't know. Don't rush to judge my mother."

Ermias paid and they walked back to Grand Central.

"Do you have any plans for the summer?" Nellie asked him on the way.

"I'll be flying to Addis. I can't wait to be with my grandmother and my dad again—miss them terribly."

"Where does your grandmother live?"

"She lives in Addis. Actually, I was born and raised in my grandmother's house."

"What's she like?"

Nellie became cheerful and lively and her eyes sparkled and the peevishness she had exhibited that afternoon disappeared for once. He was pleased to see her smile and told her about his grandmother.

"How sweet!" she reacted when he was finished, with a melancholic cadence and her liveliness having given way to a sober mood. "I envy you. I don't even know yet where we'll be spending the summer. Things are pretty tense at home."

"I'm sorry to hear that."

"It's been like this for some years now."

When the train stopped at White Plains, they hugged warmly and Ermias alighted but Nellie went on.

They had lunch together at the lounge on two further occasions, but Paul was with them both times, looking preoccupied with something and ever economising his words. On the last day of school, Ermias searched for Nellie to say goodbye and found her alone in her classroom. She was visibly upset.

"What's up Nellie?"

"Mommy wants to move out, to separate from Daddy," Nellie told him, suddenly bursting into floods of tears.

"Really? I am sorry."

"She announced it yesterday evening. Apparently, she's been waiting until school was over. She said she's been unhappy for many years."

He did not know what to say, so he sat next to her in silence.

"Listen, you'd better go now. My mother will be here any minute to pick me up and she expects me to be alone."

"All right. I just came to say goodbye."

She quickly took out a pen and a piece of paper from her bag and wrote her email address in a hurry.

"This is my private email, write me when you get to Addis and tell me everything. I'd really like to know how you're doing. I will do the same."

"I'll get in touch. Take care for now."

They hugged quickly, Nellie setting her eyes on the door.

"Paul will be joining Columbia in October, I'm very happy for him."

"That's great! I'm happy for him. He's set a good example for his little sister."

"I'm not ambitious like my brother."

"You'll make it. I've no doubt."

"Take care."

They hugged once again and Ermias went to the door.

"Wait!" she stopped him in his tracks with some urgency in her voice. "I owe you something!"

Before he had time to analyse her statement, Nellie had run to him and planted a kiss on his lips, not a soft, tentative kiss, but a proper, hearty kiss.

"It's been long overdue! Go now."

"I don't know how to thank you," he mumbled foolishly, deeply touched by her action and went out dragging his feet.

Chapter 4

With that kiss Ermias properly fell in love with Nellie and found it difficult to separate from her. Moreover, from that day on he began worrying a lot about her.

His mother had very much been divided as to whether she should send him home for the summer break, considering the volume of work awaiting him in his final year. She was afraid that Ermias would have very little time in Addis to prepare adequately. Ermias tried to put her mind at rest, but she was unconvinced. Yet she had no choice. She herself had avoided business trips the entire school year, hoping to make one or two trips during the summer break. She wanted to travel, not only because the trips were important for her organisation, but she also needed some change and freedom. And it was out of the question to leave him alone in New York whilst she was travelling. Finally, Dawit persuaded her to send the boy home for two months, promising that he himself would ensure that he studied at least three hours every day.

At the end of May, a little more than a week after Nellie's kiss, Ermias flew to Addis without his mother.

The weather in Addis assuaged his mother's fears, for it had been raining for two weeks before his arrival and never ceased raining for two consecutive weeks thereafter, so that Ermias was obliged to spend much of the time indoors studying. In early July the Holm sisters arrived to stay for two weeks and were eager to hear everything about New York and the International School.

"So, how's life in New York? Did you meet the Mayor of New York or the UN Secretary General?" Bordélique asked him as soon as they met at the airport.

"I guess they have better things to do than meeting a commonplace boy from Addis!" Ermias replied.

"Ok, did you meet any celebrities?"

"I met George Clooney once."

"Really?" the girls screamed in unison.

"Or rather, I was with my mom when she met George Clooney."

"Wow, what was he like?"

"Boring. They discussed Darfur the whole time."

"What is Darfur?" Bordélique wanted to know.

He told her.

"Still, you've met one of the most famous celebrities in the world and that makes you famous in your own right!" Rhoda declared. "Who else did you meet?"

"We visited Washington DC and went to the Capitol Building to meet some senators."

"What's interesting about meeting senators?" Bordélique inquired.

"Because they are the most powerful people in America, you silly," her sister told her condescendingly.

"The most powerful person in America is the president," Bordélique encountered with a haughty look.

But finally it was Bordélique who put the most poignant question of the day.

"Did you have a crush on a girl? Please tell the truth and don't lie."

But she did not need to wait for his answer. His eyes had already revealed what his heart wanted to hide.

"He's had his first crush already! What's she like?" Bordélique screamed in excitement.

"Dawit has heard you!" Rhoda checked her sister in whisper.

"Can we delay this question until later?" she added.

"Too late!" Dawit interfered laughing and looking at them through the rear-view mirror.

"Does your mother already know?" the father inquired cheerfully.

"Know what?"

"Oh, come on, about the crush. What's her name and what does she look like, is she pretty?"

"I don't know what you're talking about!"

The girls scrambled to change the subject.

"Were the teachers harsh at your school?"

"Some of them were."

But as soon as they we alone, the girls once again raised the question. This time Ermias told them about Nellie.

"Is this real, do you want to marry her and live in New York forever?" Bordélique asked looking very concerned.

"She is not even my girlfriend yet, silly!"

"But she kissed you! Isn't it slutty to kiss someone who's not your boyfriend?"

Barely had the words left her mouth she regretted them, because Ermias looked offended and her sister looked surprised.

"I'm sorry." Bordélique was quick to apologise.

"Do you have her picture?" Rhoda asked him.

He did not.

"How does she look like, describe her."

"She is white, slim and about my size. She has long, dark hair and greenish-brown eyes."

"That's not much to go on," Rhoda remarked, a little disappointed. "Ask her to send a picture."

"I've already asked her but she hasn't replied to my emails yet."

Rhoda and Ermias assisted Dawit in his medical centre nearly every afternoon during which time Bordélique went horse riding. From late afternoon to late evening, however, the three of them and Dawit spent much of the time outside of the city in different resorts where they met and socialised with his father's friends and their children. This amounted to a desirable and an appropriate diversion for Ermias, because the much expected email from Nellie was not forthcoming.

Sadly, the girls returned to Germany two weeks before his departure for New York and after their departure, Ermias struggled to keep up with his regular study habit and felt prosaic and tired. Indeed, the mood followed him to New York where he spent the remaining three weeks struggling to find interest in his daily activities. He called Nellie multiple times, but she never answered any of his calls. Finally, on the first day of School, he met Nellie in the lounge. She was eating with two girls and he went over to her to say hello.

"Hi, you're back? How was the trip?"

"It was good. How was your summer?"

"It was ok." Nellie spoke dismissively.

"I wrote you a couple of emails but you didn't reply."

"Sorry, I couldn't write."

"I also called."

"I know."

He was expecting her to introduce him to her friends or invite him to sit with them, but she did neither.

The thought crossed his mind: "I've been making too much of the whole thing! How stupid of me!"

He was disappointed with himself for having wasted the whole summer on account of Nellie. In the following days and weeks, he struggled with an inner compulsion to chase after Nellie, which he overcame. By the time the school was over for the Fall break, he had managed to recover from his unrequited love and was confident that the remaining school year, like the one before it, would be successful. But this confidence would vanish in less than two weeks' time.

One late afternoon towards the end of October, he was waiting for his mother in Bryant Park, idly observing the leaves of London plane trees falling down in clusters, when a cold and crystal-clear awareness of death suddenly filled his consciousness out of nothing.

"Death," he observed calmly, without lifting his eyes off the leaves. "In the end, we all die. Trees give up their leaves every year, millions of cells in my body die and are replaced every day, each year schools and universities graduate their students who never go through the same process ever again. Nothing lasts."

The observation filled him not so much with sadness or shock as with an overwhelming surprise of being. He slowly turned his eyes from the trees and cursorily studied his surroundings. Everything appeared to him infinitely unique, strange, and wonderful. That evening on the train to White Plains, sitting next to his mother and looking out of the window, he repeatedly asked himself what he was and everything that surrounded him, and what he existed for. Years later he would learn from so many existential writers that awakening into such consciousness is, at one time or another, the fate of every human being, only it fell hard upon him a bit too early.

A yearlong relentless and ferocious battle of ideas and a wild oscillation between belief and disbelief in the existence of God ensued in his mind about which it makes little sense to write. It suffices to say that as long as Ermias was conscious, even while attentively listening to his teachers and writing exams or participating in an important conversation or activity, the question of who he was and what he was doing on earth never departed from him for a minute.

At the time he was desperate for an answer and willing to do everything he could in order to regain his peace of mind, yet the preoccupation with this daunting question opened up for him a great and wide door to great books and great people, of which New York, perhaps the most secular and indifferent city on earth, could offer so many. However, the price he was to pay for admitting the untimely and uninvited guest was a steady stream of mediocre grades, which would prove finally insufficient for him to get a full scholarship in the US.

Chapter 5

Even before he sat for the final exam at the German International School, Ermias had already realised that his mother's dream that he would one day score impressive grades and secure a full scholarship in one of the elite universities in the US, would most likely never come to pass. Studying in the US as a foreign student without a scholarship would have outreached his parents' finances. So he decided to study in Germany, since education there was free. His parents would still have to cover his living expense, but, relatively speaking, this would be something they could afford. Besides, what was the purpose of spending his entire school life in different German schools if he was not going to study in Germany?

He announced his intention to his parents even before the exam results were available and began to inform himself about the entrance requirements of different universities and the cost of living in different cities. His preferred field of study was experimental physics. When the results were available, he applied to three universities and was accepted by all of them. Finally, he decided to move to Dresden, a beautiful and vibrant city on the River Elbe in East Germany.

Three factors contributed to his decision to go to Dresden. Firstly, compared to the West, studying in the eastern part of Germany was more affordable. Secondly, the university in Dresden was one of the best universities in the country, particularly, in science and engineering. Thirdly, already two years earlier he and his mother had visited Dresden for one week when she was attending a conference there and had been impressed by the beauty of the city.

In New York, Ermias had met many pupils who were eager to be independent and regarded university life as the best transition towards adulthood and freedom. As they saw it, one could enjoy the freedom of adulthood, but the associated responsibilities and liabilities were merely extensions of the responsibilities and liabilities of school life. One was only expected to pass exams with good grades and to avoid being unequally yoked. The rest, as it were, would be taken care of by the parents or the government or some other institution.

Ermias was never compelled to be independent in that sense, even though he was eager to finish school. But his eagerness had much more to do with the freedom to pursue his intellectual interests and hobbies without having to constantly worry about passing exams. He was aware, of course, that university life entailed exams as much, but had also learned from his parents that the pressure was considerably less, particularly, after the first two years.

And the first year in Dresden passed swiftly by. The lectures and tutorials were sufferable, his grades were excellent, and he had plenty of time to read, play football, and run. As far as his hobbies were concerned, he could find no better city in Germany.

Indeed, Dresden offered him more than he expected. There was the *Großer Garten,* a sprawling park in the middle of the city, around which he could run in good weather and bad weather alike, and the Elbe River, dividing the old city from the new and stretching endlessly to the east and the west, along which he could cycle when the weather was permissible. And there was *Sächsische Schweiz* and the Bohemian forests in which to take long walks on halcyon days, and cheap train tickets to Prague for a weekend trip.

As far as cultural activities were concerned, the two main theatres regularly offered plays at affordable prices. Even though, one should add in parenthesis, most of the plays were modernised adaptations of classical plays wherein the women played hysterical and aggressive roles and the men ran around on the stage completely naked. Even Ophelia and Desdemona were featured as excessively passionate, screaming at the top of their voices and smashing windows and chairs to pieces.

In his second year, Ermias was finally at ease, feeling confident and enjoying a rare sense of internal peace. He had hitherto been consumed by a persistent sense of guilt on account of his mediocre performance at the German International School and the realisation that he had let his parents down. Now he was gradually reaching the conviction that, if he was steadfast and careful, he could make his way to Cavendish Laboratory at Cambridge for his MPhil in two years' time.

It was about this time that his interest in his university's female students began to assert itself, at first in the form of a detached curiosity and then, as admiration, and subsequently, as earnest intention to possess. It was not entirely clear to him what he really wanted from a relationship, having already determined not to stay in Dresden for a long time. Still, he let the desire develop and swaddle him.

The girls with whom he attended physics lectures were very few in number. Some of them, towards whom he was attracted, were, to use the local vernacular, already claimed, and they all seemed contented with their love life, so that it was out of question to try to arouse interest in them. But the university had no deficiency of female students and there was plenty of opportunity to meet them in the cafeterias, libraries, swimming halls, and copy shops.

There was much to praise in these students, and, indeed, in the women of Dresden in general, without the danger of stumbling into the pitfalls of generalisation. Compared to the girls he knew in Addis, Heidelberg, or New York, they were remarkably fit without being either skinny or muscular. Most of them enjoyed outdoor activities, particularly, running and cycling. Indeed, had it not been for a scarcely perceptible veil of thoughtfulness they carried about their young faces, it would have been hard to find flaws in their external appearance. Ermias often described the girls he knew in Addis and New York as beautiful and lovable, but the girls of his university as voluptuous and appealing.

As his interest in the female students was stirred up to full intensity, he began also to realise that somehow his demeanour was ill-suited to capture their attention or excite their curiosity. For before their eyes could make contact, sensing his presence or intention by some mysterious power of perception, the girls always managed to avert their eyes just in time to find a diversion. When eye contact was unavoidable, and etiquette required conversation, they were always friendly and polite but he could sense that they were also on their guard, waiting for the first opportunity to excuse themselves and leave.

In the following months, through numerous encounters with a variety of women, both in and outside of university circles, he learnt that this phenomenon was rather ubiquitous, not only amongst the girls of his age but also amongst women who were much older than he. Even women who were thirty and above and were married and had children of their own seemed to feel uneasy in his presence and preferred to avoid eye contact.

As the days went by, Ermias was almost certain that spontaneous encounter with female students was the least likely avenue for developing a relationship with and "winning the heart" of a girl, whatever that meant. Therefore, he decided to approach the matter systematically.

Amongst the female students of his batch in his department who were still single, he considered two of them as "achievable goals". One of these was Sophie, a quiet and shy girl who, like himself, enjoyed running. He had seen her running around

Großer Garten several times. In her spare time Sophie worked at the students' café once or twice a week and he was almost certain that she was working Thursdays between three and five o'clock in the afternoon during which time the café would be quiet.

The other girl was Emma, who was one of the most intelligent and sympathetic students in his class. She first captured his attention when, during an impromptu discussion amongst the students in one of the physics lectures, she spoke passionately about the ruinous impact of slavery on the family of the black community in America. Almost all students admired and respected her, but for some inexplicable reason, she was still single. But that did not seem to bother her at all. She was energetic, confident, and passionate in everything she undertook. Of these two he regarded Sophie as the easiest and the less intimidating target to conquest. There was yet another single whom he really liked, but for some reason classified as unattainable target. The girl in question was named Jasmin and he was attracted towards her mainly because of her unusual placidness.

"I'm almost certain that she's single by choice and that she has a more superior goal in life than romance at present," Ermias had told himself multiple times.

Ermias was aware that under normal circumstances neither Sophie nor Emma would be his first choice. Not because he found any particular fault with them, but simply because they were very different from him. But by this time he was also beginning to feel lonely and afraid of being perceived by his peers as an isolated individual. And more than loneliness, he dreaded to be labelled as *isolated*, as if this was a gross personal vice.

His parents had anticipated some of his formidable challenges when they decided to send him to a foreign land, one of which being loneliness. Both had taken pains to prepare him for this diabolical adversary, but gave him seemingly contradictory advice…

A few hours before he departed for New York with his mother, his dad had become visibly emotional. Ermias had already sensed that there was something he wished to talk to him about but could determine what.

"Can you take a walk with me?" he finally asked him, looking at Ermias with a nervous smile.

Ermias volunteered and his father led the way out of the house through the back door. The house was full of people who had come to say goodbye or wished to accompany them to the airport.

"I can't believe time flies so fast!" his father began once they were outside, slowly walking on the left side of his son. "You're already sixteen years old and I'm nearly fifty. I wish to tell you how thankful I am that we, namely, you, your mom, grandma, and I, with all our friends here and abroad, have been together for the past many years. I've enjoyed each and every moment with you. There were occasions when I was afraid we might be separated. Your mom is to be praised for the sacrifice she's made, considering how smart and gifted she is and the number of offers she has declined. This particular decision is made for your sake, so that you can get the best education we can afford and which will one day enable you to pursue a higher education in one of the best universities in the world."

His father seemed to get confused and paused.

"It'll take you some time before you've discovered what that great city has in store for you," he continued, "since the demands of school may keep you from making friends. You should expect to be lonely sometimes. I know this from experience. At the same time, you'll have unlimited freedom to access the Internet..."

Then the father talked uncomfortably about the problems with the Internet, namely, the ease with which Internet content could be accessed, the lack of mutual responsibility and shared values, the lack of moderation, and all, but in the middle of his talk, he interrupted.

"I don't want to sound ridiculous. I know I had to talk to you about such things a long time ago..."

"Don't worry, dad, I know all about it," Ermias reassured him.

"Good that you know all about it. Perhaps you know much more than I do, which is really great. There's no greater pleasure for a father than to see his children becoming smarter than he is. But knowledge in and of itself is useless, particularly, when one is lonely."

"I'll be responsible."

"I trust you. Never take pornography as a prescription for loneliness. Don't underestimate its power either, which comes from its limitless availability."

The boy's heart sank. His father had no idea that Addis, too, had unlimited supply of pornography and that young people were more unsafe in Addis than in New York. Ermias was thirteen years old when he was first exposed to pornography both at school and outside of school. Not only that. Whereas the exposure of other young people most likely would lead to fantasy, the young people of Addis were not content with fantasy alone. Casual sex and abortions amongst pupils were so commonplace that Ermias already knew girls who had had multiple abortions before they were in grade ten. Some even had ended their lives in the process.

"Whatever you do," his father went on, "do it with a human being. I know this sounds irresponsible, but I prefer you to take a girlfriend rather than corrupt your mind, your heart, your soul. The people who produce pornography and make it freely available for your consumption over the Internet prey on your basest instincts. They expect you to consent and rejoice in the humiliation and dehumanisation of another human being, whereas taking a girlfriend at the age of sixteen may be unwise but not inhuman. Not that I'm advising you to take a girlfriend, mind you."

His mother's advice came about a fortnight before Ermias moved to Dresden. They were in Heidelberg, walking along the Neckar on a brilliant Saturday morning in the beginning of September, enjoying the magnificent view of Bergstraße at Odenwald. Ermias and his mother were trailing behind the others by about a stone's throw and Ermias suspected that she wished to talk to him about something important, so he was waiting.

"In two weeks, you'll be living by yourself for the first time," she began. "It's very likely that all the girls will have their eyes on you and make your life very busy and exciting. It may also happen that your mermaid needs some time to find her way to you, in which case you may feel lonely and forlorn. Whichever the case may be, don't settle for the second best. Everything which is alive, lovely, and honourable requires time and cultivation to fully develop. You must be patient with romance."

Ermias smiled and nodded in agreement and they walked in silence.

Now, none of these recommendations seemed to have anything to do with his pursuits and Ermias was willing to put both of them aside.

After having procrastinated for a few weeks, Ermias finally plucked up the courage and went to the students' café, which was deserted as he expected. Sophie was sitting behind the counter, alone and studying a textbook. When she saw him enter, she put her book aside and stood up to take his order.

"What would you like to order?" she asked him in English.

He ordered latte macchiato and remained standing at the counter after she had given him his drink.

"Und wie läuft's?" [b]

"Es läuft gut." [c]

She wanted to take her seat and resume with her study, but he put in his next question.

"I've seen you working here many times and decided to drop by and say hello."

"Yes, I work here twice a week."

"Does it pay well?"

"I'm a volunteer."

Sophie seemed nervous and embarrassed.

"I'm sorry; I thought you were working to earn some extra money."

"No."

"And how is the study going?"

"Good."

"Are you from this area?"

"Meissen."

"I also saw you a couple of times—you were running."

"That's possible."

"Listen, I was thinking of asking you out for tea. Do you have time next week?"

The girl grew more confused and embarrassed.

"I'm sorry, my English is not so good. Please forgive me, I have to take care of something in the other room."

Sophie disappeared into the next room and never showed up again as long as Ermias was there. After she went, Ermias too felt embarrassed. He waited for a long time in case she decided to reappear, but when he realised she would not be coming, he left without touching his macchiato.

Two days later while he was running around *Großer Garten*, he saw Sophie again. It was getting dark and cold and the park was completely deserted. As he made a turn at a corner, he saw her running towards him. They were separated by a distance of hundred metres or so. Determined to show her that he was not offended by her sudden disappearance the other day, he wanted to wave 'hello' as they passed one another by. So he kept on looking at her whilst running. It was hard to say she had not seen him, but he was equally uncertain if she had seen him. Her face was turned outwards, towards the park, at an angle of about fifteen degrees out of his line of sight. Somehow he sensed that she was self-conscious, and as a result, unable to move her face in any direction by even a fraction of a degree. She ran the remaining distance, as it were, a step at a time, as a moving wax figure, with no visible emotion displayed on her pale countenance.

Ermias delayed his next plan, which was to woo Emma, until after the New Year. He spent Christmas and New Year with the Holms and on the way back to Dresden he met Jasmin at Frankfurt Airport. They saw and briefly greeted one another at check-in but whilst awaiting boarding at the gate, she came to him.

"Happy New Year! Your name is Dawit, isn't it?"

"You can call me Ermias; it's the Amharic version of Jeremiah or Jerry."

"I'm Jasmin."

"I know."

"Do your parents live in Frankfurt or nearby?"

"No, they live in Ethiopia. I spent Christmas and the New Year in Heidelberg with friends of the family. And you, where did you spend Christmas and New Year?"

"I spent Christmas with my mother in Kassel and the New Year with my father and his partner in Frankfurt."

"I didn't know you came from the West."

"Yes, I'm *Wessi*."

"Do you like studying in Dresden?"

"I do. How about you?"

"It's alright. Why did you decide to move to Dresden?"

"My paternal grandparents were originally from Dresden. They escaped to the West after the communists took over the East, when they were still young, abandoning everything they had owned. But after the collapse of the Wall, my father was able to reclaim his parents' house which he's renovated and let out. This connection led me to move to Dresden. And you, why did you choose to study in Dresden?"

He told her.

"I've been an Au Pair in Chicago," Jasmin surprised him. "I lived for one year with a family of three—a married couple and their three-year-old daughter."

"When was that?"

"Right after my Abitur. I took one year off to improve my English and to experience life in America."

"Did you have a great time there?"

"Kind of. I'm happy to have had the experience, but it's not something I'd be glad to do again."

At this point, boarding was announced and the two checked their tickets to discover that one was sitting behind the other. Once on board the aircraft, Ermias asked the person sitting next to Jasmin to exchange places with him and the person obliged. From there the two continued chatting about life in America and the short flight to Dresden came to an end without both of them having noticed it. This was the first meaningful conversation Ermias had with anyone since he had moved to Dresden.

The following Monday the first lecture was cancelled without prior notice and amongst the fifteen or so students who showed up were Ermias and Emma, and the "bird" he was intending to charm, so to speak, came directly into his birdcage of its own free will.

"Happy New Year!" she greeted him with a firm handshake and sat behind him.

From there to turn back and strike a conversation was not very difficult.

"So how was the holiday?"

"It was hectic; I'm glad it's over. I hate holidays!" Emma answered, searching something in her bag.

"Why do you hate holidays?"

She abandoned her search briefly, folded her arms, and frowned.

"To start with, the way the West celebrates Christmas nowadays has nothing to do with the original meaning of Christmas. It's now reduced merely to excessive eating and drinking and too much waste. No one thinks of the poor and the hungry and the destitute around the world. Secondly, the Christmas season presents a great opportunity for huge American corporations to dump their junk on poor families everywhere and rob them shamelessly. Thirdly, imagine how many Christmas trees are brutally cut every year and sold at an outrageous price! Of course, our politicians will always argue that the wood will be needed and recycled anyway to make furniture and that the number of trees to be fallen will be carefully determined and there'll be new trees planted and so on and so forth, but that is not the point. As long as trees are commercialised, there'll be no way of knowing the exact effect of them being cut. Even if we accept the assertion that there are regulations in the West, this is not the case in poor countries like your own. You are from Ethiopia, aren't you?"

Ermias nodded in agreement.

"I guessed so," Emma went on with a loud and irritated voice. "In a country like yours, the forests have been mutilated for many decades non-stop and now only less than three percent of the surface area of the entire country is covered by forests. Imagine, less than three percent of a country three times the size of Germany! I know this because my father has lived in the Omo Region for many years trying to educate the natives how to protect their environment. Unfortunately, your own government is against natural conservation. In fact, it has displaced thousands of villagers in the past three years alone in order to sell their land to Indian and Arab multi-millionaires who promised to produce rice, coffee, and some spices for export. And what does the West do? Nothing but set a very bad example during Christmas."

"So you've lived in Ethiopia, or was your father living alone there?" Ermias asked Emma hoping to lead her on to a more congenial subject.

"No, I haven't lived in Ethiopia. I must correct myself; it isn't many years that my father lived in the Omo Region, but many months. Fourteen months to be precise."

"Is your father a social anthropologist?"

"My father is a pastor by profession, but the reason he went to Africa is not to evangelise people. My father believes in the importance of religion but he doesn't impose his religion upon anyone. Why in the devil is this accursed professor late today? Excuse me; I've to mind my own business now."

Emma resumed her search and Ermias decided to go out to take fresh air.

"It won't do with Emma!" he told himself on the way out. "Even if she's willing for a romance, the stats will always get in the way."

In the following weeks Ermias had multiple brief encounters with Jasmin during which the two talked about various topics: lectures, exams, the forthcoming semester break, skiing, etc., but during these encounters Jasmin wore a peculiar smile which Ermias was unable to decode. Moreover, she seemed to make an effort now in keeping a steady eye contact with him, even though she was not the sort of girl he would regard as shy or timid. Finally, he called Rhoda to ask for advice.

"Is the Wild East more benign than New York where girls are concerned?" she teased him and, then, spoke her mind. "I cannot interpret the smile before I've seen it. As to her difficulty with making a steady eye contact, I would interpret it as a lack of confidence, either in herself, in you, or in the relationship, none of which speaks in favour of the relationship. If you've noticed, girls make direct eye contact when we talk. You can take it as a sign of disinterest if you see a girl avoiding an eye contact."

"You've made your point."

"What is it you want from her, romance or merely sex?"

"Do you have to be so blunt?"

"You should be honest with yourself. What is it you are looking for in a woman? It must be sex, for I've a feeling that you're not ready to settle into a relationship yet, am I right? You've told me yourself that your immediate goal is joining Cambridge. But as far as I can tell, you're also not someone who takes pleasure in casual sex, are you?"

"I don't know yet. To tell the truth, I've been asking myself this same damn question many times, but to no avail. Maybe I want to have the experience, I mean, as an abstraction."

"But you can't have romance as an abstraction. You have to deal with real people with real feelings and demands. Perhaps you want to use a relationship as a shield to ward off loneliness?"

"Possibly."

"But in doing so, you may surrender to the wrong girl and make your loneliness even worse."

"Do you think Jasmin is the wrong girl?"

"I'm not saying she's the wrong girl. I don't know this girl, to begin with. All I'm saying is that loneliness shouldn't be the reason for entering into a relationship."

"What should be the reason then? Doesn't it say somewhere in the Bible that it is not good for a man to be alone?"

"It does say that. If you're in a good relationship, you'll not feel lonely. But this doesn't mean any relationship can be a prescription for loneliness. You should have known this two years ago, you are more experienced than I."

"There's a limited value in the knowledge derived from experience."

"Why don't you let it grow or die at its own pace?"

"What do you mean?"

"Don't make an effort with this girl. In all other circumstances, I'd have advised you to make an effort, but in this particular circumstance, making no effort seems to me the right decision. By the way, don't worry; she's by now understood that you fancy her. A girl needs only a fraction of a hint to capture your intention. If she likes you, she'll pursue you herself."

"Until then, I'll have to suffer loneliness?"

"Why don't you apply for a transfer to Heidelberg or Gottingen? I'm sure you will get a transfer."

"That will not be the way to deal with loneliness. That will be running away from a battlefield."

"A retreat is better than a senseless defeat."

So he refrained from making any effort and thereby removed from himself a considerable cognitive load. As Rhoda predicted, nothing came of his acquaintanceship with Jasmin. Indeed, the interaction between the two reduced to monosyllabic greetings in the subsequent days and eventually they stopped greeting one another altogether without this becoming an embarrassment to either of them.

Chapter 6

It was difficult to label it rejection and still less indifference. In all other spheres of university activities, whenever they felt that their help was needed, fellow female students were always ready to offer it. When Ermias missed a lecture, a tutorial, or a lab session, some of them sent him emails and attached their own notes for him to catch up.

But this nameless and abhorrent impulse to eschew intimate relationships inbred in him loneliness, lust, and, eventually, shyness, all of which he had never experienced before with such analogous magnitude. The first to dominate and oppress him was loneliness. It occurred to him that, by and large, he had been lonely throughout the first year of his studies without any awareness of the pain. But in the second year, he had felt the pain and became preoccupied with it. It was not that he did not meet students. He met students, all right, in classrooms, football fields, and labs. With some of them, indeed, he spent long hours performing experiments and writing lab reports during which they shared jokes and talked about general topics, but as soon as the work was over, they said goodbye to one another and each went their separate way.

As to lust, he could not recall how or when exactly it began to invade him, but towards the end of the winter semester of the second year, its grip was so strong and so complete and its desire so undiscriminating that he was willing to take to bed the next woman he met on the street.

"Loneliness does not make one fastidious," a woman he had once met at the Holms told him as she explained the difference between a lion, a cougar, and a puma. "The cougar, despite having many admirable qualities, is one of the most reclusive and secretive animals, which is why it preys upon lofty and humble species alike. It even devours rodents and insects."

Now Ermias understood what she had meant. Before long, he made it almost a habit to stay up far into the small hours of the night watching pornography. Then, he would wake up the next morning subdued by guilt and regret, dissatisfied with himself, and tired, both mentally and physically.

Finally, shyness took hold of him and he himself began to avoid eye contact and to feel visibly uneasy in the company of women.

He stayed the first week of the winter semester break that year with the Holms, sleeping long hours, drinking lots of tea, and reading *Crime and Punishment* undisturbed, and appreciating the much longed for serenity of mind with exceeding joy. On the last day, the four of them (Frank was travelling, as usual) went to church and after lunch, Bordélique became cheeky and provoked him and Rhoda to a pillow fight in the parents' bedroom. They were so noisy and made such a huge mess that at last Martha got impatient with them and chased them out of the bedroom and closed the door from within to take a nap. Shortly thereafter Bordélique, too, went to her room to do homework and Rhoda and Ermias were left alone in the living room.

"Will I even be afraid of Rhoda? Will I find it difficult to look into her eyes?" he asked himself anxiously and looked at her clear, deep blue eyes. She returned his gaze with a smile, unsuspecting.

There was not the slightest fear whatsoever in him. Then they played a game and talked about various issues for about an hour and finally it was time to go. They brought him to the train station, Martha driving. On the platform they talked for about twenty minutes during which time he repeated the same questions to himself and looked at the three of them alternately. There was peace in him, for there was nothing to be afraid of. The train arrived on time and they hugged and he got onto the train. It turned out that this was to be the last time he could make eye contact with them without being self-conscious or embarrassed.

Ermias spent the remaining weeks in Bad Hersfeld, packing parcels for Amazon and earning much needed money. When in April the summer semester began, he returned to Dresden, invigorated and with renewed hope that things would be different.

The city was garbed in green, the Elbe was flowing full, and the paths on both sides of the river were filled with healthy, young, and athletic cyclists, inline skaters, and runners of both sexes. There was none of the April-weather one should be apprehensive of, as it was dry, the sun was shining brilliantly, and the temperature was just right for all sorts of outdoor activities, particularly, for running. The city was swarming with tourists who came from all over Europe to populate *Prager Straße, Zwinger, Frauenkirche, Brühlsche Terrasse,* and the *Türckische Cammer.*

Ermias' grades were still in excellent shape despite a relatively poor preparation towards the end. But his greatest relief was that in the upcoming semester he would be taking experimental physics, his favourite subject, and a research project. Together, the two courses would earn him sixteen credit hours and give him sufficient relief to readjust his focus onto his studies.

Shortly after the semester kicked off, however, it became apparent to him that, unlike the courses he had taken in the previous semesters, experimental physics required frequent and direct interaction with fellow students and the tutor. Despite a good start, he became increasingly and painfully shy and uneasy. At the same time, he considered it impolite to turn away his eyes from his fellow students whilst he talked or listened to them. But no matter how hard he tried, he was unable to maintain a steady eye contact with any of them, which was confusing and embarrassing for him as well as for them. As an attempt to overcome his shyness, he became forthright, quick to answer and ask questions. Sadly, in his inexperience, he took his forthrightness a bit too far and dominated group discussions and tutorial sessions. Some felt that he was awkward, critical, eager to find faults, argumentative, and even belligerent. Some students dropped the course altogether. By the end of May, his plight was known to the entire faculty and students and professors became visibly cautious with him. No one dared to approach and ask him what the matter was, nor did he dare to approach anyone and ask for an advice or a help, even though he was perplexed and helpless.

The only social activity wherein he could take part without experiencing pain or embarrassment was football. He would arrive a minute or two before it started and leave as soon as it was over. As most of the players were not students or university graduates, he scarcely had anything in common with them except for football, so it was safe for him to avoid personal contact outside of the game.

Ermias was aware that much was at stake. If he let the course his life was taking carry on, he knew he would eventually lose his mind and interrupt his studies. He could not imagine the emotional distress this would cause to his family. Even without all of these, much had already been lost, with little hope of recovering.

His main challenge was persuading himself not to seek the company of people and not to pay attention to them or beg for their attention. His second challenge was to drop

Experimental, since this meant losing several credit hours. But attending the lecture was impossible, as it continued to be an occasion for disappointment and grief. But in the end he dropped Experimental. But he was unwilling to give up the research project, partly because this was more of an individual responsibility and the final grade was either pass or fail.

Then he welcomed loneliness as his perpetual and oppressive companion. Days and weeks passed without having any sensible interaction with anyone. By choice or design, he avoided the few international students he knew in his faculty. Most of them, in their eagerness to present themselves as the integral components of the university and to prove that they were familiar with its inner life, had succumbed to an epidemic of demeaning gossip, pretending to know which professor or scientist earned the most, which had got a prestigious job offer, which was married to whom and which was divorced, which was a homosexual, a Jew, or a gentile. Most of them had no other business in their spare time except pursuing and spreading such tidings.

Chapter 7

In the middle of May Ermias received a brief email from Rhoda telling him that Bordélique and she would like to come and visit him for Pentecost. This would be in three weeks and there would be no lecture for the entire week. The news was at once uplifting and distressing. Distressing, because he was not sure whether he would be able to conduct himself normally. His hope was that there would be such a lot to see in Dresden and in its surroundings that they would be active the whole day and, therefore, too tired in the evening to sit down for a long chat, which was his worst nightmare. In addition, he had booked a hotel room in the middle of Prague for the weekend and rented a car.

He understood that he had to take some practical steps to change his situation before their coming, the first and the most immediate being overcoming his dependency on pornography.

Since his childhood he had had an insatiable appetite for books, so he now clung to it wishing to tap inspiration from books and started reading the biographies of some of the people he admired, beginning with Dietrich Bonhöffer. Then he read the biographies of Tolstoy and Dostoevsky in succession. These people, despite the stark contrast in their intellectual disposition and temperament, were nonetheless intimately acquainted with suffering. And yet they had not permitted suffering to discourage them and to hamper them from pursuing perfection, thus compelling generations of admirers to value and imitate their commitment to selflessness, ardour, and sacrifice. Indeed, suffering, instead of inhibiting them from loving and showing compassion to others, rather enabled them to discover the potential in themselves to love and show compassion, not only to those who loved and accepted them, but also to those who opposed and rejected them.

Ermias also began to pay closer attention to the people living around him. There were many amongst them, young and old, men and women, educated and uneducated alike, who were suffering and feeling as lonely and rejected as he felt, perhaps even more so. In subsequent years Ermias would observe in many places people who were as lonely, insecure, and abandoned to their agony and fate as he was. Indeed, by the time he joined Cambridge, he was firmly persuaded that loneliness was the most pandemic and pulverizing affliction in Western Europe.

That same week Ermias received a surprise email from Nellie who wrote that after having repeated the final year at the German International School on account of her parents' separation and some personal crisis, she was now studying pharmacy at Buffalo University. Paul, who was in his junior year at Columbia, was studying theoretical physics. Nellie went on to relate that studying medicine had been Paul's dream since he was a young man and his sudden decision to study physics came as a great and unpleasant surprise to their parents. As for the parents, she wrote, they had just got divorced after twenty-four years of marriage and her mother was broken-hearted and was living alone in Yorktown, whereas her father, who had already found a new girlfriend, had moved to Los Angeles to begin a new life there with her. At the end of her email Nellie shared a poem by Aeschylus, which she said was recited impromptu by Robert Kennedy in front of a large audience on the night the Reverend Martin Luther King Jr. was assassinated:

> *Even in our sleep, pain which cannot forget*
> *Falls drop by drop upon the heart*
> *Until, in our own despair, against our will,*
> *Comes wisdom*
> *Through the awful grace of God.*

These verses forcefully smashed and broke into the wells of his tears and Ermias collapsed into inordinate and painful sobs.

Chapter 8

His condition communicated itself within a fraction of a second when Ermias received Rhoda and Bordélique from the main train station. Rhoda was unmoved but Bordélique was at first confused and after a few attempts to get back a steady eye contact, involuntarily avoided his eyes. He too made repeated attempts, but each attempt constituted a failure and a painful realisation that something had changed in him irreversibly. Then he stopped making an effort. That day Ermias learned what it meant to have a broken heart.

He took them to his apartment where they had tea. The sisters had been to Paderborn the previous day to visit the grandparents, so they told him about their visit. After the tea, they walked on foot to the *Altstadt* and visited the

Frauenkirche, Zwinger, Semperoper, and the *Katholische Hofkirche.* Then they rested at the *Terrassengasse* and drank hot chocolate, watching the ferries arriving from *Königstein* and *Bad Schandau,* dragging long and rippling shadows behind them. It was a beautiful, warm evening and the city was, as usual, full of tourists, now a large quantity of them dining below them at Münzgasse. Despite his awkward condition, the girls were glad to see him and to be in Dresden.

"So what has become of the latest project?" Rhoda asked him cryptically.

"You already knew that it was destined to fail."

"What project?" Bordélique interfered curiously looking at them alternately.

"It wasn't really a project. It was a fleeting idea."

"Am I not allowed to know about it?"

"He was about to set out to conquer the Wild East."

"What Wild East? What are you two talking about? Why are you talking in riddles?"

"Look, there was this girl I sort of fancied, but I soon gave up the idea because I realised that it was a mistake."

"Nellie?"

"No, this one was here in Dresden."

"How often do you fall in love? Are you making a hobby out of it, or what?" Bordélique sounded offended.

"It wasn't like with Nellie. This was merely a fleeting idea born of, uh, idleness, if you will."

"Speaking of Nellie, do you hear from her?" Rhoda inquired.

"Funny you should ask. I got a surprise email from her two weeks ago. She is doing fine. She's studying pharmacy at Buffalo University."

"What did she write?" the sisters asked in unison.

"Nothing in particular. She just updated me about herself and about her family. She shared both bad and good news."

"Does she have a new boyfriend?"

"What do you mean by 'new'? Did she have an old boyfriend you know of?"

"Oh, you know what I mean."

"She didn't mention a new boyfriend."

Then he revealed the substance of Nellie's email.

"What else did she write?"

"Nothing else. That was it."

"No hint that she wants to get back with you?"

"What do you mean get back with me? She never was with me."

"You know exactly what I mean."

"No hint."

"You must have been in her mind all this time."

"Perhaps."

"Do you still love her?"

"I don't know. She was the first girl with whom I really fell in love, so, yes; I still have feelings for her. But this is not something up on the security of which I can build my future. We're now an ocean apart, besides."

"Your answer is inconclusive, which means you still love Nellie."

"But he said he does," Bordélique encountered.

"What does this matter? Things will never work between us."

"So how can you fancy another girl when you still love Nellie?" Bordélique asked, still sounding offended.

"Men are capable of loving many women at the same time. Some of them aren't even real. They exist only in their imagination and still they love them."

"Look at this expert on men who never had a serious relationship with a man," Ermias teased Rhoda good-naturedly.

"I aim first and then shoot."

"You seem to aim forever, though," Bordélique ridiculed her sister.

"It is worthwhile to spend enough time studying my environment, don't you think? And then I shall settle for one. I'm a swan by nature."

"We shall see how long this theory of yours holds!" Bordélique teased her sister again.

Then she turned to Ermias.

"You should pursue Nellie if you really love her. You mustn't allow oceans and continents to discourage you."

"At your age I too have believed in the omnipotence of self-will. The truth is, I am not sure if I still love Nellie. Having feelings doesn't mean I still love her. Nellie distanced herself long before the ocean emerged which has now divided us. Moreover, I dread reliving the indeterminate swing between hope and despair."

"You cannot deserve owning a treasure you have not sought earnestly."

"The truth is that I don't know what I want in life right now."

"Really?" Rhoda asked.

"Really."

"But you are determined to join Cambridge. That's what Bordélique meant by earnestly seeking."

"So?"

"You value education more than anything else, like Aster," Rhoda remarked cautiously.

"I can't contest this claim."

"So, there is some contradiction in your statement."

"It's not necessarily a contradiction, my dear. To value something and to want something are two different things."

"You cannot want something you don't value."

"Oh, Rhoda, must we be philosophical?" Bordélique protested.

"But you should be careful," Rhoda went on, still cautiously, "that the sacrifice you make for your education isn't too much."

"What sacrifice are you talking about? I haven't given up anything for the sake of education. I'd have been somewhere else by now had I pursued education with all my strength."

"You may not be conscious of it, but you value education more than anything else."

"That can be true, I own. But I've not sacrificed anything for the sake of education. Since we're talking about romance, it wasn't I who decided to break up with Nellie. She was the one who rejected me."

"Don't we all value education more than anything else right now? I do!" observed Bordélique looking at her sister questioningly.

"We do, it's true. But that's not what I meant."

"So what did you mean exactly?"

"I raised this issue because Ermias said he didn't know what he wanted in life and I'm sure he knows what he wants."

"We shall put this matter to rest," said Bordélique and stood up.

Ermias had intended to take them out for dinner but they insisted on cooking together. So, on their way to his apartment, they went shopping. Rhoda declared that she had become a vegetarian and lectured them about the benefit of avoiding meat. So they decided to shop for vegetables and rice. In the evening Rhoda cooked and Ermias made salad. Bordélique, laying the table, shared with them her desire to take a one year break after her abitur in order to give a voluntary service in Africa. But she had not decided yet where she wanted to go.

The following day he took them to the university, which was half-deserted because of the lecture-free week and showed them around. The *Mensa*, too, was half deserted, but there were enough eyes, sufficiently curious and furtive to fix themselves upon the trio. Even King Saul when he first saw young David going forth against the Philistine giant would not have been taken by comparable surprise.

Then they drove off to Prague on Friday, late in the afternoon, and arrived shortly before six. After showering and having rested briefly, they went directly to the Old Town to visit the astronomical clock, *Josefov*, and the Charles Bridge. As they were returning to the Old Town to search for a restaurant, they eavesdropped on an old British couple who were talking about their visit to the Kafka Museum earlier that day. Bordélique was excited to hear the name Kafka, so she asked the couple where the museum was. It turned out that it was on the other side of the Charles Bridge.

"But it should be closed by now, love," the old lady told Bordélique.

But Bordélique insisted on going back and Rhoda and Ermias obliged. The museum was indeed closed, but it was sufficient for Bordélique to see it from outside, for Kafka was one of her favourite writers. Then they returned to the Old Town and found a quiet bohemian restaurant at an isolated corner, where they ate for a modest price delicious *Svíčková na Smetané* served with dumplings, cream, and cranberries.

The next day, they went early in the morning all the way up to the castle on foot and after an hour-long round visit sat inside the cathedral quietly for about half an hour. They had lunch thereafter in a cafeteria behind the castle.

It was already twenty past four in the afternoon when they returned to their hotel, following a different route. The girls decided to take shower and rest, because they had agreed to go out in the evening one more time. Ermias too retired to his room and had a nap for an hour. In the evening they went back to Charles Bridge to take pictures, engulfed by a swarm of tourists.

On Sunday they overslept and nearly missed their breakfast. But thanks to the steadfast Rhoda, they made it to breakfast just on time. They left Prague at midday and arrived in Dresden ninety minutes later, returned the car and had a snack together at the main train station. Then the train arrived and

Ermias saw the girls off. After their departure, he felt empty and abandoned and wandered aimlessly for a long time along caliginous and deserted streets, trying to decipher the graffiti scribbled on the ruins of lonely and forgotten buildings.

His condition must have had a stronger effect on the girls than he imagined, for Martha called the following day to announce that she herself would be coming to Dresden on Friday. She tried to make light of her coming, alleging that the girls were excited about their trip and had induced her to visit Dresden, but it was obvious why she wanted to come. Ermias too made light of her intention to visit him, even though he was upset and felt betrayed by the girls.

On Friday, he picked her up from the airport and after she had showered and rested, they went out to the main *Mensa* and had lunch there. Then he took her to the Old Town and in the evening they dined at Augustiner an der Frauenkirche, talking about Dresden and university life, but nothing of a particularly personal nature. As soon as they returned to his apartment, however, she came straight to the point.

"Now let's talk about you. You seem preoccupied. What's the matter?"

He was standing near the window, trying to determine how much weight she had gained and why her hips looked wider. She was sitting on a chair in front of him, next to his study table. He pretended not to have understood what she wanted to know, but she was unmoved. He stared at the table top vacantly in silence, sheepishly smiling.

What could he possibly tell her?

And we all go with them, into the silence funeral
Nobody's funeral, for there was no one to bury.[d]

On Margate Sands.
I can connect
Nothing with nothing.[e]

"Perhaps you are in love with someone?"
"Not really."
"Perhaps someone has rejected you?"
He kept silence.
"You can tell me. I don't need to tell you that you can be frank
with me."
"If you are thinking of a particular girl, my answer is no."
"It's obvious someone has hurt you and that breaks my heart."
She, too, was now looking at the table top. He felt sadness
rising from within him.
"You'll have to change university!" she said decidedly. "I'll
talk to Frank about it."
That would be a defeat, which he could not accept under any
circumstances. He would even regard securing an admission to
Cambridge at this stage as cheating. Besides, what guarantee
would there be that things would be different elsewhere.
"That won't be necessary."
"You're far away from all of us."

"That won't be necessary, really," he repeated with determination. "I admit I've a problem, but it's one from which I'll not run away. It may take me some time and require some sacrifice, but it's necessary for me to solve it here and by myself."

He was glad nonetheless she wanted to talk to him about his problem. This was the first time he had acknowledged aloud that he had a problem. As soon as the confession was made, it brought with it an immediate sense of relief. He went up to her, pulled a chair across, sat in front of her, and took her hands in his.

She held his hands tightly and silently for a while and then she said, "I know, you want me to shut up, so I'll shut up for now. But if things don't get better soon, promise me we'll talk about it frankly."

He promised.

"I'll get it sorted out quickly," he reassured her.

Afterwards she interrogated him about the university, the professors, the girls, and the people in general, trying to gather enough evidence which would enable her to arrive at a definite conclusion.

Chapter 9

Martha's visit facilitated the process for him to accept his condition in its multifaceted form. He owned, for instance, with little additional suffering that he was shy, possibly suffering from a deficiency of confidence, and that his condition was exposed to the public when he was ill-prepared. He was willing to forgive himself and to get on with his life with whatever wisdom he had acquired from the fall. In order to regain his self-confidence and to make up for his shyness, he deemed it necessary not only to be successful and to distinguish himself in his studies, but also to be downright honest with himself.

The one and only defeat he had to experience time and again was the fact that not one girl was interested in him. The reason why the struggle had become continuous and hurtful was that he was always ready to put down his guard and see hope in every accidental or tendentious smile.

Three years ago, in Bryant Park, he had equated the shedding of leaves to the death of human cells and the inevitable and irreversible dissolution of the individual. In some sense, he still saw it that way. But when he recalled his science instruction from elementary school, he also recalled that deciduous trees do not give up their leaves in vain. Anticipating a harsh and destructive winter, the trees willingly give their leaves up through the process of abscission, which enables them to conserve water and energy, so that they are able to survive the forgetful winter.

At the onset of an abscission process, the trees re-absorb valuable nutrients from their leaves and store them in their roots. One of the first chemicals to be broken down during an abscission is chlorophyll, the very sign of richness of life and splendour and the essential element which gives the leaves their power to transform carbon dioxide and water into glucose and oxygen in good seasons. Once the abscission process is completed and the leaves are shed, the trees produce protective layers of cells on the exposed areas. In a way, it is an act of palliation, a mechanism the trees adopt for protecting their wounds from cold and snow, the only skill Ermias felt he was unable to master...

One of the wisest decisions he had made that semester was dropping experimental physics in order to focus on his research project, which he pursued with all his energy. With that project, the process of redeeming his reputation slowly began. It took him a month longer than expected to complete, but it was a foretaste of the immense pleasure he would get from pursuing a research career.

His supervisor helped him to set simple and clear objectives, to define precise methods in order to achieve his objectives, to organise his time and his steps, and to render himself articulate, both in oral presentations and in written work. The two of them warmed to each other slowly, but by the time Ermias was halfway through his work, they had already managed to establish trust and to respect one another. All the same, he felt that his supervisor regarded him as a freak, but that was all right with Ermias.

After Ermias had presented the results of his project, his supervisor offered him a job as his assistant, which meant saying "goodbye" to parcel packing. Parcel packing paid well, but on occasions, Ermias had been under the apprehension that the sheer monotony and lonesomeness of the job would drive him to madness. Besides, he could now save his semester breaks for other activities.

All the same Ermias decided to pack parcels once again in summer and announced to his parents that he would not be coming to Addis. Rhoda would be joining the University of Gottingen in the upcoming winter semester. Bordélique and he were intending to surprise her with a trip to Paris in September, for which he needed some money. He was also planning to use the remaining time for self-study, because he was intending to add two elective courses in winter, so that he could write his thesis and take some additional courses in his last semester at the university.

Moreover, he did not feel ready to meet his parents and his grandmother. The news of his not coming home in the summer upset all of them, but what was to be done? One rarely suffers in isolation, for pain can never be the exclusive property of a singular individual.

Part IV
Cambridge

Chapter 1

After what seemed like an eternity of waiting and two daunting interviews, Ermias was finally admitted to Cambridge with a full scholarship. Cambridge. It was the biggest "yes" in his life. When he regarded the whole process in retrospect, what a terrible gamble it had been to invest his entire conatus in joining Cambridge, knowing how slim the chances were! Indeed, he had resigned himself to imagining what his life would be like in the most likely event of rejection. Until the first invitation arrived towards the end of April in his final year, he was able to distract himself with other things, such as books, sport, studying, holidays, and people. From the day the first email arrived, however, all of these distractions ceased to have any further appeal to him. He did not dare to dream or hope, but at the same time he could not help dreaming and hoping about Cambridge. Why he should regard studying at Cambridge as being so vital to his happiness, or how he could allow his happiness and fulfilment to be entirely dependent on a singular and uncertain goal, Ermias was unable to explain to himself then or thereafter.

The first interview took place at Cavendish Lab and was focused on his academic competence. As he was waiting for his turn outside the meeting room he was painfully nervous, his heart was pounding, his palms and his back were sweating, and he had this terrible feeling that he was floating in space and desperately wished to touch ground.

> *… I was neither*
> *Living nor dead, and I knew nothing,*
> *Looking into the heart of light, the silence.*[f]

Then it was his turn and he was admitted into a small room wherein five people sat on chairs surrounding an elliptical table in the middle of the room. He had been asked to introduce himself, explain why he wished to study at the University of Cambridge, and what his future ambitions were. After the Chairman had introduced him to the group, he offered Ermias the floor. As soon as Ermias began talking, he touched ground and felt calm.

He was hoping that the story of an Ethiopian lad who was conceived whilst his mother was competing at an international athletics event, was born before his mother had completed her study, was subsequently raised by his grandmother whilst his mother pursued a master's degree in the Netherlands, moved to

Gottingen at the age of six and returned home at the age of eleven, moved to New York at the age of sixteen and moved again from there to Dresden two years later, always because either his mother or he himself was pursuing a good education, would be interesting for the panel.

And indeed it was. When Ermias finished his talk, friendly eyes were looking at him. Then the actual interview began, lasting exactly an hour, during which time Ermias was asked to answer some specific questions in the fields of electromagnetism, statistical mechanics, condensed matter physics, high energy physics, and astrophysics. He had been warned to prepare for these subjects and he understood the legitimacy of the questions related to condensed matter physics, for that was the field he wished to specialise in, but he did not expect the questions to be at once so comprehensive and so detailed.

Some of the questions were simply beyond his comprehension, whereas others he could answer only speculatively. Towards the end, he came to the realisation that he might indeed fail the interview after all and that he should be ready to face reality. The interview finished on time and then Ermias was passed to the care of two postgraduate students and an elderly assistant to the tutor, who showed him the Lab and, after an hour's intermission, Peterhouse College, his preferred college.

As Ermias read the names of forty Nobel Laureates and some of the notable academic staff who had worked at the Lab since its opening in 1874, he was awestruck. Iconic figures such as Sir J.J. Thomson, Ernest Rutherford, and Brian Josephson, were amongst them. The two students stayed with him for twenty minutes or thereabout, explaining dutifully how the Lab was structured and functioned, how he could organise his lectures in consultation with his supervisor, and what prerequisites were required to undertake a research project. Then they wished him good luck and went back to their business.

After an hour, Ermias met the deputy tutor at Peterhouse who explained to him how the college functioned, the different opportunities and obligations pertaining to accommodation, dining halls, student clubs, and all that sort of stuff for twenty minutes, and then, he too wished him good luck and dismissed him. Ermias had been feeling hollow and pretentious all the time, but as soon as he was left alone, he was glad that it was all over. He had planned to visit the main library during the two hours he was staying in Cambridge before he had to take a coach to Stansted, but now he lost the motivation. Instead, he spent the time inside a cafeteria near Churchill College and from there he walked to Parkside to take the coach to Stansted. From Stansted he flew to Leipzig, all the time feeling despondent and nursing a vague sense of humiliation.

He endured a sempiternal suspense following his visit to Cavendish Lab, longing to relinquish his hope of a place at Cambridge and instead commence with applications to other universities, but he was not able to bring himself to do so. He had neither the motivation nor the peace of mind to submit application letters. His undergraduate thesis required lots of measurements, analysis, and writing. Whilst he could do the first two, almost mechanically, he was not able to carry out the third task. During the interminable wait, he was sleeping on average four hours a day or perhaps less. Fortunately, his strict running discipline compensated for his lack of sleep and enabled his body to suffer the stress, the suspense, and the waiting.

A week later, the second invitation arrived for an online interview, which was to be conducted by his future supervisor and two fellows. This time the focus was on his research methodology and experience. But first they gave him a brief overview of some of their research projects related to superconductors and nanosensors and explained the research background and the academic competence they were looking for in prospective applicants. Then he was asked to explain the aim of his Bachelor thesis, his experience with statistical models and tools, and his data collection and analysis methods. Thanks to his student job, he had the privilege and the opportunity of working with advanced measurement and simulation devices, so this time he spoke freely and naturally, as one who had first-hand experience. Compared with the first interview, he found this one to be congenial, to the point, and encouraging, and his hope of securing an acceptance was greatly revived.

Towards the end of the interview, however, the professor wished to know about his readiness to work in a team and subtly hinted at the apparent reservation of one of his references in this regard. Ermias suspected that the person in question must have been the professor in whose research team he was writing his thesis, for the other two could have said next to nothing about his social aptitude since he was one of hundreds of students who attended their lectures.

Ermias had met the professor once and once only, and very briefly, during a presentation he gave in front of the professor and his research team. The professor raised a couple of questions after the talk and then left the room in a hurry, apologising that he had to attend an important meeting with the dean of the faculty. Ermias never saw him again. If the professor had questioned Ermias' capacity to work in a team, he must have been reflecting the concern of his PhD student, who was the immediate thesis supervisor.

The issue was indefensible, because during his first visit to Cavendish Lab, the professor himself would have noticed his shyness and his struggle to maintain steady eye contact. After a brief hesitation Ermias told him the truth as he saw it.

"We won't be assessing your qualification merely on the basis of this particular aspect," the professor reassured him when he was finished and commented that amongst the brightest people who had studied and worked at the University of Cambridge, some were not commended for their social aptitude.

A week later the conditional acceptance notification arrived by post and, with it, so many documents to fill out and submit.

Chapter 2

Ermias recalled how his father had once argued in favour of the existence of heaven. His father maintained that there were places and people even on earth which inspired others in extraordinary ways to love and to do great and unexpected things. After Ermias joined the University of Cambridge, he sort of understood what his father meant. In some respects, his first year at Cavendish Lab reminded him of Fraulein Maria who, wonderstruck and yet inquisitive, was irresistibly drawn to those majestic and mysterious doors during her first visit to the villa of Captain von Trapp. Ermias too was in love with everything the Lab possessed and stood for and was desirous to discover and experience it intimately.

His college was the oldest college in Cambridge and relatively small, located not very far from the main college area but far away to avoid the hustle and bustle of tourists. It was also located next to Coe Fen where he could run whenever he felt like it. He would later discover, to his great delight, that the college was one of the richest and the most generous colleges in terms of bursaries. In good weather, it took him about ten minutes to cycle to Cavendish Lab, but when he had to walk it took him about twenty minutes, the only disadvantage of being at Peterhouse.

On his first day at Peterhouse, Ermias met Andrew Kakuma in the combination room playing chess with three fellow students. All of them were overseas students who had been with Peterhouse since their undergraduate years and knew each other very well. They received Ermias warmly and invited him to play, but he was novice in chess and was content to watch. Apparently, Andrew was the master player and each was eager to beat him. They called him Saint Andrew, for he was a devout Christian. After the chess, Andrew suggested going for a walk. Ermias elected to join him but the others decided to go to the College Bar.

"You are from Ethiopia, right? I've heard about your coming," Andrew began when they were going outside.

He was a good looking, slightly heavy set and tall person, about as old as Ermias was. His eyes were big and liquid and his appearance was calm and composed. His voice was base and gentle.

Ermias told him briefly about himself and his stay in New York and Dresden. In return, Andrew told Ermias about himself. He came from a small town in Kenya and had two elder sisters, both married, and a younger brother. His father was a pastor to a large Pentecostal church and his mother was a nurse. Andrew also related details of his undergraduate stay at Cambridge and some of the challenges he had faced as a newcomer. He was studying chemistry towards his MPhil. Then Andrew asked Ermias whether he had a girlfriend, and Ermias answered in the negative.

"The most important thing is not to rush into a relationship, if you can help it. Many are eager to fall in love, which is understandable, but Cambridge is very demanding, the terms are short, and the pace is fast. My advice to you, if I may give you some, is to first take time to acquaint yourself with the university's expectations and demands before you delve into something serious."

Ermias assured Andrew that he had no plan to rush into any relationship in the near future.

"This is a wise decision. You are not here by accident," he chuckled good-naturedly. "If you are prudent, you'll be all right. Many are distracted from their course on account of women."

Even though it was true that Ermias was not ready to commit himself to a relationship, he was, at the same time, dying to have a sexual encounter with a woman, but it sounded unbecoming to confess this to Andrew.

"Do you have a girlfriend?" Ermias asked Andrew in his turn.

"I have a fiancé," was his reply.

Ermias asked him where she was from and what she was doing. Andrew told him that she was in Nairobi and that she worked as an accountant.

"How long have you known each other?"

"Since we were twelve. We grew up together. Her father and my father, and her mother and my mother are friends."

"Do you love her?"

"What do you mean?"

"I was just wondering."

"Of course I love her." Andrew laughed.

"Sorry, but I know people who are engaged because their parents wished them to be."

"In our case it's based on pure love."

"Lucky you!" Ermias retorted.

He always felt jealous, and at times even envious, when he met people who were in love, for he painfully felt that this vital element was missing from his life.

"I've never been truly in love in my life. I once was nearly in love with a girl in New York but she rejected me and I got over it in less than three months. Now I'm not entirely sure if I'm capable of loving."

"Oh, you say that because you are young."

Andrew looked at Ermias kindly, as if he were much older in age and wiser.

"This sort of dilemma is common amongst young people," he added.

"When did you realise that you were in love?"

"The first time I met her, I suppose."

"This can't be."

"But it's true. They moved to our town when I was twelve. The first Sunday they came to our church my parents invited them to have lunch with us, and they accepted the invitation. Since then the two families have been very close. Since about that time I knew I would one day marry her."

"Suppose she had rejected you?"

"Why should she reject me?"

"For all sorts of reasons."

"This would never happen instantly, would it? Then our relationship would have taken a different direction and this direction would have been both acceptable and painless for both of us."

"You don't believe that one's rejection may come as a surprise?"

"I don't believe in surprises, not in this sense anyway, as long as one is honest and perceptive. Surprises happen as a consequence of self-deception."

They walked in silence and then Andrew asked Ermias whether he had friends in Dresden. He told him that he had none.

"What do you mean you had none, didn't you say you stayed there for three years?"

"That's right, but I didn't have any friends."

Andrew looked at Ermias to make sure that he was not joking. When he realised that Ermias was in earnest, he added, "That must have been difficult."

"Yes, it has been."

Ermias hesitated for a moment and then add:

"Can you imagine, often weeks and months would pass in succession without talking with a single individual. It was then that I understood for the first time why C. S. Lewis chose *The*

Silent Planet as a title for one of his books. There was even a time when I was tempted to regard my life as worthless."

"I see what you mean. The value we attach to life isn't something unassailable. Even Prince Hamlet at one point regarded the starry heavens as *a foul and pestilent congregation of vapours*."

"I sometime question myself whether I have unlearned the ability to relate with people."

"I'm sure you haven't unlearnt it, otherwise the subject wouldn't interest you. A person who's lost his appetite doesn't wish to talk a lot about food. The fact that this is your preoccupation testifies that you're still yearning for a relationship."

"But I still feel uneasy whenever I'm with people. I wasn't like this before."

Andrew stopped and regarded Ermias compassionately and was hesitant for a brief moment before he put the next question.

"Did you feel rejected?"

"It is difficult to answer. The people were invariably polite and helpful, always careful not to do me injustice. But they were shy and reserved, particularly the girls. It seemed to me, um, that they were afraid that I might misunderstand or misjudge them or take liberty of their openness."

"How did you manage?"

"I clung to the hope of one day joining Cambridge. But it was very tough. I cannot tell you how many times I questioned the purpose of my suffering and the meaning of my life. Loneliness is a vicious foe. It makes you forget all the beautiful and great things in life and forces you to fix your attention on a singular need, namely the ceaseless yearning to have someone beside you.”

“Loneliness can really be vicious, as you rightly put it, I know this from experience.”

“There was this woman I knew. She was the sister-in-law of my landlord, about fifty years old. She had no children and her husband had died some years ago, before I came to Dresden. For some reason, she wasn’t admitted into the landlord’s house, but kept trying in vain. I sometimes met her on the streets and many times in the university library and in the library cafeteria. When she read books or drank coffee she looked like any other person, but when she was on the street, I could tell that something wasn’t right with her. She was always alone, always well dressed, though her clothes were a little shabby and unironed. I felt very sorry for her and often wondered what reason she had to wake up in the morning every day and face the day. Then I asked myself whether I was by any measure any different from her. It was a heart-breaking experience.”

“Life is an onerous burden for the lonely,” Andrew agreed and added, “But this is the cost of civilisation, don’t you agree? The more human beings strive to be civilised, the more elevated becomes their self-consciousness. Elevated self-consciousness in return magnifies their deficiency rather than their surplus of resources. And the sense of deficiency always repels people from one another as well as from God. Deficiency is never a unifying trait, as some would like to believe.”

"But if we accept the assertion that human beings are given free will, doesn't this entail consciousness?"

"Paradoxically, it does." Andrew replied thoughtfully.

Ermias had so many questions to ask Andrew, but he did not want to overwhelm him in their first meeting. As they were approaching the river, Andrew stopped.

"Listen, in half an hour I'm going to my room to practice guitar with a brother. If it doesn't bore you, you may come and watch us. But we won't be communicative, we have to concentrate."

Ermias did not have anything to do, so he accepted the invitation. They spent the remaining time walking along the Backs by the River Cam, now talking about the upcoming semester.

Chapter 3

Andrew had been absolutely right in maintaining that the pace at Cambridge was fast. In less than two weeks, Ermias had more than enough on his study table and, to his consternation, he realised that his background in random vectors, which was indispensable for almost all the courses he was taking, was not strong enough. This realisation had distressed him for a few days when he met Andrew at supper one evening. Andrew asked him how he was coping and when he heard the trouble Ermias was experiencing, he recommended a lecture on random variables and stochastic processes.

"I know a certain Dr. Masson who lectures on this subject. He is a little peculiar and his lectures are not frequented by so many students, but I recommend that you attend one of his lectures. As far as statistics is concerned, you will find no better person."

And so on Friday afternoon Ermias went to attend the only lecture Dr. Masson was offering that term. Just as Andrew purported, there were only four students: a female Erasmus student from Portugal and three other male students, two Chinese and an Indian.

Dr. Masson was in his mid-forties, short and scraggy, with a relatively big head and poorly kempt, long, curly brown hair. His ears were large and protruding. From his red, bloated, and unshaven face Ermias suspected that he drank heavily. His dress was formal, but he wore no tie. His clothes, particularly his old grey coat, appeared to be a size larger on his body, as if they were not his own.

He was about to start a new chapter that day, having already summarised probability theory the previous week. He began his lecture by claiming that there was no device or instrument on earth which could measure the temperature of the room or the distance of the earth from the sun or the weight of a person with a hundred percent accuracy. He explained that if one were to use a highly sophisticated device and repeatedly measure with it a fixed parameter, each time when the measurement was taken one would obtain a different value, even though some values would be more likely to be observed than others.

"We can approach reality but never touch it. Our perception of reality is an approximation containing an error. At a quantum level, this error obeys Heisenberg's Uncertainty Principle, but as we move away from quantum reality and towards macro reality the error accumulates. Fortunately, it rarely attains a magnitude so as to make existence intolerable. It is this uncertainty we wish to characterise as a random variable."

Dr. Masson went on to describe a random variable.

"But when we say random, we don't mean haphazard. The value of a random variable is governed by an underlying probability density function which assigns a probability to each possible outcome."

In the subsequent weeks, Dr. Masson seemed to oscillate between the ideologies of Albert Einstein and Werner Heisenberg as far as his understanding of uncertainty was concerned. Einstein maintained that existence is essentially deterministic and obeys a set of fixed and immutable laws. Thus, our uncertainty arises due to our ignorance or lack of evidence. Heisenberg, on the other hand, maintained that uncertainty is inherently embedded in Creation and, therefore, we are uncertain, partly because Creation itself behaves in a random fashion, even though the randomness appears to be bound by probabilistic laws.

One day, after the lecture session was over and the other students were gone, Ermias approached Dr. Masson and raised this issue. The lecturer was collecting his old papers and putting them back into his old and faded leather briefcase. He listened without interrupting his task, but when Ermias was finished with speaking, he raised his head and gave Ermias his full attention.

"Call me Brian," he offered before addressing the concern Ermias had just highlighted. Since he had left New York, Brian was the first authority Ermias could recall, who was willing to be addressed by his first name. In Dresden the professors addressed their students with great formality and expected them to return the favour.

"You've correctly observed my dilemma," Brian went on, closing his briefcase and standing erect. "Oscillation is the fate of living by faith, for no one knows exactly how Creation actually behaves. All are but plausible explanations."

Then he explained for about twenty minutes the different theories of randomness in Nature and their merits and demerits. Ermias quickly realised how profound his understanding was in this area and how, by comparison, shallow was his own knowledge.

"You must read Baruch de Spinoza's *Ethics* in order to fully appreciate why Einstein committed himself to causal determinism despite his inability to disprove Heisenberg," he encouraged Ermias.

Ermias promised to read the book and left. This was the first time in many years that he found someone with whom he could discuss a serious issue without being self-conscious or superfluous. From then on, whenever Brian had some spare time, the two discussed similar issues after the end of the lecture and Ermias felt that Brian was enjoying the discussion as much as he did.

But his lecture was not making appreciable progress as much as Ermias had hoped. Despite his depth of knowledge or, perhaps, just because of it, Dr. Masson exhibited the tendency to wander off course during his lecture. At times, Ermias had difficulty following him and often he was anxious that the much needed knowledge was trickling so slowly that he might not be able to benefit from it that term. By comparison, all the other lectures were moving forward at a frightful speed to the extent that Ermias was worried and even thought of dropping his lecture course altogether. But he decided against it, for Brian was a great lecturer. Ermias asked him, instead, to offer him a consultation hour, to which Brian readily agreed.

The next day Ermias went to Wilberforce Road to see Brian. He was not expecting much from their first meeting thinking that his immediate problem was too specific for Dr. Masson to offer a direct answer without prior preparation and that he might digress as usual. But to his surprise and great relief Brian came straight to the point and wished to know the difficulties Ermias was facing. Ermias explained his difficulty with functions of multiple random variables:

"Determining the probability density functions requires multiple integrals for which there's no simple solution, if there is one at all."

Brian asked Ermias to show him some specific examples and when he showed him, he studied them carefully.

"Um, you need to remember two or three facts about random variables," he began at long last. "Unlike the integration of functions dealing with normal variables, the geometry of integration, in the case of random variables, is never a fixed region. Its structure changes according to the specific range of values the random variables take. Secondly, when, as a result of a given geometry, the equation becomes difficult to integrate, you can take advantage of the fact that the probability of an event plus its complement is always one, which means the probability of an event can be expressed in terms of its complementary event, which means, again, you can alternatively integrate the complementary region. But the most important thing is to remember how to determine the limits of integration."

Brian began with the examples Ermias gave him and skilfully demonstrated how the geometry of an integral changed when the domains of the random variables changed. As soon as he had explained the changing nature of the geometry of an integral and the complementary feature of probabilistic events, the veil was lifted up and Ermias was able to see clearly. The problem which had daunted him for more than a month thus suddenly vanished.

As their session was drawing to a close, there was a knock on the office door and in came two men. One of them was a white man whereas the other was of mixed race. The former, whose name was Jason Brown, was about the same age as Brian, but the other, who introduced himself simply as Bishop, was much younger, most likely in his early thirties. Ermias learned later that his mother was English and his father was either from Zimbabwe or Zambia, he forgot which.

"He read English at King's," Brian told Ermias, referring to Bishop, but he did not mention what he was now doing. Jason was a mathematician and a fellow of Christs College. From the way they had entered the room and had taken their seats Ermias conjectured that the three were friends. He thanked Brian for his help and was about to leave, but Brian invited him to stay.

"We are going out to a pub; you can join us if you wish."

Ermias first thought he was joking and looked at him in bewilderment.

"Or, perhaps, you have another engagement?"

"Oh, n—o. I'd be glad to come. I just hadn't expected the invitation."

"Why not?"

"Never mind," he mumbled still a little bewildered. "I'd be happy to join you."

The quartet went to The Eagle and Ermias stayed with them for an hour. Brian and Bishop discussed American politics and Ermias and Jason listened. Jason seemed rather taciturn, but listened to the conversation with interest.

Chapter 4

The next time Ermias met Brian outside of the lecture theatre was some weeks before Christmas. He went alone one evening to Fitzbillies to have tea and there, sitting at a corner, he saw Brian having coffee. Bishop and Andrew were also with him. Ermias greeted them and was going to sit somewhere alone but Brian invited him to join them.

As it happened, Brian and Andrew were arguing about the afterlife. Bishop, stretching his left leg out leisurely and setting his right leg in constant motion, was listening. There was a faintly visible mocking smile forming at the right corner of his lips, but he seemed to be enjoying the argument. After Ermias had placed his order, the two continued on from where they had left off.

"Everything I am is stored in my memory," Brian began, "my likes and dislikes, my virtues and vices, my skills, my good and bad experiences, my knowledge of people, everything. Indeed, it can be said that my memory is who I truly am. If something is removed from my memory permanently, some part of me dies forever. I cease to exist when everything in my memory perishes permanently. So, if God resets my memory in heaven after my earthly death, then the earthly I no longer exist. Which means no part of me exists in heaven, and in this sense alone, it can truly be said that I'm a new creation. But God can and, indeed, should also do this to everyone, regardless of his past, should the past have absolutely no part in the future. If he has to reset a person, then no virtue or vice should serve as the basis for it. In which case, it doesn't matter whether one has been good or evil on earth in order to be deserving of an afterlife. If, on the other hand, my identity should matter and be preserved in heaven so that I may continue to exist as I'm known to God as well as to myself and others, then God should leave my memory intact, that is, he mustn't selectively remove a part of my memory which doesn't fit into his plan in heaven. In which case, there'd be no essential difference between my earthly life now and my life in heaven in the future, which also means that death and an afterlife don't make sense. Whichever way you see it, the justification for an afterlife doesn't hold water."

"You're assuming, of course, that the meaning you attach to the data you store in your memory persists forever, which isn't true even here on earth. Even if we assume that the data persist forever, they may have an entirely new significance under a different light. What makes bad memory offensive is often the shame and pain associated with it. I believe shame and pain are earthly properties. Who knows, if God somehow destroys shame and pain as well as time, the human memory can be redeemed and made useful. I believe that God can redeem not only the future but also the past, only I don't know how."

"In which case, all shall be saved?"

"Again, God will not take away human freedom, for otherwise love and fellowship would be impossible. The redemption of memory requires human freedom."

From there the two branched off into an argument about the significance of human freedom, but Ermias stopped listening, because Bishop had presently asked him how he was doing with his studies. Ermias told him he was doing fine.

"I saw you a couple of times running near Coe Fen," Bishop remarked without looking at Ermias.

For some reason Ermias suspected that Bishop was a proud man. Perhaps this was because of his languid voice or the haughty look he always wore in his sharp face or the mocking smile lingering in his sensual lips.

"It's possible you've seen me." Ermias replied imitating his voice.

"I also saw you at Waterstones the other day, in the French literature section. You didn't see me, I suppose?"

"No, I didn't see you."

At this point Brian interjected to ask Ermias whether he enjoyed reading French literature. Ermias already knew that Brian enjoyed reading French literature, for he had seen a pile of French novels on his working table in his office and, besides, Brian always carried in his bag a novel which was, more often than not, a French novel.

"I do enjoy reading, but I don't have a particular preference for French literature. I don't know French, for a start."

"What sort of books do you read?"

"I'm not sure if I've any preference. Sometimes I get recommendations from the people I know and read those books."

"What do you like best in books?"

Ermias deliberated briefly.

"I like authentic characters as opposed to characters which are purely fantastical."

"That wasn't exactly the answer I was expecting. Let me rephrase my question: Why do you read books in the first place?"

"I don't have a single answer to this question. I read books for all sorts of reasons. Sometimes I read simply to occupy my mind."

Bishop drew his right leg back and sat properly and gave Ermias his mocking smile, thereby opening his mouth briefly, so that Ermias could be able to see his clean and white teeth, which were also large and remarkably even.

"Often I read books in order to peer into other people's mind," Bishop put in, "so that I can say, 'I'm not that different from all the rest after all', or 'this writer is not that different from me after all'."

"You mean you read books, so as to justify your way of life?" Ermias asked Bishop.

"So to speak, if you put it this way."

"This raises an interesting question," Brian observed looking at Bishop. "Why do people write books? I don't mean, of course, those who write merely to make money."

"Different people write for different reasons," Bishop said, "but the good ones write chiefly to make sense of their life, their feelings, and their thoughts. Others write to make sense of their surroundings insofar as they are affected by them."

Ermias was impressed by Bishop's observation as well as by the ease with which he expressed his mind.

"You seem to prefer reading French literature, though," he remarked turning to Brian.

"Incidentally, yes," Brian answered. "The books I have read have this authenticity about them: The characters are portrayed as they are, as opposed to how they should be and without the need to explain or psychoanalyse their very being and essence. This style of writing avoids the danger of the writer being perceived as a hypocrite. But more importantly, the books pay equal attention to the realm of thoughts and the realm of emotions. They are neither mistrustful of the faculty of emotions, as the British are, nor are they vulgar, like the Americans. The French seem to agree, in their own way, with Spinoza, who purports that both thoughts and emotions are expressions of one and the same source."

A little put off by his persistently mocking smile, Ermias asked Bishop what sort of books he read. Like Brian, he too happened to enjoy reading French literature. This partly explained why the two of them were close. Whilst Bishop was telling Ermias what sort of books he was reading, somehow Brian and Andrew had started off with a new subject, for he heard Brian explaining the difference between an American soul and a European soul.

"The European soul is a typical example where the cord binding the mind and the body is getting weaker in every generation. The only reason the mind still retains a set of ideas about the body is simply because it's fearful of total dissociation and that without these ideas there'll be no justification to keep the body and the soul from going asunder. The American soul, on the other hand, still retains the cord, which I call religion, but this cord is highly sensitive to noise and magnifies out of all proportions every idea it takes hold of."

Ermias stood up to say 'goodbye', but Brian brought out a slim book from his jacket pocket and offered it to Ermias to read. The book, *A Certain Smile*, was written by a certain François Sagan. Ermias was about to decline, giving his tight schedule as an excuse, but considering its volume, decided to accept the offer. Then, he apologised and left.

Later that same evening he met Andrew, this time in Peterhouse combination room, where Ermias expressed his appreciation of Brian's versatility.

"The unfortunate man." Andrew observed calmly but as if unintentionally.

"Why unfortunate man?"

"He feels like he's trapped."

"Trapped in what sense?"

"In life."

"Why?"

"I can't tell. It was just his expression."

"But why does he think he's trapped?"

"Maybe he feels that he can't change his situation."

"He seems to have many things to interest and occupy him. He's a voracious reader, for a start. I've seen him immersed in books several times."

"You see, he's the sort of person who needs some space. He's intelligent, inquisitive, and voracious, as you correctly observed. At the same time, he likes to be with people. But finding the right distance is not that easy, both for him and for the people concerned. He's been married and divorced twice. Then he lived with another woman on and off for three years, but she too left him recently. Now he's living entirely by himself. As he grows old, he finds it increasingly difficult to connect with people, which is why, I think, he feels like he's trapped."

"How do you know so much about his private life?" Ermias asked Andrew, but immediately regretted asking.

"Brian is an open book," was Andrew's reply.

Ermias finished the book that same evening, but was disappointed. For to him the characters, as well as the theme of the book, appeared to be rather prosaic and he could not ascertain the balance between thoughts and emotions to which Brian referred. The story was about a young and inexperienced law student who fell in love with an elderly, married lawyer, the uncle of her boyfriend. To make sure that he had not overlooked anything, he reread the book the next evening, but his impression of the book did not alter.

Three days later he arrived unannounced at Brian's office in order to return the book. Brian was sitting behind his work table with dishevelled hair and a pair of red eyes, still wearing his winter jacket and a scarf around his neck. He was visibly displeased to see Ermias and objected to his coming to see him without an appointment, adding with a resigned voice that he was ill-disposed for entertainment. Ermias apologised and told him the reason he had come, whereupon Brian pointed to the table carelessly and asked Ermias to leave the book there. It was obvious that he had been drinking, but Ermias saw neither a bottle nor a glass on his table. He put down the book on the table and left.

In the middle of the Lent term Ermias met Brian in London by accident. He was going to see *Endgame* at the Duchess theatre that evening. After having taken the tube from Finsbury Park, he alighted at Covent Garden and in front of the station he spotted Brian in the crowd. He was surprised to see him there but his first impulse was to avoid him and mind his own business. Apparently, Brian too had seen Ermias and came towards him.

"Hello," he greeted him with careless voice.

Ermias returned his greeting with a self-conscious smile.

"I'm awfully sorry for coming to your office the other day without an appointment."

"Never mind," he said, casually glancing at the people passing them by in both directions.

Then he asked Ermias how he found the book.

"I read it twice," Ermias replied evasively.

"I see that you didn't like it."

"I didn't have much time to properly analyse the book."

"The quality of the book lies in its prosaicness, in the struggle of the main character to make the most of a dull life, and in her ability to put a finger on her suffering and assign a cause to it."

"I recognised that much," Ermias reacted, pleased that Brian, too, saw the prosaicness of the story.

"Life is essentially prosaic for all of us, only our coping mechanisms are different."

Ermias watched Brian closely whilst he was speaking. He seemed to be absent-minded, as though he were forcing himself to speak. His hair was dishevelled, as on the previous occasion, and his clothes were creased and untidy, as if he had slept in them the previous night on a dry, uneven bench. His eyes too were inflamed and watery. Ermias wanted to ask him whether he was all right, but he lacked the courage.

"Anyway, what are you up to?" Brian asked presently.

Ermias told him.

"And you complain of a prosaic story?" he chuckled, for once being interested in the conversation. "All right, I don't want to keep you. Bye for now."

They parted company.

But Ermias had not gone three hundred metres towards the Duchess when he felt a tap on his shoulders. It was Brian.

"I'm sorry to bother you, but I need your help," he said.

"How can I help you?"

"I need to borrow some money. I lost my wallet two hours ago. It took me sometime to reconcile myself to the idea of borrowing money from you, my former student."

"How much do you need?"

"I need about two hundred, two hundred fifty pounds."

"Oh, I don't have that much money," Ermias replied, making a swift calculation in his mind. Having unwittingly replied *that much*, he felt obliged to offer Brian some money.

"Will a hundred do?"

"That will do, thanks. It should get me to Cambridge."

Of course, it will get you to Cambridge, Ermias retorted to himself. He himself had paid eighteen pounds to take the train from Cambridge to Finsbury Park ninety minutes ago. He was annoyed at himself for having been so generous since he was dubious as to whether Brian would pay the money back. But it was too late to change his mind, so he gave him the money and Brian returned to Covent Garden.

Chapter 5

On the first weekend of the Lent break, Andrew, Bishop, and Ermias had lunch together at the Eagle. Ermias had not seen Bishop since the evening they had met in the café. Bishop was dressed exquisitely and radiating virility and freshness and seemed to be quite pleased with his life. He told the others that he had been to Paris for six weeks, working for a publishing company and talked the whole time of the women he had met in Paris and how sophisticated and open-minded they had been.

Ermias did not know that Bishop and Andrew knew each other so well that he would have no qualms over bragging about his success with women in front of Andrew. This was also the first time he had spoken freely in the presence of Ermias. Andrew listened to him, apparently out of politeness, but Ermias was burning with jealousy and envy. Bishop must have understood his feelings, for after lunch, as Ermias was going to the lavatory, Bishop came after him.

"Hey, what are you doing next Saturday?"

Ermias thought briefly and told Bishop that he had not planned anything yet.

"There's going to be a hot party going on in Leicester. I'm going along with a friend. Do you fancy joining us?"

"I'd be delighted."

"We can give you a lift if you wish."

"What kind of party is it?"

"Hot university chicks will be coming from all over the UK. Maybe you can try your luck."

"Do I need a ticket?"

"Admittance is by invitation only. Entrance fee is seventy-five. No dress code. Just dress casual and be cool. You'll get a welcome drink for free but the rest you'll have to pay yourself."

"The entrance fee is damn expensive," Ermias complained.

"It's a classy party."

"Mmmm, I'm not sure…" Ermias lingered.

"I suppose you've been living a monk's life so far, so why not give it a shot this time?"

"I'll think about it."

Bishop gave Ermias his mocking smile and went to relieve himself.

"What does seventy-five pounds mean to me?" Ermias wondered in silence. Undoubtedly it was a handsome amount, almost sufficient enough to cover a one-month coffee expense. At the same time, however, his curiosity was already aroused.

But what type of a girl would he meet there? Who would be willing to pay money to meet a young man like himself?

"Do the girls pay that much?" he asked Bishop when the latter was done.

"Entrance is free for the ladies, but it's by invitation only."

"Who invites who?"

"The organisers, well-connected people."

The truth was that Ermias had not met a single girl in Cambridge so far, not for want of opportunities, but also because there was no spare time. He was unwilling to entangle himself into a committed relationship yet, being uncertain as to where his future lay.

"Why shouldn't I experience the world for seventy-five pounds, once in a lifetime?" he asked himself.

"All right, I'll come with you, thanks for the invitation," he said aloud.

Nevertheless, he gave Bishop his consent, for some reason, not gratefully, but grudgingly.

"Great!" Bishop exclaimed, ignoring the tone of the consent, and left without Ermias.

As soon as Bishop left, however, Ermias felt a microscopic pinch in his conscience and his peace was clouded with a vague consciousness of wrongdoing. He closed his eyes and tried to determine the reason. Was he being stingy or was there something else to it? What harm was there in enjoying a night out with friends after working hard for six months? What if this led to meeting "a chick", as Bishop had put it? Was he still being afraid of girls or beginning a relationship or even romance? He was unable to determine the cause of his pain.

Was this the sort of ability Brian was referring to when he spoke of Dominique and her ability to put a finger on her pain and assign a cause to it?

That evening Ermias received a brief email from Bishop telling him where and when he should wait for them on Saturday. Bishop also asked him to be punctual. The remaining days passed with Ermias feeling uneasy about his decision, during which time he also read *War and Peace*. The book gave him the distraction he needed and the excuse to avoid Andrew, who was a good friend.

Saturday arrived finally and Bishop and his friend too arrived by car at the appointed time and place. It was a cold, misty, and rainy evening and Bishop was driving. Sitting next to him was his friend, a middle-aged, short, fat man, possibly an Algerian. As Ermias took his seat at the back, Bishop greeted him with his languid gesture and feeble smile and asked him the usual questions about his studies.

As soon as they had left the city and joined the A7 motorway, however, they all fell silent, only the stereo, which was playing Simon & Garfunkel, was to be heard. Ermias removed his jacket, leaned back, and began to listen to the music. Since he was not driving, somehow he was able to appreciate the darkness, the rain, the silence, and the music, all of which collectively had such a swaddling, melancholic effect on him that he did not want the drive to end. But the drive, which took about two hours, came to an end when they arrived at their destination at ten minutes past eleven.

It was not really Leicester city that they had driven to but a village located some twenty-five miles south-west of Leicester. Bishop pulled the car up in front of an old villa which was too big to be a private house but at the same time was too small to be anything grander. They got out of the car. Bishop and his friend, who had not introduced himself for the entire duration of the journey nor had spoken a single word with Ermias, went forward and Ermias followed them.

"Oh, by the way," Bishop turned back and addressed Ermias, "audio and video recordings and taking pictures is strictly prohibited once we are inside. Eyes only."

Two elderly women with heavy makeup on their faces received them at the entrance and collected the entrance fees. The old villa was a one-storey house with a spacious foyer. A set of huge sofas was placed at each corner and four or five tall cocktail tables were standing in the middle without chairs or stools around them. There was a bar along one wall, on the left side of, and adjacent to, the entrance, for serving drinks and snacks. A long, wooden, winding staircase led directly to the first floor where there were many rooms, around seven or so, surrounding the foyer below in a circle. There were also some rooms on the ground floor. Ermias saw about twenty-five people in the foyer, most of them young, good-looking women, standing next to the tall tables and the bar.

Bishop entered the villa as one who was entering familiar territory. Girls swarmed in from different directions to greet him. His friend too was greeted in a familiar fashion. There were no formal introductions, only greetings. Then the newcomers proceeded to the bar and ordered their drinks.

Ermias was ordering lemonade when Bishop came up to him from behind and whispered into his ear.

"If I might make a suggestion, order something cheerful. Even if you don't usually drink alcohol, just order one and sip it slowly. Otherwise, you'll be a big bore."

"Then order something for me," Ermias retorted into his ear, suddenly irritated by Bishop's patronising attitude. But Bishop ignored the tone and ordered a cocktail of some sort for both of them. Ermias took a step back and stood next to the Algerian, who already had ordered his own drink. Whilst waiting for their order, they chatted, or rather Bishop chatted, with two young women, but as soon as their order was ready, the trio retreated to one of the corners and sat down on the empty sofa. Bishop and his friend talked about some article published by *Times* that day and Ermias listened. After twenty minutes or so, the two women from the bar joined them, bringing another woman with them. All of them had a drink in their hand.

The two women sat on either side of Bishop and started questioning him about Paris. Bishop told them about *Chicago*, which he had watched at the National Theatre in Paris. Apparently, the women knew Bishop very well. The third girl and the Algerian, if indeed, he was an Algerian, also engaged in a conversation, sitting side by side, and Ermias was left alone.

It was not the sort of party he was expecting, for there was neither music nor fancy lights. Nor was there any host who welcomed the guests. The guests simply entered the room, ordered their drinks, and mingled with one another, most of them preferring to stand. Shortly after their arrival, additional people arrived, most of them young women. Now there were plenty of women in the room, almost at a two-to-one ratio, all of whom were conspicuously young, whereas the men, except perhaps Ermias and Bishop, were conspicuously older, fifty or above. Ermias was on the verge of feeling out of place when he spotted a young woman standing next to a tall table in apparent isolation. She smiled at him when she saw him watching her. He smiled back and stood up and went over to her.

"Hey, what's up?"

She had a heavy accent. Still smiling, she extended her hand. He shook her hand and told her his name.

"I'm Tanya, nice to meet you."

She was not beautiful, but had a pair of well-shaped long legs. By contrast, her torso seemed shorter. Her face was round like a full moon and plain, neither attractive nor repulsive. She had short, fine, white blond hair, and was wearing a short, light-blue denim skirt with a pair of black leggings and a light-green blouse. Her chest was bare and the shape of her small breasts traceable beneath the blouse. He liked her plainness.

"Where are you from?" she asked him.

He was about to say *Cambridge* but people usually wished to know where he came from originally. So he told her.

"What do you do in the UK?"

He could tell that she was East European but could not tell which country she came from. Perhaps from Bulgaria or Romania, he guessed. He told her he was a postgraduate student at Cambridge.

"You look like an honest man," she commented, though her comment seemed out of place.

He put aside his intention to ask her where she came from and what she was doing. Then she said sweetly that she wanted to order a drink and he volunteered to accompany her. As they went to the bar, she told him that she was studying Business Management at Manchester University to obtain a Bachelor Degree. She said she had already a Master's Degree in the same field, but it was not recognised in the UK, which was why she was now studying the same subject, so that she could finish her studies and find a job as quickly as possible. This explained something, for Tanya seemed a little older than a typical undergraduate student.

She was easy to talk to but avoided talking about anything in particular. She placed her order and they stood near the bar talking about life in the UK as overseas students. When ten minutes later her order was ready, she suggested sitting down somewhere. Ermias agreed, but did not want to sit near Bishop and his friend. So, he took her to another corner and the two sat close to each other on a sofa and talked for a while. She liked to gently touch his arm, his wrist, his chest, and his chin whilst she talked. Ermias felt her warmth and smelt her perfume.

After midnight, the bright light was finally turned off and a disco ball went on rolling. Shortly thereafter, the tall tables were pushed aside and a samba began to play and people began to dance on the floor.

"Do you like it here?" whispered Tanya into his ears, very close to him.

He swallowed under the influence of her scent and warmth and nodded.

"This is your first time, am I right?" she asked him melodically.

Ermias had the same question on the tip of his tongue.

"Yes, and for you?"

"This is my second time."

"How did you end up coming here in the first place?"

"A friend invited me."

"Did you like it from the start?"

She laughed affectedly.

"It was strange but exciting. You'll enjoy it too, just you wait." As they watched the dancers in silence, Ermias became conscious of Tanya's burning hands touching his thigh. But he tried to fix his attention on the dancers. The men on the dance floor were very good at dancing, whereas most of the women appeared to be rather amateurish.

"Do you know how to dance a samba?" Tanya wished to know.

"I've never danced before," he confessed stupidly.

"Come let's dance!" she stood up cheerfully.

"I'll embarrass you," he warned her, but she pulled him up gently to his feet and led him to the dance floor.

He followed her reluctantly, at the same time, being irritated with himself for being so passive. She was not a good dancer herself but she did not care. She tried to imitate a nearby couple and furtively beckoned Ermias to do the same. Fortunately, the music faded, and the two returned to their seat.

"Can we order something to eat?"

Ermias agreed, and they went to the bar. She ordered a snack and another drink and Ermias ordered a snack and paid for both of them. In the meantime, another samba started and the floor was full once again with dancers. This time, however, the dancers were kissing and caressing one another freely, the men unbuttoning the shirts and blouses of their women and fondling them openly. When Ermias and Tanya returned to their sofa, they found a couple sharing their seat and kissing passionately.

"Wicked Cupid has sneaked in!" whispered Tanya suggestively into his ear, standing very close to him.

He felt her warm breath caressing his neck. Harnessing all his courage, he embraced her. She received his embrace with a feeble plastic smile but without moving. Then Ermias held her tighter and felt his own heart pumping hot blood into his entire body.

"Your heart is racing wild!" she whispered.

"I'm awfully galvanised. Do you mind if I kiss you?"

"You don't need to ask, you idiot," she replied laughing and encouragingly.

His lips searched for hers in the dim light and he kissed her softly. Then, he closed his eyes and held her tight and kissed her once again.

"Your lips are deliciously moist and fiery. Are you a virgin, may I ask?" she whispered.

He did not reply, but swallowed hard.

"Come, we do dancing," she said cheerfully and pushing him back gently, she led the way. Ermias followed her.

After the kiss, he had difficulty in detaching his body from Tanya's but she did not mind. Besides, all the couples surrounding them were more intimate and assertive than they.

"Listen," Tanya whispered seductively into his ear in the middle of things, "I got to go shortly."

Ermias stopped involuntarily.

"But why, we've only started to have fun."

"I know, but I've another appointment and it's getting late."

"At this time of the night?"

"But if you can send me by a taxi, I can stay with you for another hour. Then we can have a great time."

"Where do you want to go?"

"To Manchester."

"How much will that cost?"

"It'll be a little expensive because it's late and I only ride with a taxi driver I trust, because otherwise it can be pretty dangerous."

He was already worrying about his spending habit, having already noticed how expensive the drinks had been. A taxi to Manchester would most definitely be expensive.

"Tell me," he encouraged her nevertheless.

She came very close to him, draped her arms around his neck and talked in a whisper. He was already wondering why she always whispered.

"Four hundred."

"Dear me!" he exclaimed, completely taken by surprise. "That much money I don't have."

"You see, I'm a lady and I've to be very careful. But by way of compensation, if I stay with you, we can find a place where I can make love to you."

He closed his eyes in both pain and excitement and tried hard to think.

"So what do you think?" she whispered presently, her warm and toxic breath brushing across his face.

"But where can we go?" he asked in spite of himself.

"We shall sneak into one of the upper rooms. I'm sure we can find a place. My friend has told me that these rooms are available for guests."

She was right. He had seen couples going up into those rooms. He was in turmoil to the extent that he could neither concentrate nor decide what to do. Part of him was for it, but part of him was well aware that it would be sheer recklessness on his part to spend so much money on a woman of questionable standing.

"Look, I truly can't. I don't have that much money."

"How much can you afford?" she asked with a disappointed tone.

"I don't know. I guess I don't have the right to keep you..."

"I understand."

She stopped dancing and moved slowly to their place. He followed her, immensely relieved and feeling free and triumphant.

"I really began to like you."

Tanya turned back to face him and looked at him reproachfully. Meanwhile, an old gentleman came to them and invited Tanya to dance with him.

"Sorry I can't, maybe later," she rebuffed him, taking Ermias' right arm lightly and drawing closer to him. The gentleman apologised and retreated. They stood in silence for a while, facing one another closely.

"Well then, I'll take the risk. I'll take any taxi. Can you afford that? You can imagine how much courage this is costing me." He felt terrible but kept silence.

"Say something. You kissed me, you touched me, you put my body on fire, and then you want to let me go?"

'If I were to take her to a hotel,' he reasoned in the meantime, 'it would cost me half of the sum.'

He was surprised and a little shocked by his cold and matter-of-fact reasoning.

"I can afford a hundred and fifty, how about that?"

"Two hundred and we have a deal," she said looking at him appreciatively. Then she added, "You are a gentleman, I knew it."

Without waiting for his consent, Tanya stood in front of him and kissed him. She was a skilful kisser. His body reacted instantly and he felt the sudden rush of blood into his entire body once again.

"Come, why should we wait?" she said and led the way to the staircase.

None of the rooms was locked or free. None of the rooms was occupied by a single couple only. In one of the rooms, he saw Bishop in bed with the two women. His friend, the placid Algerian, was sitting on a chair in front of the bed, watching, and the little woman who was with him sitting on his lap, her upper body fully naked.

"We can share the room with them, if that's ok with you," Tanya looked at him mischievously.

Despite the electric current flowing through his veins, Ermias felt shocked and disgusted.

"Are you crazy?" he nearly shouted in disbelief.

"Look, all the rooms are occupied and we are impatient. Besides, if you are willing to put aside your prejudice, love-making is so commonplace. There's no shame in sharing it amongst friends."

"Sorry, I differ with your philosophy of love completely. I have to say no and goodbye."

"What do you mean 'goodbye'?" she shouted angrily.

He removed two twenty and two five notes from his purse and handed them to her.

"This will compensate for the time you wasted on me. I'm going."

Without waiting for her reaction, he turned back and descended the staircase in haste and left the house, but Tanya followed, running behind him.

"Come back, please. I'm sorry. I was only trying to be of help."

"Please go back. I'm done here."

"But where are you going at this time of the night?"

"I don't know, but I'll be fine."

"It's dangerous to walk in the streets alone, please come back."

"I appreciate it, really. But I'll be fine."

"At least let me relieve you."

Tanya quickly knelt down in front of him and tried to unzip his trousers, but he pulled her up.

"Thanks, but that won't be necessary. Here, take this."

He added another twenty-pound note, for at that time he was asking himself why he was leaving. Was it because it was expensive or was it because he thought it was inappropriate? Tanya turned back and Ermias was left alone. It was ten past two and the streets were completely deserted. He decided to go to the train station and wait there for the first train to Cambridge.

"What a waste, what a grand waste!" he scolded himself with extreme disconcert.

He stood indecisively for a long time, hesitating as to which direction he should take. Meanwhile, he was shivering with the cold, but he felt deeply offended to go back to the villa. Finally, he forced himself to take one of the directions.

He had walked for about forty minutes, as it turned out in the right direction, when he saw a taxi coming up behind him, which he then stopped. It was from the taxi driver that he learned where he was and from where he had come. To his great relief, the taxi driver asked only thirty pounds to take him to the central train station, which he instantly agreed to. As soon as he got in, he closed his eyes and felt the pulses in his temples throbbing.

"What a waste, what a grand waste!" he kept repeating.

Now that he was out of the villa and alone, he felt ashamed. Not only because he had nearly had sex with a prostitute but also because he was numbered in the league of those old people who had more than half-exhausted their lives. None of them seemed honourable to him now. And the women, all of them relatively young and foreigners, how badly must have they needed money to so abandon their dignity, he thought. But he felt wretched and disgusting in pronouncing judgement upon others knowing that he himself had behaved badly.

"How dishonest it feels to regard the whole situation from a false pedestal! I am a sick man ... I am a spiteful man. An unattractive man."

He tried to remember the book where he read the last verses, but could not recall.

"This is aimlessness. I wish I could stop thinking!"

He closed his eyes but opened them immediately.

"Oh, dear! How I wish that my mind would stop thinking and that I could forget everything!"

But his mind was alert and the entire scene in its monstrous detail was being vividly replayed in it. He remembered Ivan Karamazov, who had desperately wished the past to have no part in his life as he escaped to Moscow the evening preceding the murder of his father.

"Away with the past. I've done with the old world forever, and may I have no news, no echo, from it..."

Chapter 6

Ermias lay in bed for three days, because he had caught cold whilst sitting outside the train station in Leicester, waiting for the train to Cambridge to be ready. Andrew nursed him graciously with oranges and bananas and home-made Kenyan soup.

During the time he was lying in bed, his mind and his body functioned in the most bizarre and exasperating manner. The lust he thought had left him for good after he moved to Cambridge suddenly resurrected itself and took hold of his imagination once again with irresistible force. He was consumed with regret at not letting Tanya relieve him that night as she had suggested. His mind was persistently filled with her image, her smell, her sound, her touch, her warmth, and her whisper. The remembrance of their kisses and the caressing of her small breasts and her buttocks, the taste of martini in her lips and the scent of her warm breath, all drove his imagination wild such that he was unable to sleep or concentrate at anything else.

Freud must have been right when he wrote: "To touch is the beginning of every act of possession, of every attempt to make use of a person or a thing". Little did Ermias suspect that by touching Tanya and by accepting her touch, he was making his imagination captive. Now the money she had asked for appeared to be all too insignificant and those rooms into which she wished to take him not only inoffensive but also inestimably desirable and exciting.

He had intended to search for a research topic during the break, but now he lost the motivation as well as the energy for it. Furthermore, he was suffering from a headache and lack of sleep. Why was he always prone to stumble at the last step of a crucial phase in his life, he wondered. This time, he decided to retreat to Rhoda, who was studying Economics at the University of Gottingen. To his great relief, she was delighted to have him as her guest.

"Bring Saint Andrew with you!" she begged him.

Rhoda and Bordélique had been to Cambridge with his father during the previous break and had met Andrew, whom they had liked very much. But Andrew had already made other plans. On Wednesday Ermias flew from Stansted to Hannover and from Hannover he took the Regional Express to Gottingen.

Gottingen, sweet Gottingen. He was always filled with powerful emotions of affection and nostalgia whenever he visited Gottingen. Only Addis could evoke similar emotions in him. Rhoda received him at the train station, looking pleased to see him, but greeted him with her characteristic calmness.

She had grown to be tall and attractive, with a pair of kind and deep blue eyes and long, abundant brown hair. But she was hopelessly ectomorph, like her father. Bordélique, by contrast, had enough meat on her bones, like her mother.

Rhoda was living in a student apartment at Bühlstrasse, not very far from where they had lived when they were children. They walked all the way to the high hill, Rhoda pushing her bicycle; on the way they talked about their childhood and quizzed each other on whether they did remember this place or that. Ermias was at once glad and sad to be in Gottingen and with Rhoda. There was gladness and peace in knowing that he was accepted and trusted here. But he was also sad, because he felt like a fugitive who had been on the run for many years— From the time he had left Addis at the age of sixteen, some part of him had steadily and irresistibly been drawn into something murky and solitary. He anxiously wondered whether he would remain separated from all the people he loved and cared for. Or would there be a redemption and wisdom to be had in the end?

As soon as they arrived at Rhoda's apartment, he realised how exhausted he had been. Rhoda gave him a fresh towel for the shower and left for shopping. By the time he had finished taking a shower, Rhoda had not returned from shopping. He was intending to wait for her, but was unable to keep his eyes open. He must have fallen into a deep and heavy sleep, for he woke up the next day after nine o'clock in the morning and Rhoda was lying next to the bed on a mattress, reading a book. They stayed at home the whole day and only left the apartment in the evening to attend a guest lecture by a retired Oxford professor. It so happened that for the second time in less than three months, Ermias found himself in a venue where the afterlife was the subject of interest, for the title of the lecture was *The Epicurean philosophy of Death*. [g]

They arrived at the university on time, but the lecture hall was already full, the audience consisting mainly of elderly people. Even before he saw the audience, Ermias was wondering how Rhoda had become interested in death. They took two of the last seats available in the last row and shortly thereafter, the professor took to the podium.

He was a tall, well-built and handsome gentleman, in his late sixties or early seventies. He dressed impeccably and had his long grey hair loosely held at the back of his head in a bun.

"The subject of my lecture is death," he began. "Death, after all, is the final end of all our interest and one of the things in life of which we can really be certain."

Then he went on to explain that of all the ancient philosophers, the Epicureans were by far the least apprehensive of death. The professor quoted Lucretius to highlight his point:

> *So, when our mortal frame shall be disjoined,*
> *The lifeless Lump uncoupled from the mind,*
> *From sense of grief and pain we shall be free;*
> *We shall not feel, because we shall not Be.*

The Epicureans were unafraid of death, according to the professor, because they believed that in the same way the body disintegrates and eventually vanishes after death, so does the soul disintegrate and vanish. So, there would be no life after death and nothing nasty or unpleasant can happen to the dead. Here the professor quoted Epicurious himself:

> *Why should I fear death?*
> *If I am, then death is not*
> *If death is, then I am not*

Therapeutically speaking, the professor went on, the Epicurean philosophy was as good as any cure which any ancient doctor would offer to any ordinary disease. His concern, however, was not the ethical merit of the philosophy, but rather whether the philosophy made a decent argument.

"That is to say, does it reach a true conclusion by valid argumentation from true premises?"

The professor listed four basic premises upon which the Epicurean philosophy rests and contested the soundness of the conclusion following each premise. Finally, he concluded his lecture by claiming that the Epicurean philosophy failed to reach a true conclusion, but it seemed to Ermias that he had made this conclusion mainly on account of ethical rather than logical fallacies, for he pronounced one of the premises as selfish and inconsiderate of those who might be affected by the death of a person.

After the lecture, Rhoda and Ermias went to Cron & Lanz and thereafter walked around the Kiessee for about an hour. It turned out that Rhoda did not have a particular reason for attending the lecture. She had merely found the title interesting.

But the professor, through his repeated reference to Lucretius and his book *On the Nature of Things*, inspired Ermias to read the book. The next day Rhoda brought the book from the library and Ermias started to read it. The book took him by surprise right from the very beginning with its remarkable lucidity of thought, wit, and poetry. The elderly professor might have disagreed with the Epicurean philosophy of life, but it was difficult not to be captivated by the genius of Lucretius, the variety of the arguments he made, the sobriety of his tone, the simplicity of his ideas, and the harmony and beauty of the verses he committed to paper. Lucretius wrote about atoms, vacuum, the speed of light, and how the effects of invisible particles can be observed, themes which even today occupy seasoned physicists. Lucretius occupied Ermias for five peaceful days, then he returned back to Cambridge.

Ermias had nearly given up the hope of pursuing a PhD at Cambridge, because securing a placement was very competitive. But one day, towards the end of June, whilst he was still in the middle of his research project, his supervisor sent him a brief email requesting a meeting.

"What's your next step after you have completed your study here at Cambridge?" the professor asked Ermias when they met.

Ermias was not prepared for this question, as he was expecting to discuss project results. He thought for a moment and confessed the truth.

"I'd very much like to pursue a PhD but I also see that the chances are slim here."

Then the professor asked him which subject he was interested in to take up as a PhD research, should there be a possibility of pursuing a PhD. Ermias told him without much deliberation that the experimental aspect of condensed matter physics was his interest.

"There may be a slim chance here in our group." The professor scribbled something on a piece of paper which was lying in front of him. "Have you ever heard of a Marie Curie fellowship?"

Ermias told him that he had. The fellowship was a European Commission's initiative with the aim of fostering research collaboration amongst European research and academic institutions.

"We've submitted a project proposal and shall know of the decision in the beginning of August. If the proposal is accepted, I might be able to offer you a position, assuming that your research project is successful, of course, but you have to be willing to spend some time in continental Europe, either in Germany or Switzerland. A research visit to one of our European partners is mandatory in the program."

Ermias assured him that his project would be successful.

"The success of your research will be measured by the publication of your results in a highly reputed journal," the professor underlined.

Ermias accepted the challenge and left the office, filled with a sudden surge of an uplifting hope. The professor had chosen a favourable time, for the hope suddenly boosted the much needed energy Ermias had been slowly exhausting over a period of many years and helped him to endure the lonely and trying days of the remaining months of his final year at the University of Cambridge as a graduate student.

Konstanz

Chapter 1

At the beginning of August, the project proposal was approved by the European Commission and three weeks later, three days after the defence of his research project, Ermias was awarded a four-year studentship in order to pursue a PhD. In September, he travelled to Addis for a one month holiday, the longest holiday he had enjoyed with his family in four years.

On the third of October the project officially kicked off. The consortium consisted of two academic and two research institutions, namely, University of Cambridge, ETh Zurich, the European Organisation for Nuclear Physics in Switzerland, which was otherwise known as CERN, and the Röntgen Institute for Experimental Physics (RIEP) in Germany. Altogether twelve PhD students and four postdoctoral fellows were directly involved in the project. For Ermias, the transition was seamless, as his research would be a continuation of his MPhil thesis project. Moreover, the postdoctoral fellow who had hitherto supervised his thesis would continue to be his immediate supervisor.

The focus of the research project was on developing and characterising a new generation of superconductor nanosensors which were intended for receiving very weak infrared signals from celestial bodies. These signals were expected to reveal some vital information about the nature of celestial bodies in addition to their position and state of motion. Considered individually, the nanosensors would be unreliable, but when they formed an array of sensors, they should produce highly reliable and reproducible results.

Ermias was assigned the responsibility of developing a model which would efficiently combine the output of the nanosensors. As his research required extensive measurements, analysis, and modelling, his supervisor advised him to divide his time into three periods. In the first period, which should have duration of approximately six months, Ermias should stay in Cambridge, establishing the groundwork for his research. In the second period, which should have duration of one year, Ermias should visit either CERN or RIEP, to conduct a series of experiments and to gather sufficient statistics pertaining to the nanosensors. In the remaining period, he should return back in Cambridge, to develop, refine and test the model and to write his thesis.

For several days Ermias was undecided as to which of the European partners he should select. CERN was a highly respected research institute and almost all his colleagues had spent some time there, but its focus was more on high energy physics rather than on condensed matter physics. RIEP, on the other hand, was a relatively small institute, but specialised in condensed matter physics and had some of the most advanced fabrication facilities for superconducting nanocircuits. Moreover, he felt closer to Germany and the institute's proximity to the Holms made it attractive for him to go there. Finally, he decided to go to RIEP.

The first six months at Cambridge went rather fast, almost like a whirlwind. Indeed, Ermias was forced to postpone his research visit by three months because there was so much to do.

In November that year he travelled to New York to present a paper at a scientific conference which was held in White Plains, the Crowne Plaza Hotel. Three weeks before the trip he had written Nellie an email to let her know that he was coming to New York. Since he had received her surprising email in Dresden, he had not contacted Nellie. Back then, he had felt that she had always been in charge of making the rules which governed their relationship and that more often than not they had been unfair to him. Nor had Nellie sent another email. He was not sure what he had expected from her, but after he had sent the email, he waited impatiently for her reply and found himself yearning to see her. Nellie delayed her reply for three days, but when she replied, she was candid to express her eagerness to see him in New York.

It was early in the morning when he arrived at the hotel and he was very tired. He spent much of the day sleeping, but shortly after four o'clock in the afternoon, someone from the front desk rang and informed him that a young lady wanted to see him. It was Nellie. He hurried to meet her, his heart suddenly pounding wildly.

She was sitting on a black leather couch in the reception area wearing a pair of black jeans, an orange sweatshirt and a pair of shoes with high heels matching the colour of her sweatshirt. Her once long brown hair was now cut short giving her a sophisticated look. She stood up when she saw him coming and gave him a lambent smile. She had changed a lot. The formerly slim Nellie had now a full figure and looked quite attractive. Only the paleness of her face had remained faithful to her past. They hugged warmly and he regarded her with unconcealed fascination.

"You look criminally attractive!" he declared.

"You've become rather handsome yourself. Look at you!" she complimented him cheerfully.

"Don't worry, you can tell me the truth. University life has its price."

"You look like your mother. I haven't forgotten her beauty, you see. I'm so happy for you that you made it to Cambridge."

"Do you want to come up to my room? I've a present for you."

"Sure," said Nellie a little taken aback. "But I haven't brought you a present. I haven't even thought about it. Are you trying to embarrass me?"

"Don't be silly, I don't expect a present from you. You are the present."

"An honourable lady mustn't receive any gift if she doesn't intend to reciprocate it."

"It's not a big present. I must confess, it's not even something I deliberately purchased for you. I received some gifts from my family for my graduation, most of which I'll never need. Which is why I decided to pass one of them to you. Now you know all about it."

On their way to his room and in his room they updated each other about their family and studies. She told him about Paul, who, after having distinguished himself at Columbia, had moved to Caltech to pursue a PhD in theoretical physics, she had a baby step-brother in California, and she and her mother hardly saw each other or talked to each other over the phone on account of her mother having felt betrayed when Nellie flew multiple times to Los Angeles to visit her father and his young family. He briefly told her about his undergraduate life and the difficult time he had left behind.

Speaking of his undergraduate life, much to his great surprise, he was completely uninhibited by shyness when he talked to Nellie and could look into her cheerful hazel eyes without any fear or embarrassment whatsoever. His shyness had receded somewhat since he had moved to Cambridge, but people were still aware of it and would gently shift their gaze every now and then when they talked with him. Interestingly, he was less shy of brown or black eyes than of transparent eyes, partly because when he looked into the former, all he could see was a pair of bright beams, whereas the transparent eyes reflected no light, and appeared as infinitely long, unknown hallways into which he must peer. For some reason, he was frightened of those eyes. He was aware, of course, that his fear was irrational and for himself a constant disappointment.

Nellie found his room small but Ermias, coming from Europe, thought his room was rather spacious. Then he opened his travel bag and handed Nellie a small, cream-coloured rectangular box.

"Are you proposing to me, Ermias?" she joked and laughed affectedly.

"Open it."

She opened the box and there was a solid gold chain necklace in it with a small cross attached to it.

"Oh my Goodness! I can't accept this gift; I've no right to take it."

"You'll make me happy if you accept it."

"Why should I accept it? I am nobody to you. As far as I can remember, I've mistreated you badly. I-"

Nellie could not continue, for her eyes were suddenly filled with tears.

"You were unhappy, Nellie, I gathered that much."

She carefully placed the box on the table standing next to her and sat on the bed and covered her face with her palms.

"I'm very sorry," she whispered.

"Why should you be sorry?"

"Oh, you know..."

"I was never mad at you, you should know. Even when I was tormenting myself for wasting my time, my heart refused to be angry with you."

"Wasn't I the reason for your sudden departure to Europe?"

"What on earth makes you think you were the reason?"

"I couldn't help thinking that I was to blame."

"No, you were not."

"So why didn't you answer my email when I tried to contact you?"

"I saw no future in that email."

"That was my sentence."

"Do you remember that much?"

"You were very kind to me from the very start," she said, ignoring his question.

"Will you accept my gift?"

"I don't know, let me think about it."

"Good."

"So what is your plan for today?"

"I thought of spending the evening with you. We can go out together and eat somewhere."

"Do you want to eat Ethiopian food? Someone has shown me a nice restaurant in Harlem. We can go there. It's a walking distance from Columbia University."

"Since when have you become a connoisseur of Ethiopian food?"

"Since I met you."

"Then let's dine in Harlem."

As they were preparing to leave, Nellie made up her mind to accept the present.

"Alright, I'll accept it, on one condition," she said, taking the necklace out. "You'll have to help me put it on, and dinner's on me."

"This is the easiest condition I've ever been bound to."

He removed the sterling silver necklace she was wearing and replaced it with his. Then she turned to him and gave him a soft kiss on his lips.

"This kiss is more precious than a diamond."

"I'm not ungrateful, you know."

"And it's typical of you."

"I don't know what you mean."

"But one more kiss and everything will be forgiven."

"Really?"

"Yah," he nodded, smiling shyly.

She put her arms around him and kissed him once again. This time he responded by returning her kiss with a passionate kiss of his own. From there, despite repeated attempts, both were unable to detach themselves from one another. His hands held her cheeks gently while they kissed, and then greedily caressed her temples, her eyes, her hair, and found their way down to her breasts. She accepted his caresses and kisses and kissed his nose, his forehead, and his neck in return. Finally, he gently led her to the bed and laid her down and undressed her. She helped him. Both were lying on the bed and kissing. He, too, was now completely naked, and their eyes closed, when Nellie, between her breaths, spoke.

"I must tell you something."

"What is it?" he asked her without opening his eyes.

Nellie sighed deeply.

"I'm still a virgin."

Ermias opened his eyes in disbelief and looked at her. She was already looking at him.

"Are you kidding?"

"No kidding."

"You never had sex before?"

"It's a complicated story. I just thought you should know. But I'm happy to do it with you now."

He untangled himself from her embrace involuntarily and forced himself to a sitting position.

"Nellie!"

"What?"

"I can't Nellie."

He shook his head, for a reason he could not explain, in sadness.

"What do you mean you can't?"

"It's such a huge responsibility…"

"What are you talking about? I'll never be your responsibility. I'm an independent woman."

"I don't mean it that way."

"So what do you mean?"

"It's hard to explain…"

"What's the difference between making love to me if I'm a virgin and if I'm not? You were ready to make love to me just now, weren't you?"

"Perhaps there's no difference, but to my primitive mind, the difference seems to be enormous."

Nellie became visibly angry and she too sat on the bed crossing her legs.

"You told me that you're a virgin because it matters to you."

"Yes, I told you so that…"

She could not complete her own sentence.

"…I thought… that you should know."

He looked at her silently, conscious of the sexual tension within him quickly subsiding.

"Haven't you had a boyfriend in all this time?"

"Why does this come as a great surprise to you? How many girlfriends have you had in the past, perhaps ten, fifteen?"

"None."

She opened her mouth instinctively intending to protest or object but his response took her by surprise. She studied him tentatively and then spoke with a deflated tone.

"There you are."

"I never had a girlfriend because I was rejected many times. But you're not like me. You are such a desirable, beautiful, precious gem..."

Nellie kept silence and fixed her gaze at the white duvet up on which she was sitting.

"Come, cover yourself, you'll catch cold."

He removed the duvet from under her, laid her down on the bed and lying next to her, covered both of them with the duvet. They both were silent for some time, Ermias not quite sure how to proceed.

"You were right in saying that I was unhappy," Nellie began. "But not for the reason you might think. You see, since Paul and I were quite young, we kind of guessed that our parents did not quite love each other. Since I was twelve, I knew very well that my parents were staying together because of us and that it was only a matter of time before one of them moved out. I was expecting Daddy to move out, but it was Mommy who first moved out in the end. But the primary reason I was unhappy when I met you was a different one. Even the year before, when I was fifteen, I had a crush on my personal tennis trainer and gave myself completely to him. He was fifteen years older than I was and obviously more experienced with the opposite sex and the way of the world. To my great shame I realised quite late that he was merely interested in having sex with me. And no matter how hard I tried to please him, I couldn't bring myself to have sex with him. I permitted him to do lots of things with me but my whole body would shake and tremble when it came to having sex, I didn't know why. At one point he nearly raped me in a changing room, but I managed to escape from him. Then Mommy got suspicious of him and cancelled his contract and I was very upset for many days. And yet, that same year a friend of Paul set his eyes on me. He was turning eighteen and we started to meet in secret, sometimes in my room. But he too was only interested in sex. It was about this time you and I met. Given the circumstances, I still wonder how I could have warmed up to you. I'll not hide this from you. At some point, I really began to like you very much, but I also saw that there was no future in our relationship, partly because I was tired of living on a rollercoaster."

"And afterwards, in Buffalo?"

"Well, even though I foresaw my parents' separation, the experience, nevertheless, hit me hard. Everything just summed up to make me insecure with men."

Ermias turned to Nellie and put his arms around her and caressed her hair compassionately.

"Nellie…"

"I don't want your sympathy. I don't want anyone to feel sorry for me."

"I feel very close to you."

"You are, at least physically."

"I feel ve—ry close to you," he repeated meaningfully and softly kissed her lips.

"Well, I've spoilt everything, I suppose."

"That's not quite right."

"Let's get up now and have something to eat."

They took the train to Harlem and dined at Abyssinia and stayed there until late in the evening. She stayed the night with the family of one of her high school friends. The following day they went to the German International School, which was a mere three-miles distance from his hotel, and paid a visit to their old teachers, who seemed genuinely pleased to see them and to know that they were doing great. Some of them could not conceal their astonishment when they learned of Ermias' success. Apparently, none of them had expected that he would make his way to Cambridge let alone pursue a PhD there.

After the visit, Ermias and Nellie drove by train to Grand Central to watch a movie at Times Square. The next day Nellie flew back to Buffalo and two days later Ermias returned back to Cambridge. Immediately thereafter Ermias wrote Nellie and the two began to correspond by email almost daily, but gradually their correspondence slackened and in less than six months, the two had ceased to correspond altogether, for no apparent reason.

Chapter 2

Ermias moved to Germany at the end of May and took up residence in one of the institute's fully furnished apartments for guest researchers, located about a kilometre north of the institute.

RIEP was situated in a small, beautiful village, approximately eleven kilometres northeast of the city of Konstanz. The village was surrounded on the west side by a chain of gentle hills running uninterrupted north-south and upon which vineyards grew. On the east, it was surrounded by the Lake Constance.

The institute was named after the Physicist Wilhelm Conrad Röntgen, who discovered the x-rays and had won the first Nobel Prize in Physics. Compared to Cavendish Lab, the institute was smaller with regard to the number of its employees, but consisted of three big, sturdily built and neatly placed buildings and a spacious and pleasant compound. One other conspicuous difference between the two institutes was that whereas at Cavendish Lab the lawns were meticulously mown and the trees were regularly trimmed, in RIEP neither was touched. For the former, the art was in cultivation whereas for the latter, it was in letting nature freely express itself.

The institute's director, Professor Thomas Steinbrecher, whom Ermias met only once, was a slender, medium-sized, friendly-looking man in his early fifties. Ermias was told that he was, politically speaking, one of the most influential persons in the state of Baden-Württemberg. By training, he was an experimental physicist and, in addition to being the director of the institute, he occupied a Chair at the University of Konstanz.

It was not entirely clear to Ermias why the professor had assumed two great responsibilities when one of them alone was heavy enough for one professor. Equally puzzling was how he managed to separate the research agendas of the two groups from one another. Indeed, all the other professors who headed the research labs at RIEP, six of them altogether, all males and Germans, each had his own Chair and multiple research groups at different universities. RIEP had seven labs in which around two hundred full-time researchers worked. About one third of these researchers were, like Ermias, pursuing a PhD.

Ermias already knew that unlike in the UK or the US, professorship in Germany was not necessarily a title bestowed upon one as a result of an exceptional academic merit. One was called by a commission to be a professor, as it were, in a fashion akin to the calling of the biblical prophets, such as the prophet Jeremiah or Amos. Moreover, under normal circumstances no two professors belonged to the same research Lab or Chair, for to be a professor was equivalent to having one's own kingdom (some had empires), and no two kings could reign in one and the same kingdom at the same time.

Ermias was associated with the Nano Sensing Lab, the head of which was a tall and heavily built elderly professor in his early sixties. In this lab there were thirty full time researchers and the lab was subdivided into three research groups. One of which, and with which Ermias' research was aligned, was the Nano-Scale Magnetometry group.

Ermias was not the only researcher visiting the Nano Sensing Lab that year. Michel Durand, a PhD student like Ermias from Grenoble, and Dr. José Gabriel Lorenzo, a professor from Brazil, had already arrived two weeks earlier. The team leader, Anne, the only woman in the group, was a petite and soft-spoken young woman of twenty-seven, originally from Luxembourg. She had a pair of big, innocent-looking grey eyes and short, dark-blonde hair. She had received her PhD with *summa cum laude* from LMU Munich when she was twenty-four years old and spoke Luxembourgish, French, German, and English, fluently.

Ermias was given an apartment on the second floor, the view from which encompassed the full expanse of the lake. It had two rooms, one of which he used as a study and a living room, the other as a bedroom. Other than these rooms, the apartment had a separate kitchen, a bathroom, and a small balcony. Compared to his Peterhouse apartment, this was sheer luxury.

For the first time in a long time, Ermias was enjoying a deep sense of peace and a rare sense of reassurance, of the sort which someone who has been climbing a difficult mountain for a long time might experience upon seeing the mountain top from nearby—The climber is weary but firmly convinced that he has sufficient strength within him to go on. It was not that Ermias was already sure of conquering the mountain top, not at all, but he was persuaded that from here onwards it was a matter of exercising strict mental discipline and working hard in order to successfully complete the vital race he had chosen for his life. The self-doubt which had plagued him three years ago was now kept at bay. Of course, this newly acquired confidence would be put to the test time and again in the following months. But each time, the doubt would inhabit him only briefly. There was something in him which had crystallised for good.

Two days after his arrival at RIEP, he went to the office of the institute director to deliver two bottles of Cabernet Sauvignon on behalf of his professor at Cavendish Lab. The director was not in his office but there he met Seble Wongel Zemariam, one of his personal secretaries (the director had three secretaries). Ermias learned later that she was an Eritrean but born and raised up to the age of thirteen in Addis.

In many respects, she reminded him of his own mother, except that she was more beautiful and a little darker in complexion. Like his mother, Seble was of medium size, slim, and agile in her movements, had long and smooth black hair and a small, angular face. His heart missed a beat when he saw her but she received him coolly.

"Perhaps I am not the first Ethiopian she has received or met at RIEP or, perhaps, she didn't want me taking liberties on account of our shared background," he thought swiftly.

He was pleased to see her nonetheless and gave her the wine bottles. She thanked him and asked him if there was anything else he wished her to convey to the professor. Ermias told her there was nothing else, whereupon she thanked him once again and carried on with her work.

A little disconcerted by her aloofness, he left. Thereafter he did not dwell on Seble for too long. Indeed, he nearly forgot her, until one day, two weeks after their first encounter, when he met her once again in the corridor of his building. She stopped when she saw him and smiled and asked him in Amharic how he was doing. Ermias beamed a smile back at her when he heard her speak Amharic, and told her that he was doing well. Then she asked him whether he was getting accustomed to the institute and whether the difference between Cavendish Lab and RIEP was too big.

Apparently, she already knew he was from Cambridge. He told her that his knowledge of Cavendish Lab was not that great, since he had merely been a graduate student and known the Lab mainly from outside. In her turn, Seble explained that even though RIEP was comparatively small, it had established a solid reputation in Germany for its focus on practical experiments. She did not speak perfect Amharic but had the sweetest accent Ermias had ever heard. He guessed that she was older than him, but not much older, perhaps by two or three years. They agreed to have lunch the following day at the *Mensa* and went to their respective offices.

The following day they paid for their meals separately and took a table with two chairs at a corner. In the middle of their conversation Seble asked him whether he knew who she was.

"You seem to be the right hand of the boss." He replied jokingly in German.

"I mean do you know who I was, who my family was, in Ethiopia?"

"I've no idea. Why should I know?"

"Does the name Zemariam ring a bell?"

He tried to remember the name but could not. There seemed to be no entry in his memory associated with the name.

"My father was a stationary distributor in Addis. We had a business in Arat Kilo."

With this hint, the name struck a bell, a powerful bell.

"Are you…?"

He stared at her with disbelief. She nodded with a smile on her face, but in that smile there was a lot to read, namely, a complex mixture of nostalgia, sadness, and defiance. If not every Ethiopian, every inhabitant of Addis should know who her father was. He was a multimillionaire stationery importer and distributor during the time the Eritrean People Liberation Front was waging war against Ethiopia to secede Eritrea. There had been a strong suspicion that he was secretly helping the gorillas financially. The communist government had tried its best to set a trap for him, but it could not find any evidence which could implicate him.

The man was a devout Catholic and a fanatical supporter of Ethiopian athletes, known for his extravagant gifts to some of the impoverished musicians and artists, and nationally admired and respected. He died of a heart attack five years after Eritrea seceded from Ethiopia and the family buried him in Eritrea, because that was his wish, even though the man had never lived in Eritrea in his entire life. That same year the Eritrean government awarded him, post mortem, the highest medal of patriotism, stating his unprecedented support and exceptional sacrifice for the cause of the Eritrean people. Since then it had been made public that the position Italian and German politicians had held for a decade in the 1980s towards Ethiopia and Eritrea had, to the most part, been due to the influence of her father.

The Tigrean gorilla group, which ousted the brutal communist regime in Addis Ababa by fighting alongside the Eritrean gorillas, nearly idolised the man in the beginning and gave all his grown-up children and siblings critical government posts at the ministries of custom, transport, and foreign affairs, even though they were by then officially Eritreans.

Nevertheless, not even a decade had passed when the covenant between the two rebel groups was shattered for some inexplicable reason and a terrible war broke between Eritrea and Ethiopia in 1998 to claim nearly a hundred thousand lives in less than two years. The irrational group in Addis shamelessly expelled all the Eritreans living in Ethiopia overnight, forcing them to leave behind everything they had toiled for their entire life. They were hunted far and wide on a massive and frightful scale and were swiftly removed from the country. No one knew how and where they disappeared to. The Eritrean government, which, eight years prior to the war, had expelled a large number of Ethiopians from Eritrea and upon their exit removed all precious stones from their body, including from their teeth, now returned the favour in kind by blindly imprisoning thousands of Ethiopians and by deporting yet additional thousands.

Ermias looked at Seble not knowing what to say.
"Does it disturb you?" she asked him with a weak voice.
"What do you mean?"
"I mean, to know me. I was only a little girl at the time and I hardly understood what was going on."
"I was merely a boy myself. The war has nothing to do with you and with me. Besides, you are not the first Eritrean I've met."
He told her how happy he was to meet her and expressed his wish to get to know her better. Seble had a Master's degree in physics from the University of Stuttgart and was married to a German. The couple had a four-year-old daughter and lived at the outskirts of Konstanz. Her husband, who was an electrical engineer by profession, worked for a small company which developed navigation systems for Audi.
"Why do you work as a secretary when you have a Master's Degree in physics?" he asked her.
"I studied physics to test myself, but research was not my primary interest."
"Isn't it boring working as a secretary?"

"Sometimes it is, but I'm content with my life. I'm not ambitious by nature, you know. The main thing is that the family is staying together."

"Do you have contact with your family, I mean, with your mother, brothers, and sisters?"

"My mother passed away three years ago. I have five brothers and a sister. Some of them live in the US, some in Canada, and one in Australia. We hardly see each other these days. You know how things are when everybody has their own family and occupation."

"What happened to the business in Addis?"

She released a big, painful sigh.

"The government confiscated much of it. The rest simply died out. The buildings and the trucks are still standing empty and rusting. No one dared to rescue them, because everybody was afraid of retaliation. According to current political developments, however, there's some hope that we might be able to sell them."

Ermias could not imagine that such a vast establishment could simply evaporate into thin air, but he did not wish to dwell on the subject, lest he distressed her.

"I heard that you can speak German fluently," she observed after a moment of silence.

He told her his story briefly.

"Interesting. Your chances of becoming successful in Germany are considerable, if you wish to stay here."

Ermias did not comment, for he did not have any plans for the future beyond completing his PhD. Besides, the first question he was always asked by the natives, by one and all, upon their first introduction, was how long he was planning to stay in Germany, which made him a little sick.

Seble and Ermias talked for an hour as people who had known each other for some time. Unlike the coolness with which she had received him upon their first meeting, she was now unreserved and easy to talk to.

Shortly after she had moved to Germany, the war broke out. For, as if anticipating the great divorce between the Eritrean Liberation Front and the Tigrean gorillas, her eldest brother, who by then had assumed the responsibility of managing the family's affairs, had decided to send her to an all-female Catholic boarding school in Black Forest. The war scattered the family around the world and she never returned to Ethiopia.

"Many a time I've been attacked by a grinding nostalgia, during which my life seemed to have no meaning at all. In the beginning it was really worse, but since the birth of my daughter, it has gotten better. I still miss Addis and all my friends and my home, but I'm learning step by step to let go of the past."

"My journey is very different from yours, but I, too, experience the grinding nostalgia to which you just referred."

"You don't go to Addis regularly?"

"I do, once or twice a year, but then I don't stay long there. I have a sweet grandma whom I miss terribly."

They talked about food and coffee and she told him where he could find Ethiopian restaurants in Konstanz. Then it was time to go to their respective business. Before they depart, Seble extended an invitation.

"Come and visit me whenever you can."

Her office was in the administration building, on the second floor, amongst the most powerful people in RIEP, so he was not keen to be seen there. He sent her a short email after he returned back to his office to thank her about the lunch and to express his hope of meeting her occasionally to have lunch together.

A week passed and one Wednesday afternoon Ermias felt a little tired, having no motivation for work. But he did not want to go to his apartment, because he would be alone there, as Michel and José decided to stay late and work in the Lab. He considered going for a run but for that, too, he had no motivation. Suddenly, he remembered Seble and her invitation, so he went to her office unannounced. She was alone and smiled when she saw him entering into her office and stood up to greet him. They greeted Ethiopian style, with a cheek kiss.

"I remembered your invitation and decided to say hello. I hope I'm not disturbing you."

"You're not disturbing me. I'm glad to see you, sit down."

He sat on one of the chairs in front of her table. Her office was more than twice the size of his and had another door at the opposite end adjoining the director's office. The other two secretaries had a separate office on the other side. There was a full set of leather sofas and a long glass table in the middle of the room. A big shelf for periodicals and books was standing at the right hand wall and next to it, a big cabinet, displaying some of the significant discoveries of the institute, both old and new. Seble's big mahogany table was at the left hand wall, approximately in the middle of it. All these he had seen during his first visit but had not perceived them properly.

"It's frightful here," he said almost in a whisper.

She laughed softly.

"Even the professors feel the same when they come here," she remarked, sitting back in her chair. "Some even think that the room was made big deliberately so as to intimidate visitors."

"Is the director here?"

"No, he's hardly ever here, you know."

Ermias felt relieved. He saw a small decorated Bible lying on her table, which she must have been reading when he entered.

"I see you read the Bible," he observed idly.

"I love reading the Bible. Do you?"

"I used to read the Bible when I was in New York, since then I hardly got the time or muster the concentration."

"One has always time for the things one loves or regards as important."

"I can't contest that."

"What do you do in your spare time?"

"I barely have any spare time."

"That's one of the reasons I gave up physics," she told him, putting her Bible in a drawer next to her. "Some people spend their entire lifetime studying the characteristics of cooper-pairs whilst those studying cosmology spend endless hours searching for holes in the universe. In real life, these people are the most ordinary and boring human beings one can meet. When I come face to face with some of the brightest physicists, I find that they don't know what to do with me, a fellow human being. Then I have this image of a father who spends his entire life building a splendid villa for the children with whom he never spent an hour in his entire lifetime."

"Most physicists embody Ivan Karamazov's philosophy of love. Ivan maintains that in order for him to love his neighbour, his neighbour must hide his face. As soon as the neighbour shows his face, love is gone for Ivan."

"How absurd it sounds," she mused, "to love humanity as an abstract entity."

"Physicist or not, most human beings are ordinary and boring."

"You're rather cynical," she encountered smiling.

"It's true, isn't it? Prince Hamlet has a reason for saying man delights him not."

"My dream as a girl was to be a nun."

Ermias was about to make a joke thinking that she too was joking, but she was in earnest.

"What do you mean to be a nun?"

"Exactly that. But my family was opposed to the idea."

"What on earth induced you to want to become a nun?"

"From my childhood, I've been strongly drawn to the church. I feel inexplicable peace when I'm in a church. This is not something I consciously sought or attained. It just came naturally. Then when I left Addis, I felt like being uprooted from my foundation. Even before that, what happened in my surroundings was too complex for me to grasp. There was fear everywhere, and mistrust, too, and there was disappointment with one another, I mean between the peoples of the two countries. It was very upsetting to me. From all that was going on I learnt that nothing on earth was permanent. When I moved to boarding school, the girls I met were from rich families. Most of them were absorbed by the things of this world, which they mistook for something permanent and worth striving for. Ironically, most of them were from broken families or from families which were falling apart. There I came to the conviction that my true place should be in a convent."

"But now you are married and have a daughter of your own."

"Man proposes, God disposes."

She folded her arms together and leaned back in her swivel chair. She looked more beautiful when she rested her head gently on the chair.

"How did you meet your husband? How did you decide to marry him?"

"We knew each other for a long time. My father and his father had known each other for a long time already. Then my father-in-law was on the Board of Trustees of my boarding school. My husband used to come to the boarding school regularly in order to assist his father."

"I've heard that your dad was a powerful man here in Germany."

"I'm not sure how accurate that statement is," she said in dismay. "But my father was a religious man and that was also the basis of the friendship between him and my father-in-law."

"But why did you abandon your plan of becoming a nun?"

"It was a long and gradual process. It's taken me nearly ten years to change my mind. In the end, my husband's honesty and selflessness persuaded me to trust him."

Then Seble changed the subject to literature.

"Do they still have good plays in Addis?"

"I'm not sure. Going to the cinema seems to be the latest fashion. But I'm a bad witness, really, since I don't reside in Addis."

"I remember once going to the National Theatre with my uncle. Shortly before I moved to Germany, it was. Tsegaye Gebre-Medhin's translation of Hamlet was being played. I didn't understand a single bit of it, but I liked Ophelia very much. She was young and very beautiful, but distraught, as if the burden she was carrying in her soul was too great for her to bear and was about to crush and destroy her with its immensity. I was moved by her misfortune and felt very sorry for her. I remember being sad for some days afterwards. A few years ago my husband took me to Hamburg to watch Hamlet, but it didn't move me as much."

"What else did you watch in Addis?"

"Nothing. Remember, I was only thirteen years old when I left Addis. But I have this."

She opened her drawer and withdrew an old but neatly kept paperback. It was *Esat wey Abeba*,[h] a collection of the selected poems of the poet Tsegaye Gebre-Medhin.

"Do you understand his poems?" Ermias asked her in amazement.

"Some of them, yes. My favourite poems are the ones he wrote about his grandmother, the martyred Bishop, and the butterfly."

"You surprise me, really."

"Why?"

"Because the poem about the bishop celebrates the bishop's sacrifice of his life for his country, for Ethiopia, a country which many Eritreans consider their enemy."
She brushed his stinging comment aside and explained.
"What I like about the bishop is his total submission to the will of God and his total trust in the Virgin."
"Did your family approve of your reading Tsegaye Gebre-Medhin?"
"I've always been an independent woman and will remain so. Apart from that, my father must have enjoyed reading the poet, since his collection of books included all of his works. I was told that he detested his post-revolution works, but his pre-revolution poems and his translations of Shakespeare, particularly, Hamlet, he regarded as good works."
Then Seble suddenly looked at her watch and stood up in alarm. "How the time flies! I've to collect my daughter from kindergarten, I must say goodbye now. But please come and visit me whenever you have time. I've enjoyed our chat."
He promised and left her. The time was twenty minutes to four. He had been with Seble for more than an hour.

Chapter 3

Ermias visited Seble on an almost weekly basis. They talked for about an hour each time and occasionally even longer. As their acquaintance developed, Seble talked freely about her religion and the Bible, perhaps the only interest, next to her immediate family, she seemed to have in life. Her knowledge of the Bible was more than ordinary. She knew many names and places and their history in detail. Whenever he tried to make a joke about her saints, she was very upset with him and never held back from scolding him.

Another thing which Ermias noticed was that her recollection seemed to have contained almost no reminiscence of her past life after the age of thirteen. She talked scantily of her university life in Stuttgart and the few things she mentioned about her boarding school primarily consisted of its strict lifestyle and how some of the girls were observed in trifles and frequently squabbled out of rivalry and jealousy and played hurtful practical jokes on each other. But she talked gladly about her childhood, particularly about her Sunday school experience when she was between the ages of ten and thirteen. This period in her life coincided with her discovery of her love for mathematics. She had rarely experienced significant problems with mathematics or any of the other subjects previously, but her performance at school had been average hitherto. But one day in her fourth grade, as she was returning home from school, sitting inside the school bus, she was solving some division problems in her mind. She solved all the problems with unusual quickness of mind and, in doing so, experienced an explosion of great joy.

In the following days and weeks her propensity for solving mathematical problems and the sharpness of mind improved steadily, thus giving birth to her exclusive devotion to mathematics, which stayed with her all through her high school and university life. She ranked fourth in her class that year but in her fifth and sixth grades, she stood first. When she moved to the boarding school in the Black Forest, education, except for mathematics, became a conscious effort and even with mathematics, she rarely experienced that same explosion of joy.

The first time Seble and Ermias met outside of the institute was towards the end of July when the institute organised a weekend trip to Zurich, Munich, and Strasbourg. The three secretaries were in charge of organising the trips. Michel and José joined the group going to Zurich but Ermias decided to join the group going to Strasbourg because Seble was in charge of this group.

They set off to Strasbourg early in the morning on a brilliant and warm Saturday, Seble and Ermias sitting next to each other. She talked much of the time during the drive and he listened with interest. She told him about a childhood friend with whom she used to take horse riding and swimming lessons and with whom she attended a Sunday School in Addis. This friend of hers, who had happened to be an Ethiopian and was from a respected family in Addis, was now a famous model in New York, but had never met or spoken with Seble ever since Seble had left Addis. Seble still thought of her friend and cherished her memory, but somehow did not make any attempt to re-establish contact with her.

In Strasbourg, the group was further divided into three sub-groups and went to different places by tram. Seble and Ermias stayed together, all the time talking about Addis and standing a step or two behind the rest and hardly listening to their guide. The group reconvened and had lunch together at *Au Crocodile*, but was divided once again after lunch.

In the afternoon, they were dismissed for three hours, so that they could visit the city by themselves and shop for souvenirs. Seble and Ermias went to *Parc de l'Orangerie* and sat there the whole time and talked. But when the group reassembled once again at six o'clock for dinner at *Hotel Maison Rouge*, where some of the people, including Seble, were staying, they were separated, for there was a table protocol. But they regrouped after dinner during a boat tour on the *Batorama*. After the tour, Ermias went to his hotel, having enjoyed his time with

Seble very much and feeling unusually happy. The next day, Seble and Ermias were not able to enjoy the privacy of the previous day, as there were colleagues in their company. Perhaps, they too unconsciously sought the company of others, in order not to attract attention.

Four days after the trip to Strasbourg, as Ermias was returning to his office from the *Mensa* with a couple of colleagues he met Seble in the corridor. He thought she was there by chance and was about to pass her by when he noticed from her look that she wished to speak to him. So he lingered behind and greeted her.

"I'll be staying late today, because there's a meeting which will go until six. Thereafter, I'll be working for an hour or so. You can drop by and keep me company if you have time."

She spoke in a low voice and in a hurry.

"What about your daughter?"

"My husband will pick her up and will take her to her grandparents. She'll be staying with them tonight. Will you come?"

"I'll come," he reassured her.

She gave him a sweet smile and hurried to the staircase. Suddenly, he was flooded by a strange joy. For each time he had been to visit her, his conscience had been pricked, because he thought that he was intruding on her privacy, and that she was receiving him out of mere politeness. He was equally bothered by the thought that he might compromise her reputation.

The meeting must have been an important one, for he saw through his window, five shining black Mercedes, the type used by the diplomatic corps, parked in front of the admin building. He waited eagerly until it was over and all the cars had gone and, then, went to Seble. When he entered her office, she and two young ladies were clearing up the director's office. Seble saw him coming and came out to greet him.

"Are you hungry?" she asked him after they greeted.

"I can't say that I'm not."

"Sit down, I can offer you something to eat."

Ermias sat on a sofa. Seble returned to the director's office and came back with a plate of food. He did not feel comfortable to be seen eating in that office, but she did not seem to notice.

"Have you ever tried this food?"

Looking suspiciously at the plate, he told her that he had never seen its kind before.

"It's called *Coquilles Saint-Jacques*. It's a French dish, made of scallops, fish, and mushroom. And these," indicating with a fork, she explained, "are the scallops. Try it, it's delicious. I won't offer you wine, because out of principle, I disapprove of wine. But I can offer you *Apfelschorle*."

"Will you join me?"

"I'm afraid, I won't. I've some pressing work to do."

The food was indeed delicious. He was hoping that the ladies would clear up quickly and leave, but they took a long time. Seble, too, was busy at her desk, so he was left by himself. Then he finished eating and waited idly. Shortly before seven the ladies finished and left, but Seble worked until eight. Then she stood up.

"I'm sorry, I didn't have the time to chat with you. Will you accompany me to my car?"

He too stood up.

"I miss my daughter and feel a little guilty for not being able to say good night. I know she has also missed me. By now she's already in bed, fast asleep."

"Why do you feel guilty?"

"I don't know, I feel a little guilty whenever I miss her, knowing that the feeling is reciprocal. There is some pain in missing someone."

"Old Freud asserts that human beings feel guilty either because they are afraid of punishment or because they are afraid of losing someone's love," he remarked.

Seble deliberated for a moment.

"I'm not sure if either of them is applicable here, or may be a little bit of both. But is it really possible to compress such a complex feeling as guilt, so as to fit it into one of these two compartments?"

"Freud maintains it is."

"We shall leave Old Freud to rest in peace," she said with a mocking smile.

Presently, they came to her car in the garage. She was driving a fat Audi SUV which Ermias inspected with reverence and admiration.

"On second thoughts, I can take you home," she offered noticing his fascination.

"Don't worry, I can walk. It's not very far from here."

"Come on, you'll enjoy the ride."

He was intending to go back to his office to collect his laptop before he went home, but now he did not want to keep her waiting, so he got into the car and they drove off.

"This is sheer luxury for someone who wished to be a nun!" he commented jokingly.

"Either all or nothing," she joked in return. "This was my husband's gift. He drives a humble car himself."

"Humble, indeed. I haven't seen a single person in Konstanz who drives a bloody humble car. The BMWs I saw in this small village alone very likely outnumber the BMWs in the entire city of Cambridge."

"The Germans love driving expensive cars, particularly, in the south."

"So what was the meeting about?"

"RIEP has applied a proposal for a two hundred million euros funding in order to upgrade its measurement and simulation infrastructure. The proposal should be approved by the German Research Foundation and the State of Baden Württemberg, and the process involves multiple local inspections, face-to-face interviews with the director and the heads of the laboratories, and also negotiations."

"Isn't the professor responsible for the measurement and simulation systems a computer scientist, the short, fat guy?"

"Yes he is."

"I suppose he's a powerful man?"

"What do you mean exactly?"

"I heard Anne and the others talking about him. According to them, he's a close friend of your boss and enjoys his confidence. They accused him of meddling a lot in other people's affairs."

"He gets things done, which is why my boss likes him. All the others talk but don't achieve much. He brings in money."

"They also said that he has an exceptional love for cheese and wine," he added, for some reason lusting for gossip. "Is it true that his approval is indispensable for securing a professorial position at RIEP or elsewhere in Europe?"

"I can't answer that question, partly because I'm not a professor."

But from her suppressed smile Ermias could tell that the claims had some foundation.

"What exactly does a computer science professor do here?"

"I don't know exactly, but, as you just said, he's indispensable for our institute. Through experience, he knows very well what we do and what type of computer assistance we need. Admittedly, he also maintains a strong network in the industry, the academy, and the realm of politics, both nationally and Europe-wide."

"Do you think the proposal will be approved?"

"I hope it'll be approved. It's taken us five years to prepare. But such proposals aren't approved or rejected merely on the basis of their academic merits."

"What are the other criteria?"

"Oh, you know, many."

In the meantime, Seble parked the car in front of the guesthouse. Ermias thanked her for the ride and got out of the car.

Chapter 4

The following week Ermias travelled to Meyrin and missed his weekly meeting with Seble. This was the first time he had missed their meeting in several weeks and he felt a little void. He strongly wished to phone her but, knowing that she disliked receiving phone calls and emails, he refrained. Yet he repeatedly checked his email the whole week in case she dropped a line to let him know how she was doing or feeling. But there was no email.

He returned to Konstanz on Friday evening and learned that José and Michel had gone to Baden-Baden for the weekend. He felt lonely and restless. After a brief rest, he went running and covered twenty-one kilometres in ninety minutes. That evening he could not get anything done. Instead he spent the time aimlessly surfing the Internet. Feeling unsatisfied with himself and wishing to have some distraction, he spent the weekend in the lab, all the time missing Seble.

"Where am I headed, where do I expect this whole thing to lead?" he asked himself repeatedly.

"It's a fact that I'm lonely, but I should be careful not to do anyone any harm."

The thought of hurting Seble or her relationship with her husband was at once difficult to imagine and frightful. On Monday and Tuesday the desire to see her was strong, but he resisted going to her office. The next Wednesday he deliberately stayed at home, determined to break the habit of seeing her. When he thought calmly and at length about how emotionally attached he had become to her, how quickly he had developed this attachment, and the possibility that it might have devastating and lasting consequences for her marriage, made him shudder.

On Thursday he persuaded José and Michel to have dinner in an Ethiopian restaurant in Konstanz, so they left the office early. He slept late on Friday and went running as soon as he got up. By the time he had returned from running, it was past twelve. He took a shower and went to the *Mensa*, finished lunch at half past one and went directly to the lab, feeling fresh and motivated to do good and what was right.

Every time he came back from running, not only did he feel refreshed and invigorated, but he also found the strength to accept the possibility that his toil, loneliness, pain, unfulfilled yearning, and all, might someday have some significance and even some specific purpose, even though this optimism usually lasted only a day or two, after which he would revert to his, now habitual, reflection on the aim of his loneliness. He was forever thankful to his mother for introducing him to this wonderful gift of running (and to his dad for his gift of appreciation of the Alps in winter).

The afternoon went swiftly by without the slightest temptation to go to Seble. Indeed, he was so engrossed in his work that he hardly realised how the time went by. He stayed in the lab until ten o'clock in the evening and returned home fully satisfied with himself.

The next week started off as usual, with a team meeting at nine o'clock in the morning and a telephone conference with the Swiss and Cambridge partners at eleven. The conference was supposed to take not more than an hour, but it dragged on until half past one and Ermias ended up going for lunch alone. On his way, he saw Seble in the building as she was coming down the staircase from her office. He was very pleased to see her, but was checked by her coolness. Subdued, he waited at the foot of the staircase to greet her.

"Why did you disappear suddenly? Did I do something wrong?" she inquired coolly.

He was hoping to get a cheek kiss, but she stretched a lackadaisical hand for a handshake.

"I was in Meyrin the week before and last week I had some pressing deadlines," he lied. "But I'll admit it, I missed you."

"You don't have to lie. Tell me what wrong I've done."

He looked at her straight in the eyes, searching for some clue that she, too, had missed him.

"Do you know that you're beautiful?" he confessed to his great surprise and consternation.

For some seconds she did not shift her eyes nor did she blink, but looked at him as if he had not said anything in particular. Then she blinked.

"What are you talking about?"

"I'm sorry, I don't know what I'm saying, but you look awfully beautiful and I thought I should tell you."

"That's why you ignored me for more than two weeks, for no apparent reason!"

At that instant he suspected that the feeling was shared. He felt at once exhilarated, anxious, and sad.

"Can I come and see you later?" he asked her by way of an apology.

"I'll be leaving early today, but I'll have time tomorrow. Come at three."

He felt like a child who had received its choicest gift for Christmas. He did not try nor wish to hide his happiness. But Seble left him where he stood without saying another word and went out of the building. As soon as she left, his joy was once again checked by that sting of conscience and he entered into the *Mensa* anxiously and having already lost his appetite.

"Where does all this lead to?" he asked himself repeatedly.

"I don't know, I don't know," was the only answer he could whisper each time.

For some inexplicable reason, he had been haunted much of his adult life by the fear of one day behaving shamefully or cowardly. And like Oedipus, he, too, had been dreading the fulfilment of this ominous oracle. Would he, in the final analysis, escape to Cambridge, where his privacy and reputation would be safe, after all was said and done, leaving her alone with all the troubles he would bring upon her, her family, her marriage, her reputation, all of which were now at stake? How could he save her? Or did he not care for her? It was no use, he told himself, this endless, idle and impotent reflection.

"I am helpless. I should know my limits."

He had already started missing her terribly and time seemed to be standing still. He returned the meal untouched and went to the lab instead of his office, for he had no concentration to work on a concept. But in the lab he felt so impatient and restless that even Anne noticed his demeanour and startled him with a bold and unexpected question.

"What is the matter with you, are you in love?"

"No, God forbid!"

On Monday evenings he and Michel played football with the university students in Konstanz, which began at six o'clock when the weather was permissible. Now he yearned for the time of action to arrive and glanced at his watch repeatedly, but time was moving ever so slowly whilst he sat in front of a computer and tried to visualise the measurements he had taken previously. But he could visualise nothing, understand nothing. He was restless and impatient and consumed by an unlawful desire to see and be with Seble.

He blamed and resented the institute for confining him and making him lonely and desperate. In the city he would have a wider range of choice, he thought. But the truth was that New York was big. Dresden and Cambridge were big enough. And yet he was not presented with a wide range of choice in any of these cities. Perhaps what made him impatient and restless was not so much being in love with Seble or the desire to be with her, as being in an indefinite position and wishing to make it definite, regardless of the specific shape and direction the relationship was supposed to take on. After all, he thought, she was as much responsible as he was.

"Maybe she's capable of controlling the whole situation. Maybe she is stronger than I."

But he did not wish to make her responsible. He felt compassionate towards her in the same way he had always felt compassionate towards Bordélique.

"But what can I do if she dislikes my disappearance and if I'm unable to control myself when I'm with her?"

The afternoon passed. In the evening football kept him busy and distracted. After football, the students decided to eat gyros and watch thereafter a Woody Allen film at the Unikino and invited Ermias and Michel to join them. It was past midnight when they returned to their place and Ermias was both mentally and physically exhausted and went directly to bed.

I awoke with the painful sensation of having an urgent problem to solve. He once read in that slim book of Francoise Sagan, which, by the way, he had reread many times and had come to appreciate its remarkable simplicity and candidness.

On Tuesday morning, he too, awoke with the same painful urgency to make his relationship with Seble definite and irreproachable. All through the morning, whilst he showered, breakfasted, walked to his office, and worked, he was pressed by the same urgency, even though it was not hundred percent clear to him what he meant by irreproachable, and how he was intending to make his relationship irreproachable. Around eleven o'clock his conviction began to disintegrate as he started to be impatient and restless once again and his eyes yearned to see hers.

"Four more hours," he sighed.

When, after four interminable hours had passed, he went to see Seble, she came rushing to the door as soon as he had finished knocking. She opened the door and stood at the threshold.

"I'm sorry; I can't entertain you now. My boss is in and he's asked me to prepare something for him urgently. Come at six, I'll be here."

His heart sank with dismay and she saw it. By contrast, she was sober. Ermias quickly forced a smile.

"Of course! But we can also postpone it, you know. I'm sure you want to see your daughter before she goes to bed."

"Don't worry about my daughter, come back at six."

The whole time she did not release his hand, which she had taken to shake, but she became conscious of it and released it quickly. Ermias had this explosive desire to kiss her on her lips then and there, but he let it implode.

"I'll see you later," he said dutifully endeavouring to appear composed and casually slipping his hands in his trousers' pockets.

"See you later," she said and closed the door.

"I'll kiss her tonight, come what may," he told himself resolutely.

Then he went back to his office.

Chapter 5

At six o'clock the admin building was deserted and Ermias found Seble collecting her bag, ready to go out.

"Let's go to the lake," she suggested after they had greeted, as if she had already made up her mind.

This was a generous offer considering how late it was, and one for which he had not prepared himself. They went in silence to the lake through the side gate. A gentle wind was blowing and the midsummer air was pleasantly warm. His heart was beating wildly and he was pleading with himself not to do or say anything stupid or regrettable, despite his resolve to kiss her. There was no one on the shore in their immediate vicinity but farther away they saw a group of people barbecuing, most of whom were probably employees of the institute. They found a wooden bench next to a giant redwood and sat down on it. For some reason, they both were still silent.

"How beautiful!" Seble was the first to break the silence.

"Yes," he agreed without understanding what she was referring to.

"I suppose you have read *Fikir eske Mekabir?*"[i]

"Yes, when I was fifteen."

"How do you like it?"

"Should I answer this question?"

"My father liked it very much, which was why I was named Seble Wongel."

Upon hearing this, he recited a long poem from the book, written by the departing lover, which he had learnt by heart when he was fifteen years old. She listened to the poem with disbelief, her eyes full of tears. He had never seen anyone so beautiful and so absorbed. His heart was moved with a painful compassion. When he finished, she turned her eyes towards the lake and gazed blankly in silence for a long time. Without knowing the reason, he felt very sorry for her.

"Are you unhappy?" he asked her at long last, without understanding the reason for his own question.

"I'm always a little unhappy, but that is my natural disposition. But, no, I'm not particularly unhappy."

"Do you regret our meeting?"

She thought briefly and then said: "Not really. What a strange question you ask. Besides, it's not for human beings to decide whom they should meet and whom they should avoid. God brings people together for them to build a temple."

"It'd break my heart to see you unhappy."

"I'm under God's protection, don't worry."

"I wish I could be that confident!" he thought.

Then they were silent again. He began to sing softly:

> *Tell me no secrets, tell me some lies*
> *Give me no reasons, give me alibis*
> *Tell me you love me and don't let me cry*
> *Say anything but don't say goodbye.*

"You have a beautiful voice. Why don't you use it for the glory of God?" she said, trying to suppress an irritated tone.

"What's the matter with you, Seble? Can't you say anything without involving God?"

"I can't." She whispered. "I'm frightened."

"I'm sorry."

He took her hand in his. She did not resist but kept looking at the lake.

"Why do you study physics anyway? Why didn't you study literature or something similar, instead? You seem to love literature and, apparently, you are gifted."

He was about to say, 'I love literature as one loves his mistress', but swallowed the sentence at the very last second. Instead, he answered: "I've been struggling between pursuing science and pursuing the arts most of my life. I suppose this struggle will never cease."

"I'll never be your mistress; do you understand?" she was saying in the meantime, still gazing at the lake.

Even though he was loath to hear these words, he was exceedingly pleased that she had perceived his innermost thoughts. This was particularly important for him knowing how easily Ethiopians could be tempted to be false or pretentious. "We should accept the possibility of falling in love without falling into sin. If you insist that this is absurd, so be it."

He did not say a word, for he was happy and ready to accept any terms she wished to introduce.

"I've got to go now."

She got up from her seat without a hurry. He followed suit and accompanied her to her car. The underground garage was empty and dark. Neither of them attempted to talk until they arrived at her car. She did not seem to be disturbed or fighting off her thoughts, whereas he was fighting with himself over whether to try to kiss her or not. His heart was beating wildly once again and he felt that he was not ready to let her go. But he did not wish to distress her or embarrass himself, so instead he watched her get into her car. She started the motor and opened her window to say goodbye.

"In a fortnight we, that is my family and I, will be going on a fortnight's holiday. Just to let you know, because I don't want to disappear without a trace like you did last time."

"Suffering!" Ermias uttered the word involuntarily.

"I cannot change it."

"Drive carefully," he said, so as to change the subject and turned his face away from her and towards the exit.

"Wait!" she urged him.

He stood but without turning his face towards her.

"Are you angry with me?"

He was not. How could he be angry with her? How could anyone be angry with Seble? He turned his face to tell her that he was not angry with her.

"All right, you may come and give me a goodbye kiss. On my cheek." She pointed with her left index finger at her left cheek. He was very pleased with the proposal and went to her and kissed her on her left cheek, but he found it impossible to detach himself. It would have been a thousand times better for him to have stayed away from her in the first place. Now his desperate lips searched for her lips and he finally kissed her greedily. Her lips were on fire.

"That is enough," she whispered and pushed him gently. "Go for now."

He obeyed and she drove off.

He felt light after she had left and returned to the lake and sat on the wooden bench, gazing at the water blankly. He was in a state that was difficult to classify, for it was neither rest nor restlessness, neither elation nor despair. He did not know whether he was fine or unwell. He could have sat there, as it were, indefinitely, but with no particular urge forced himself to stand and walked northwards, following the lake for about an hour and thinking of nothing in particular. By the time he had returned to his apartment, it was already getting dark but he met Michel and José outside the building, playing table tennis, evidently waiting for him.

"Where on earth have you been?" José shouted at him.

Michel was visibly disappointed. It dawned on him that they had agreed to cook together, but he was late by more than forty minutes.

"You should be thankful that I returned now by sheer accident." He told them off.

José came to him and asked if he was all right.

"I'm all right. I wish to be left alone. Please go ahead and cook without me, I apologise."

He went to his room and lay down on his bed, with all his clothes and shoes still on. He must have been very tired, for he fell asleep instantly.

Chapter 6

He woke up at two o'clock in the morning, his mind filled with the scene of the previous evening, which he now replayed in minute detail without opening his eyes or moving his body. But he did not wish to dwell for long in the past. Indeed, the only thing which was important for him was to know the final outcome of his relationship with Seble, not the past as such. Then he got up from bed, undressed, and went to take a shower, asking himself again and again the following question: "What will happen in the end, what do I want to happen in the end?"

From the very outset, he knew that his regular visits to Seble were not entirely innocent. He liked her and had made his feelings known to her on various occasions and in various ways, albeit with great subtlety and caution. There was no denying that he had acted deliberately to win her approval and, perhaps also, to take advantage of her vulnerability, her loneliness.

"But there's no sense in tormenting myself now," he pleaded with himself. "I too am lonely and vulnerable. Now the main thing is to establish some normalcy and to be willing to accept the consequences. Only I should be careful not to torment her or drive her to despair."

That much he was ready to do. He was also determined to not let himself be swayed by torrents of emotions. With this determination, he came out of the shower and went to the kitchen in search of food, for he was starving. And yet he had neither the motivation nor the strength to cook. So, he ate an apple, two bananas, and fruit yoghurt, and made himself tea. Then he sat down to work until dawn.

At five o'clock in the morning he lay down to sleep but his mind was alert, occupied with a succession of lines of thought, none of which he was able to develop to a logical conclusion. Towards six o'clock, he drifted into an uneasy sleep, but this too was interrupted around eight o'clock by the irritating and monotonous noise of a boring machine drilling in the corridor. He awoke suddenly, the nauseating sound having succeeded in both probing his temples and causing a burning sensation in his eyes. The noise persisted for about five minutes and then disappeared, but Ermias was unable to fall back to sleep. At last, he got up and decided to go to the institute and to have breakfast at the institute's cafeteria.

It was Wednesday. Habitually, he would go to Seble in the afternoon, but was not sure if that was what she wanted. Besides which he had developed a certain apprehension towards visiting her office, to approaching the entire building, as a matter of fact. But there was no way of avoiding it, for there was no other opportunity to meet her alone.

"I shall wait in my office until two thirty," he thought. "If she doesn't communicate in some way that I shouldn't come to her office, then I'll go and see her at three."

To his relief, he worked with relative peace the whole morning and went for lunch with the group. After lunch, Michel invited him to go out for a walk with him and they went to the lake.

"You were moody yesterday," Michel remarked on their way to the lake, glancing at Ermias sideways with a mischievous smile.

"I know, I'm sorry," replied Ermias still thinking whether or not he would be able to see her that day.

"What is the matter?"

"Oh, you don't want to know. I don't even know or want to know what exactly is happening to me."

"I can guess, though." Michel surprised him.

"You can?" Ermias regarded him with suspicion.

"I saw you yesterday sitting by the lake with someone."

"I see. If you saw me, it also means, you, too, were late for our appointment, which also means that you were a shameless hypocrite in being mad at me for coming late."

"I wasn't late. I saw you from a distance as you were just sitting. I was speeding on my bicycle towards the guest house."

"Well, what else did you see?"

"Just that. I shouldn't be meddling with your private life, but I should also tell you as a friend what I think about it."

"Feel free!" Ermias gave him his full attention.

"You know she's married?"

Ermias shuddered involuntarily but kept silence.

"I also heard that the director has personal interest in her family."

"What do you mean?"

Michel hesitated.

"I don't wish to alarm or frighten you, but they said that there's some familial connection."

"Wow!"

Ermias released a sigh and looked at Michel in despair.

"Who are these people you're alleging to?"

"What people?"

"I mean the people who told you about the familial connection."

"Some people in our team."

"Who exactly?"

"Anne, for example."

"So, we're already a subject of discussion? Do they already suspect something?"

"I'm not sure."

"If you've caught on to it, there's a likelihood that they also suspect what's going on."

"I didn't have a clue until yesterday evening when I saw you behaving distractedly like Prince Hamlet. So there's chance that they haven't figured it out yet, which is why I wanted to talk to you about it, since you may wish to exercise some caution."

"Thank you, Michel. But I feel helpless right now."

"Why don't you meet her somewhere else, in some hotel away from here? The people are gossip-mongers."

"I'm not yet clear about the precise nature of our relationship."

"Why, don't you like her?"

"I suppose I do."

"And does she like you?"

"I suppose she does. But you yourself just said that she's married, didn't you? Besides, she doesn't want to be my mistress. Neither do I want her to be my mistress."

"So why on earth do you keep going to see her in her office?"

Michel looked confused.

"You're aware of that as well?"

"Aware of what?"

"Aware of my regular visits."

"Oh, come on! Of course, I'm aware of that! We sit in the same office."

"I'm afraid I can't answer your question."

"Only don't go to the director's office. It will compromise her. Particularly, when you're not certain about what you want from the relationship."

Ermias agreed.

As they returned to their office, they passed the admin building by and saw Seble and the two elderly secretaries strolling towards the building. It was obvious that they, too, were coming back from a walk. The elderly secretaries were, Ermias supposed, possibly counselling her about the dangers of falling in love with a lonely and desperate bachelor from Cambridge. Since their paths were parallel, Ermias was determined to ignore them but Seble called him by name, so he stopped, but Michel went on. Seble left her companions and came to him.

"How are you?" she asked him anxiously.

"I'm fine, and you?"

"You look tired. Your eyes are red. Let me guess, you haven't slept well?"

"I've had enough sleep, but I was also working."

"Will I see you later?"

Ermias bit his lip and looked at her doubtfully.

"I understand. What shall we do?"

"Can we meet somewhere else?"

"Shall we go to Mainau?"

"Is it all right for you?"

"Yes, I'll pick you up, say at four?"

"How about your daughter?"

"I'll ask her grandmother to pick her up."

"Are you sure this's a good idea?"

"Then suggest something else. Shall we meet on Friday afternoon? It's my free afternoon and I usually go swimming after work."

"I like that better."

"See you on Friday, then. I shall meet you in front of the guesthouse. Be punctual. I don't want to stop there for too long."

"I'll be there."

There was so much worry and pain to read in her countenance. He was moved by a strange compassion which tempted him to draw her closer and hold her tight. He said goodbye instead and went on his way with a heavy heart.

Chapter 7

Aeschylus was back again. The following two days Ermias worked and carried out his usual obligations whilst persistently suffering from the pain of missing Seble and the uncertainty of their relationship. On Friday, Seble arrived on time in front of the guest house as they had agreed.

"What have you done to me?" she asked him when he got into the car.

"I've missed you!" he confessed.

They did not greet properly. She drove off as soon as he took his seat.

"It occurred to me that we haven't decided where we should go," she remarked.

"Konstanz is your city; you may take me wherever you like."

"Do you want me to show you around?"

"I'd rather we went somewhere, where we can't be disturbed."

"You mean, where we can't be spotted? To tell the truth, I don't know Konstanz very well myself. My life is pretty boring. Perhaps we should drive to Mindelsee. Can you check the Navigator to see how far it is from here? It should be about twenty kilometres."

He had no idea how the navigator functioned, so he took instructions from her.

"Is this the sort of navigator your husband develops?" he asked her.

"Among others. Let's not talk about my husband for now, please. I'm already nervous and upset without making my husband the subject of our conversation."

"Of course."

"On second thoughts, let's talk about him. There's no reason why we shouldn't be talking about him. We're not doing anything wrong, are we? We won't be doing anything wrong, will we?"

She looked at him anxiously.

'There may be no kiss today,' he thought, dolefully.

"That kiss was a mistake," she spoke, as if reading his mind. "Oh, God! What am I doing and saying!" she added in apparent agony.

She was momentarily silent, striving to maintain her focus on the road ahead as tears began rolling down her cheeks.

"It's twenty-three kilometres," Ermias told her.

"It'll take us about twenty minutes to get there and another twenty minutes to bring you back and fifteen minutes to my place, how much time is that altogether, can you calculate? I can't concentrate on two things at the same time, especially when I'm nervous."

He told her the answer.

"Good, we shall have an hour and a half by the lake."

He tried to cheer her up but was not successful. So he let her drive in silence.

"When I get back from holiday, I'll introduce you to my family. My birthday is on the 9th of October. Mark and reserve this date. We usually barbecue in our garden. Everybody will be there, including my in-laws."

"I won't be coming."

"Yes, you will. If I'm allowed to make a wish, please order one of Kebede Michael's poetry collections from one of those second-hand bookshops in Mercato for me. It would make me very happy."

"I'll certainly buy you the book, but I'm not coming to your place—all eyes will be on me. Everybody will be able to read me like an open book."

"They'll see that you love me as a sister. I wish our love to develop into something pure and honourable."

'There'll be no kiss today,' he concluded and remained silent.

A week ago it would have been impossible to imagine that Seble and he would be talking about love. Even though he had been studying the characteristics of dynamic systems most of his university life and was aware that they were subject to great and sudden change, he was nonetheless fascinated by this incredible development.

Apparently, Seble mistook his silence for sulking.

"I don't wish to be difficult," she said. "Nor do I wish to upset you. But I wish to keep our friendship pure. I can't do so unless I avoid doing anyone any harm, you know whom I've in mind, otherwise we'll never discover true happiness in one another."

'It's really possible that she'll be able to control the situation,' he let the thought float in his mind.

"Why don't you say something? I like you most when you are cheerful. Dolefulness doesn't suit you."

"I agree with all your proposals."

"It's not that I'm cruel or..." she let her sentence hang and wiped her tears away with one hand.

Then both were silent. Suddenly he felt sad. He closed his eyes and leaned his head on the headrest. Then Seble broke the silence with a different tone.

"Yesterday evening I watched an Ethiopian lady giving an interesting interview on a German TV. The interview was first given in English to BBC, but they translated it into German."

"What was the topic?" Ermias asked her opening his eyes.

"It was about the challenges of sustainable development in Africa. I tell you, the woman was very impressive. She made a dull topic quite funny and interesting."

"That must be my mother. I've heard her mentioning giving an interview to the BBC some weeks ago."

"What do you mean 'my mother'?"

"She gives that sort of interview every now and then. She is an economist and works for the UN."

"No, that can't be. This woman was around my age."

"Do you recall her name?"

"No."

"Was she the slim, cheerful, long-haired, Liya Kebede type?"
"That is a little exaggerated, but yes, she remotely resembled
Liya Kebede."
"Then that must have been my mom."
Seble looked at him to make sure he was not joking.
"I was convinced that she was around my age or perhaps a
couple of years older than I."
"Believe me, that was my mom."
"I don't believe you. How old is your mom?"
"Forty-three."
"If indeed she's your mother, you are really lucky. You have a
smart, young, and beautiful mother."
"And I feel lucky."
After a brief silence Seble looked at him with astonishment and
gently hit the steering wheel with the palm of her right hand.
"On second thoughts, she must be your mother! It just hits me
that you look very much like her when you smile."
He was pleased that she was distracted. So he told her about
his childhood. Then they arrived at the lake.
They both were apprehensive lest they should meet a lot of
people, but to their great relief they found that the lake,
flanked on the east side by farm fields and on the west by
forest, was lonesome and quiet. Seble drove the car slowly in
order to come as close to the lake as possible and parked it on
the side of a street where a footpath branched off from the
main street, leading to the lake.
They sat in the car for some time, each desirous of the other.
His heart started to pound wildly as he searched for her hand,
taking it in his. But she gently withdrew it and got out of the

car. He stepped outside to join her. He was about to torment himself for taking her hand, but Seble dispelled the cloud by taking his arm in hers, and led the way.

"How strange, how awesome, how exciting! I feel very close to you; do you know? Since I left Addis, I've never lived in any one place for more than five years either," she said.

They walked arm in arm down to the lake. It was a small, clean, beautiful lake, and they could see a pair of swans peacefully floating on one side.

"If I remember correctly, the lake is under natural protection. It contains some rare and endangered species," Seble told him.

It was a warm, windless late afternoon, very pleasant to the senses. He felt serene and wished for time to stand still. They followed the footpath towards the north, commenting on the beauty of the area. She told him that she lived nearby, in a small town called Allensbach, about fifteen kilometres from RIEP.

Then she stopped suddenly and looked at him straight in the eye.

"Promise me you'll come to my birthday party. It would make me happy."

How could he say 'no' when she insisted in earnest and, particularly, when there was the reward of being with her, near to her, the whole afternoon and, perhaps, the evening too, even though there would also be anxious and unfamiliar eyes all around him furtively scrutinising him, inquiring who he was and what he was doing there.

"But what of it?" he asked himself, "Haven't I had to deal with such scrutiny before?"

"I'll come."

"For this, you deserve a kiss."

She softly kissed him on his cheek and laughed nervously, now walking ahead of him a little faster, her arm still locked in his. They walked for about ten minutes, and shortly before they reached the forest, she suggested sitting down on the meadow which overlooked the lake. They sat, and Seble talked about her childhood friends, her Sunday school in Addis, and some of the songs she used to love then (she sang a couple of songs and her voice was sweet). He listened to her eagerly, but could not help asking himself the questions that had been in his mind for some time. Was it Addis, the past, or the childhood she had lost in Addis that she loved in him? What was it she really liked or was searching to discover in him? But he was too happy to dwell on these questions.

"The first time I was allowed to stay the night in church, I was nine. It was a Christmas Eve. I was feverish with excitement. We left home in Daddy's car around ten o'clock in the evening. I remember that there was a security alert in Addis and everybody was talking in whispers and walking cautiously. Already eleven hours before more than five hundred anti-government protesters, many of whom were young people, had been gunned down in the street by British trained special sharpshooters. It was dark and the streets were completely deserted. We saw armed patrols monitoring the deserted streets. Mind you, our house was in Bole and we drove all the way to Churchill. It was a long and exciting drive. Once we were in the church, the children, who came from all walks of life, were put together inside a small, pink, bright room, full of comfortable mattresses and pillows. There was a big picture of the Virgin and Child hanging on the wall. Otherwise, the walls were empty. The contrast between outside and inside was great, for inside it was peaceful whilst outside there seemed to reign impenetrable terror and fear. We spent the night telling each other stories, mostly undisturbed by the adults. I remember deeply wishing that the night would never end like that girl in *One Thousand and One Nights*."

"I was wishing that time would stand still just a while ago," he confessed.

She looked at him keenly and then she applied both her palms on the ground and brought herself closer to him and cuddled him. He put his arm around her shoulders and kissed her left temple.

"How frightful!" she said barely audibly. "The only way I can permit a love of this magnitude is if I can hold you forever without feeling divided inside, do you understand?"

"Yes."

Then they were silent, feeling the pressure of one another's bodies. She was wearing a simple short-sleeved orange dress with lots of coloured butterflies on it, appearing to fly in different directions. Her well-shaped legs were modestly exposed. She was wearing neither ornament nor makeup, like many German women. In short, she was natural and beautiful.

"We may not be able to see each other so often at the institute," Seble broke the silence.

He could not help thinking that this had indeed been the topic of discussion between her and the two elderly secretaries during the after lunch stroll on Wednesday. He was neither surprised nor annoyed. Indeed, on the contrary, he was relieved. That hideous admin building had been a menace to him for some time, exercising passive aggression on him. He gently massaged her head to express his agreement.

Then he said, "What is the point of seeing you in your own home when our relationship is already under suspicion?"

"Who suspects us?"

"I suppose the two secretaries and, perhaps, your boss."

"How do you know?"

"You just implied it yourself when you said that we might not be able to see each other at the institute."

"That is because some people thought that it would be, how can I put this correctly, ah, necessary, imperative, to separate our personal, private affairs, our relationship, from our professional affairs, that some of the professors may feel uncomfortable with one of their employees frequenting the director's office. Do you understand? That doesn't mean they suspect anything. I can understand if this is upsetting to you. It is upsetting to me, too."

"It's not upsetting to me at all. Perhaps, they were right."

"You think so?"

"I think so."

"But where can I see you then? My life consists of my home and the institute only, and the church. Nothing else in between. I don't have many friends and it's not in my nature to sneak around, it's humiliating to me."

"Let's not burden ourselves with such questions and live one day at a time."

"But what does it mean to 'live one day at a time' and how does it solve the problem? Where shall we see each other?"
"We shall see each other when the situation permits, when you can. I'm always ready to see you."
Thoughtfully she studied him in silence knowing that he too was helpless like her and did not have an answer to her question.
They stayed at the lake for about an hour and finally it was time to get up.
"No kiss today?" he asked her shyly.
Her face contorted with pain and she shook her head in disagreement. He sighed deeply and got up.

Chapter 8

The following Wednesday Ermias stayed away from Seble, but the prospect of not seeing her for the remainder of the week, indeed, for the coming two weeks, distressed him and made him overtly miserable. Despite his agreement with the idea that he should not visit her in her office, he now felt upset with the people occupying the admin building, particularly, the professors, whose disapproval was to be feared and avoided. The symptoms of bitterness manifested themselves in the form of his fixation on their foibles.

He saw in the institute's website, for instance, the list of journal articles the director had co-authored in the past six months, twenty-nine in all, three of which in *Nature*. In other words, the director had been publishing more than one paper every week, which seemed absurd. It was very likely that he had read none of those articles let alone written them. Besides managing a complex research institute and a Chair of his own, he served as the editor-in-chief of two outstanding journals (one of which was a theoretical physics journal whereas he himself was an experimental physicist), sat on the board of directors of a couple of research foundations, advised the German government on various matters related to nuclear physics, and served as the chairman of a project review panel for the European Commission. In addition, he gave keynote speeches regularly. All of these activities required frequent and tedious travelling, which strained the body, the emotions, and the mind. Yet the harvest of his decades of research was impressive, and from the sheer volume of papers he published every year, one would be tempted to think that his scientific genius exceeded the combined genius of Max Planck, Albert Einstein, and Paul Dirac.

His malady had compounded by Friday morning and Ermias struggled to decide whether or not to go to her office. The past days had, to a certain extent, been bearable knowing that she was in the same compound as he was and that, had he wished to, he could have simply gone to seen her. Somehow this prospect had given him the strength to endure the pain and to abstain from going. But on Friday, the realisation that in less than a few hours she would be gone and that he would not be able to see her for two weeks became oppressive.

Indeed, it was not just the anticipation of not seeing her which was unbearable. He was also dreading the possibility that once she was away from him and from the influence of his presence, she might get the strength to reject him and to disentangle herself from their unwholesome relationship. He was willing to accept her desire for chastity, but at the same time, he disliked being rejected. A rejection of this kind he would regard as a pronouncement of his betrayal of her trust.

After lunch Ermias grew visibly doleful and stood immobile in front of his office window for a long time, his hands inside his trousers' pockets.

"It's her, isn't it?" Michel asked him at long last, coming forward and standing next to him.

Ermias nodded in agreement without turning his face towards Michel. They stood side by side for some time in silence and Ermias was conscious that Michel was trying to say something, but each time he was unsure of what he wished to say. But in the end, Michel cleared his throat and made a suggestion.

"It's Friday, we should go to the movies tonight and eat somewhere afterwards."

"Why, don't you have a date already?" Ermias asked him with a little impatience.

"What do you mean?"

"Oh, shut up! I too have eyes that can see in the dark."

"I've no idea what you're talking about."

"You're lucky and I envy you."

"Ah, I don't know. It's like torture, you know, when you can't make up your mind what to do."

"Why do you say that?"

"Well, when two people working together are attracted towards one another and one of them happens to be the supervisor of the other, many questions will pop up in their minds as well as in the minds of those working with them."

"What of it? She's worthy of it. She's beautiful, smart, and kind. Besides, she'll be your supervisor only for a few months."

"But I wish to stay here, because I like working here and the pay is great."

"Don't tell me she isn't the main reason behind this wish to stay."

"She is, perhaps. But do you see my problem?"

"There is no problem but human prejudice."

"You infidel!" Michel mocked, half in jest. "You will accept anything to justify your unlawful affair."

"There's no unlawful affair, as far as I am concerned, for there's no affair."

"I'll not judge you," Michel stated gently.

At that moment, there was a knock at the door and in came Seble.

"I'm leaving." Michel whispered rapidly and hurriedly left the room. Ermias admired his instinct for discretion.

Ermias turned his back to the window and rested his body lightly on the window frame. Seble stood at the door for a moment looking at him steadily and then she walked towards him with measured steps. They hugged in silence and Ermias felt the pressure of her body. She was slightly shivering. He held her tight and felt his anxiety, his doubts, and his cynicism evaporating instantly and a warm compassion for Seble taking place in his heart. At length he gently detached himself from her embrace and studied her face with concern. She too looked at him, but was unable to speak. She was still shivering.

"All is well," he tried to calm her down taking both her hands with his.

"I'm sorry if I have embarrassed you by my coming," she said with a subdued voice.

"Nonsense, I'm infinitely glad to see you."

"I can't stay long. I came to say goodbye to you. I shall see you after two weeks."

"Yes."

"God bless you. Take care of yourself. And work hard."

"I will."

She hugged him once again, studied him briefly, and appeared to be hesitating.

"I so much want to give you a kiss, but I mustn't. Please forgive me for all the confusion and agony I've brought upon you."

"There's no agony," he lied. "I'm unworthy of your love, but I'm infinitely thankful for it. It means a lot."

"I'm consumed by guilt, because I know you're suffering."

"So are you. We suffer because we've discovered that we have the capacity to love. You yourself once said that even the lowest type of love is better than not being able to love."

"I didn't fully grasp what I was saying."

"So what do you think now?"

"Love is suffering, love is painful and cruel, love is incomprehensible; love is untimely. In short, love is everything but peace."

"That's not entirely true!" he objected passionately. "There's solid peace in love, underneath everything. If we remove the carnal desire from our love, we find nothing reproachful in the compassion and care we have discovered for one another."

Upon hearing his response, her eyes radiated brilliantly and her face gleamed with a broad, sweet smile. His response was partially designed to assuage her, but whilst speaking, he himself believed in its truthfulness.

"I'm sure there's some wisdom in what you've spoken just now," she observed, gazing at him lovingly. "But how is it possible to remove the carnal desire, as you put it, and call what remains "love"? By carnal I don't mean sexual, necessarily. I rather mean the unyielding desire to see and be with you? How can we remove this desire and still define our condition as love?"

Upon a brief reflection, now his statement sounded hollow to him.

"The truth is, I've no idea what I was talking about."

"Still we both feel that there's something in our love which should be transformed," she put in emphatically.

He was listening to her words with interest from where he was still resting his body and was intending to say goodbye to her when suddenly he was overpowered by such an irresistible force surging up from within that he pulled her into his arms and started to kiss her passionately. She tried to resist but changed her mind and submitted completely. As he continued to kiss her, his hands caressed her voraciously. But when he tried to advance into her, she resisted forcefully, disentangling herself from his embrace.

"That's enough!" she reproached him with her usual gentleness.

"Please forgive..."

"I love you, but I'd better go now. Please take care of yourself."

He did not want her to go but he also knew that if she stayed longer, it would be impossible for him to detach himself from her.

"Goodbye, then."

She hugged him quickly and rushed out of the room.

Billions of neurons in his cerebral cortex were still firing and flooding his blood with epinephrine long after Seble had left, such that it was impossible for him to focus on his work. He felt restless, and, for the first time since he had left Dresden three years ago, he experienced the very same loneliness, fear, and anxiety working in him in unison. He walked back and forth in the room energetically, like a lion bereft of its partner and locked inside its cubicle in a zoo, without focusing his attention on anything in particular. Was this the first stage of madness? He wondered.

"What does it all mean?"

At long last, he decided to leave the office and go for a run, but he was also afraid of going out, afraid of bumping into someone, anyone. Irrationally or not, he felt that everybody in the institute was aware of, interested in, and disapproved of his illicit affair with Seble. But staying inside the office was a torture he could not endure. He waited until the corridor and the one below were empty, sneaked out of the office cautiously, and took a half-deserted back street to hurry to the guesthouse, still haunted by those oppressive emotions. Paradoxically, he dreaded being alone. When he arrived at the guesthouse, he checked on José and Michel, half suspecting that they were still at the institute and, he had guessed right, their apartments were locked.

His usual running route, around the Bodenseeufer, would be deserted at this time of the day. So, he decided to take the bus to the Seeufer, which was near to the old town. The route was relatively short, but there he would be amongst people, and the journey, there and back again, would help reduce the lonely hours of the evening, the coming of which he was now dreading. When he boarded the bus twenty minutes later, he took an empty seat at the back, wishing to be left alone. His desire to be amongst people oddly excluded an interaction with them.

He ran for two hours and ended up being alone in front of Schloss Seeheim where he threw himself on the meadow and lay down on his back, fixing his gaze on the clear sky. He was sweating all over. The day was warm, but after a while he felt chilly, because there was a cold breeze coming from the lake and his body had cooled down.

"This has to end!" he told himself with cold resolution.

There he rested for about twenty minutes and decided to return to the guesthouse.

Chapter 9

Like Dickens' Dr. Alexandre Manette, who reverted to shoemaking in times of great emotional distress, Ermias too reverted to viewing pornography on Friday evening and stayed up far into the night. On Saturday, he woke up at eight with a bitter taste in his mouth, a headache, and a dull spirit. But his body was tireless and light. Wishing to compensate for a wasted time, he left his apartment quickly, grabbed two croissants and a latte macchiato from a nearby café and went to the institute. He worked with concentration until four o'clock in the afternoon, but always indwelt by the familiar pain of missing Seble. At four o'clock, however, he found his situation intolerable and decided to retreat to Heidelberg.

Frank and Martha had returned to Heidelberg the previous evening after having stayed in the US for two months.

Bordélique, too, who had taken a one year break after her *Abitur* to work as a volunteer assistant librarian in a Christian college in Nairobi, had returned to Germany two days ago for a fortnight visit, after having stayed in Nairobi for three months. She and Rhoda, together with their three cousins, had arrived from Gottingen five hours before Ermias. Martha's eldest brother Thomas and his wife Henrike had been staying at the Holms for the past two months, taking care of the house and working on a joint book project. The project, however, had not been making progress as much as they had hoped and the couple was on the verge of frustration and feeling trapped when Frank and Martha arrived in time to set them free.

After eight o'clock visitors began to call. By half-past eight the house was filled with them. Shortly thereafter, following a delivery of Indian food, the guests were admitted to a buffet. There was loud chatter and laughter and everybody was glad to see everyone else again. Ermias, too, was glad that he had come.

The guests stayed until very late, the older adults talking around a big round table in the living room and the young people playing Monopoly in Bordélique's room. Around two o'clock in the morning Ermias felt exhausted and sick and was suffering from a headache, but had to wait until all the guests were gone because he was supposed to sleep in the living room, now that the study had been taken by Thomas and Henrike. The last guests left at half past two and Ermias was finally permitted to make his bed on the couch.

He was awakened at noon by the chatter and laughter emanating from the kitchen, where, he gathered, everybody was congregated. Before long, Bordélique approached him and started to tell of her adventures in Nairobi—She had already been to many places in just three months' time, including to Saint Andrew's birth place by the Lake Turkana, Mount Kilimanjaro, and a three-day safari in Mombasa.

"So much for being a humble volunteer," he teased her.

"What can I do about it? It's in the nature of the call. They all treat me like a child and everybody wishes to take me here or there. I'm very fortunate. I didn't go there expecting all this, but if it comes with the package, why should I refuse to enjoy it?"

Meanwhile Rhoda joined them, she, too, coming from the Kitchen.

"Anyone special yet?" Ermias teased Bordélique again, but she blushed deep this time and turned her face away.

"I see! There must be someone then."

"If you say anything to Daddy and Mommy I'll kill you, but..." She paused for a moment, choosing her words. Ermias looked at Rhoda who was looking at him with a mischievous smile.

"Spit it out."

"Oh, I don't know. There's this Canadian who seems to like me."

"And you, do you like him?"

"I don't know. I can't imagine living in Canada. I mean, I've never imagined that I might one day live in Canada..."

"The question is not whether or not you can imagine living in Canada. The question is whether or not you have feelings for him."

"I don't know," she lamented, dragging her words, her face displaying signs of distress. "He's such a kind and smart type, but…"

"I told her to wait," interjected Rhoda. "Three months is too short a period to decide anything."

"I'm just surprised that you are already old enough to be seriously contemplating being in a committed, romantic relationship," Ermias remarked.

"One has to begin at some point, don't you think? Some of us started when we were sixteen or thereabouts, setting such a splendid example for the rest of us!"

"You wicked kitten!"

"Now it's your turn. What's new? Don't lie."

It was impossible to talk about Seble. What could he tell them? That he was in love with a married woman and the mother of a four-year-old daughter? Now when he thought about it in a different light, away from RIEP and the influence of its confinement, away from Seble, and in the presence of the most innocent girls he had ever known and cared for, the whole affair appeared to be grievously wrong and shameful. Yet, he was unable to make up something instantly, so he covered his face with his palms and considered what he was going to say.

"I'm in a mess," he confessed after a pause. "But I don't have the courage to tell you about it, partly, because it's not yet clear to me what I'm doing or what I should be doing."

"Does it concern a woman?" Bordélique asked.

"Let's say it does."

Upon hearing this, the sisters, particularly Bordélique, nagged him to tell them, promising not to be judgemental. He was distressed by their insistence but was left with no other option. "How can I say this without shaming myself? No, I can't tell you. I'm embarrassed to admit it. Please give me some time, a few weeks, until the picture has become clearer in my head, and then I'll tell you. But right now, I lack the courage to tell you about it."

"It must be real bad," said Bordélique becoming serious. Then, turning to her sister she added, "Do you think?"

"I suppose it is," Ermias interjected. "Particularly, when I regard the whole thing in the light of your presence."

"He's being sensitive," said Rhoda, regarding him calmly.

"Have you hurt anyone?" Bordélique asked him in earnest, she too, scrutinising him closely.

"I can't say. I might have."

"If you were to leave Konstanz today and never return again, will the mess follow you?"

He admired her style of questioning and looked at her meaningfully.

"Now that you put it that way, I don't think it would follow me. Somebody's heart may break, though. But that exactly is the problem. I'm not leaving Konstanz today."

"I see. This means it's not that messy yet, but it could get messy. Let's say you're on the threshold."

"That's a very good way of summing up the situation. The agony lies in that I'm not leaving Konstanz right now and I'll return to the situation tonight."

Ermias found himself feeling miserable.

"A clear-headed decision is required here," stated Bordélique firmly and decidedly.

"In the same way your affair with the unfortunate Canadian requires a clear-headed decision," he teased her.

"So what are you going to do about it?" Rhoda interfered.

"I don't know. I really don't know."

Rhoda deliberated for a moment and looked at him with uncertainty.

"Shall I ask you one simple question?"

"You can always ask me any question."

"But promise you'll give me a simple answer."

"Is there such a thing as a difficult answer?"

"There is such a thing as a complex answer," she replied mocking.

"Well, go on, let's hear your simple question."

"Why did you stop communicating with Nellie?"

"Now what has Nellie got to do with the present discussion?" Ermias looked at Rhoda reproachfully.

"Well, we shall find out."

"The communication faltered on its own. Nellie was equally to blame for that."

"Why did you re-establish communication with her in the first place, knowing well that it would be difficult to maintain?"

"Why, she was an old friend, wasn't she?"

"More than an old friend."

"Where are you leading up to, Rhoda?"

"Well, you seem to have a strong ambivalence when it comes to women and romance."

"Really Rhoda? What are you talking about?"

"This is just my observation, think about it."

"Professor Rhoda Holm, you said you wanted a simple answer, but you're the one who came up with a complex theory," Bordélique came to his defence.

"Thank you, precious."

"So how is our researcher doing?"

It was Martha, descending the stairs, coming down from the bedroom. She came into the living room and sat on the edge of the couch upon which Ermias was still lying.

"I'm fine," he replied automatically wearing a cheerful mask.

She began to interrogate him about his life in Konstanz and his research at RIEP. The girls, afraid that the interrogation might lead towards an awkward theme, distracted her by saying that it was time to eat something, to which Martha instantly agreed. They all went to the kitchen and joined the others.

They stayed at home the whole afternoon and Ermias took the six o'clock train to Konstanz. During the drive, he remembered the discussion he had had with Rhoda and Bordélique and how terribly he had felt about his relationship with Seble. He pleaded with himself to end the relationship and to set both Seble and himself free from the predicament in which they now found themselves. He was eager to see Seble again, so that, so he thought, he could announce his decision and draw their liaison to an official conclusion.

The two weeks went by peacefully and uneventfully. Ermias neither received, nor wished to receive, a message from Seble. Yet, in the course of the third week, his desire to see her and his restlessness increased gradually but steadily, now that he knew she was in the institute. Nevertheless, he resisted going to her office and worked in the lab much of the time. The following Saturday was her birthday and, until Wednesday, he was undecided whether or not he should accept her invitation. After lunchtime on Wednesday, as he was returning to his office with the group, he met Seble, who apparently had been waiting for him outside of the *Mensa*. She looked strikingly beautiful, but a little tired or sad.

"Can I speak with you for a second?" she inquired after they had greeted one another.

His heart began to pound instantly and felt a strong desire to possess her. Nevertheless, he stood tentatively, as if he wanted to hurry to his work. Seble, however, asked him to take a walk with her.

"You look beautiful," he confessed once they were alone outside, despite his wish to remain neutral.

"Thank you. You look great yourself. Not at all like someone who has missed me."

Ermias released an involuntary sigh.

"I understand if you wish to be free, not that I've kept you captive," she said sulkily.

He wished to announce his decision to end their relationship but the setting was unpropitious, he felt. In addition, he was not really sure whether he was ready for it after all.

"All right, you can keep your peace. But I'll see you on Saturday. Here is the address, I've written it down for you. But I want us to meet at the bus stop; it will calm me down if I meet you at the bus stop first. There I shall wait for you at three. If you arrive earlier than that, wait for me there. There's a bus leaving from your place every half an hour. If you're late, it's all right; I shall come back and check for you half an hour later."

She handed him a piece of paper upon which she had neatly written down her address and the bus stop where he should alight. Then she left without waiting for his reaction. He stood there and watched her approaching the admin building.

His heart ached. He felt very sorry for her. Her entire constitution invoked in him profound pity. Helplessly massaging the left side of his forehead and his left eye with his left palm, he tried to think what he should do next. He was hoping that she would stop at the revolving door and turn, but she did not. He watched her disappear into that monstrous building.

He then went to his office, feeling sad and disdainful, and spent the rest of the day in the lab, the pain of missing her never leaving him for a minute.

"There's no use lying about it, I'm missing her so awfully right now," he lamented.

On Thursday morning Seble surprised him. He was alone in his office when she entered without knocking and holding a proper Ethiopian *agelgil* in her hand. He could not contain his joy when he saw her.

"A relative of mine from Frankfurt brought it from Addis," she told him reservedly and lifting the *agelgil* up. "I decided to give it to you. I suppose you don't get traditional food that often. But the *agelgil* isn't mine; you'll have to return it to me when it's empty."

She put the *agelgil* on the table and turned towards the door, ready to go.

"Please don't go!" he begged her rising from his seat hurriedly and coming forward. She stopped. He stood in front of her and took her hands in his. She looked at him with a look which was at once sympathetic and defiantly aloof.

"I've missed you."

"You had the chance, but didn't show it yesterday," she replied reproachfully.

"I wish you could know how my heart ached and is still aching."

His words were received with agony, for she contorted her face painfully. This was not what he wished to say, not only because he mistrusted the sincerity of his own words, but also because it pained him to add an additional burden on her misery by suggesting that she was the cause of his suffering.

"So you'll come on Saturday?"

"Yes, I will."

She hugged him and he held her tight and felt her heart racing. He also felt the gentle pressure and touch of her warm and naked arms on his shoulders, and the caress of her warm, gentle breath lingering on his neck. This hug was to him as vital to his existence as the air he was breathing. Was this the sort of need Elizabeth Barrett Browning was referring to when she wrote of every day's most quiet need in her sonnet? He wondered. He so much wanted to tell her how much he loved her, but the words refused to come out of his mouth, for he thought it was wrong to say them to a married woman. She had once told him that she loved him, but he suspected that she, too, was conscious of the gravity of this forbidden declaration.

"I've got to go now," she whispered, as if she did not wish to disturb anyone.

He released her. She regarded him in silence for a moment as he watched her eyes rapidly shifting left and right. Then she left without a word. He was dismayed to see her leave, but he got a huge boost of energy and encouragement from her visit. Indwelt by a joy he could hardly conceal or contain, he worked hard for long hours.

Chapter 10

Indeed, the joy lasted until Saturday, but on Saturday, she met him at the bus stop, as she had suggested. She too was cheerful and hugged him tightly. But as they approached her house she suddenly stopped.

"What is it?" he asked her instinctively alarmed.

"I'm a little nervous, hold me."

She turned to him and he held her. They stood in silence for some seconds. She was shivering like an autumn leaf troubled by a mindless wind.

"Are you sure you want me to come with you?"

"Yes," she whispered.

They stood for some more seconds in silence and then she said she was calm and he released her. When they arrived at her place, there were about fifteen people in the garden. The house was a big two storey villa with a modest front lawn and a small playground, the sort of traditional family house one frequently encounters on the outskirts of many German cities. Three people were working at the grill. One of these happened to be her father-in-law, a sturdily built tall elderly man in his early seventies. The rest were clustered into four or five small groups, talking leisurely. There was a big table next to the grill upon which salad, cold food, drinks, and fruits were placed. Seble's husband, her mother-in-law, and her daughter were playing Frisbee, a little isolated from the rest of the groups. He was introduced to each of the guests.

Two of these were her sisters-in-law; both married and with grown up children of their own. One of the two, he was told, had four children and the other had two. The sister with the four children was married to an American businessman in the aluminium industry and was living with her family in Fort Lauderdale, Florida. She was taking a one-week holiday alone. The other, who was married to an Italian banker, was living with her family in Zurich. Her entire family was there.

"A mixed family like the Bonhoeffer family," Ermias thought.

Wishing to have some occupation, he joined the three at the grill and volunteered to help. Presently, they were joined by Seble's husband, who offered Ermias a bottle of beer. He was a very attractive, tall, muscular man, thirty years old or thereabouts, with a pair of deep blue eyes and a slightly balding head. His beard was unshaven but his thin blond hair was neatly cut short. He was wearing a pair of khaki jeans and a white polo t-shirt with a pair of white sport shoes. His dressing style was similar to that of Seble's.

"I've heard that you are from Cambridge?" he remarked in accent-free English.

Ermias answered in the affirmative, feeling like those wretched Israelite spies who had regarded themselves as grasshoppers when they first saw the Amalekites in Canaan. For he, too, felt like a dwarf and insignificant in the presence of the husband's imposing figure. It was so strange; not once had Ermias imagined or tried to imagine what he looked like, and not once had he asked Seble to describe him or to show him his picture. As far as it was possible, they both had avoided mentioning him in their conversations. It was there that Ermias learned for the first time that his name was Stephan.

He was easy to talk to and eager to please and asked Ermias about his family, his research, and his hobbies, and expressed his admiration for Ethiopian athletes. His own hobby was riding expensive motorcycles. He took Ermias to his garage and showed him two massive and shiny BMW motorcycles, and eagerly described their construction detail and the differences between them. One of them, he explained, was popular for reasons of comfort and safety, whereas the other was more powerful and faster and was constructed from a light and expensive metal. The comfortable one was inherited from his father, who had also enjoyed riding motorcycles when he was young.

Then Stephan took Ermias to the house and showed him around. It seemed bigger and wider from the inside and was a demonstration of wealth and good test. There was nothing in the rooms which was misplaced, superfluous or accidental.

Ermias saw an old, polished August Förster piano standing in the living room and asked him which of them played.

"I play. Seble plays too," he answered simply. "Do you play?"

"No, I can't play any instrument, regrettably. But I didn't know that Seble plays the piano."

"She does. She must have forgotten to mention it. Do you meet her often?"

"Once a week or so."

"So, there isn't enough time to talk about everything, I suppose."

"That is right."

"But she's told me a lot about you," he stated simply.

"Has she?"

"Yes, she has. She told me the other day about your mother. I liked her interview, by the way. She looks young for one so successful, but Seble said she was over forty, forty-two?"

"She is forty-three."

"What is her secret for staying so young-looking?"

"She must have shared from the magic drink of Endymion."

"Who is Endymion?"

"In Greek mythology, he's a handsome shepherd who is granted eternal youth by his father Zeus."

"I see. Do you like reading mythology?"

"I do, whenever I've time."

"I suppose reading the classics is the mark of belonging to Oxbridge?"

"You'll be much surprised to find that the majority of them do not read books, let alone the classics."

"Really?"

"Why, it's the age of social networks, audio bites, video clips, talk shows, comedy centrals, and all."

"I suppose these things have always been the diets and addictions of the majority, albeit being delivered in different forms."

They went out and joined the party outside. At the grill they met a newcomer, a young girl of about twenty, whilst greeting the three gentlemen. Her name was Liselotte and she was Stephan's cousin, a student of law at the University of Konstanz.

"I've heard about you," she told Ermias when they were introduced.

"Seble must have been talking a lot about me," he observed with a tone faintly containing regret.

"It's natural, don't you think? You're her countryman, after all. Aren't you Eritrean?"

"I'm Ethiopian."

"Forgive me," she was quick to say, a little taken aback.

"What for?"

"For mistaking your national identity."

Nothing about her appearance featured Stephan. She was slim and of medium height and, except for her dense, wavy brown hair, she was plain-looking. She had dressed in a plain red skirt and sleeveless, white coloured cotton cambric shirt.

In his eagerness to sustain the conversation by teasing her, he took the joke a little too far when he claimed that lawyers earn their living at the expense of the misfortune of others. But Liselotte subtly changed the subject. Perhaps assuming that he was more apt to talk about his own immediate activities than topics about which he had little idea, she asked him to explain to her in plain terms what research he was doing. Ermias was counting the seconds before she made a polite excuse and left him as the girls in Dresden used to do, but she stayed and listened to him with interest. He too decided to be wiser this time and kept his story short.

"Why did you come to RIEP and not go to CERN, as most physicists do?"

He told her the truth. The sausages were ready by this time and Stephan called for everybody to come forward and help themselves. Liselotte and Ermias went forward and took their share: sausage, bread, and salad.

"Would you care to go to the swings?" Liselotte asked Ermias on their way back to their place and he agreed.

He was thankful for her companionship, for coming just as he was beginning to feel out of place in the company of Stephan and the three men at the grill, for none of the topics they chatted about were appealing to him. They sat on the swings and talked about various things. Then Ermias apologised for his blunder.

"Were you in earnest when you said that lawyers prey upon the misfortune of others?"

"In a way yes, but so do doctors and technicians. There's nothing particularly vicious about lawyers."

"What profession is holy in your opinion, experimental physics?"

"It too is a dishonest profession."

"Are you a nihilist?"

"I'm not sure what I am. I'm a little unhappy with myself."

"Why?"

"Youth is full of troubles, don't you think?" he replied and sighed.

"Do you have relationship troubles, by any chance?"

"You are asking a rather personal question."

He was certain this time that he had screwed-up for the second time and it was a matter of time before she stood up to excuse herself. Instead she made an observation.

"You are either a nihilist or in a bad relationship, or both assertions are true at the same time."

He was quick to throw her off the train.

"No, it's just that since I left my homeland at the age of sixteen, I've felt rootless and lost. It's been a long time since I felt at home with myself."

"And you are anxious, too. You don't like to displease people."

He looked at her but turned his eyes away quickly. He had been trying to look her in the eyes but was frustrated multiple times by his old foe.

"You've observed me closely. It's my first time to hear such a genuine evaluation of my psychology, and after such a brief encounter."

"I'm also anxious when I'm with other people. I'm mortified when people disapprove of me. Paradoxically, I have a rebellious nature. You, on the contrary, seem to me rather tame."

"What are you rebelling against?"

"My parents, to begin with. Church. God."

"Wow, you have a long list of formidable foes!" he declared.

She smiled and nodded in agreement and continued eating her food in silence. Ermias too focused on his food. Presently, Seble came to them with her daughter.

"Salem wishes to show you her room," she announced.

He thought he could detect a look of disapproval in her face, but he was not sure why. He got up quickly and gave his right hand to the little girl who had already stretched hers.

"Will you join us?" he asked Liselotte.

"I'll stay here. Little Salem may wish to have you all for herself."

"You can come," intervened the little girl innocently.

"It's all right," said Liselotte kindly. "Go and show him."

Salem and Ermias went to the house and Seble remained with Liselotte.

Salem was just the right kind of distraction for Ermias. He did not have to make an effort to please her or to choose topics which might be interesting to her. Moreover, their bonding came naturally. She showed him almost everything that was in her room and did the talking much of the time. Then she invited him to play with her puzzles and Lego, which he did gladly. After they had stayed together for about thirty minutes, they were joined by Liselotte who also got along with Salem very well and the three of them played a game called "catch a fish". Around six o'clock Seble and Stephan came upstairs to see how they were doing and invited them to come outside and play Kubb.

They all went out. Freshly grilled, delicious sausages and potatoes were being served, from which Liselotte and Ermias ate with appetite.

Then two teams were formed in each of which were four players. In the first group played Stephan, Seble, Liselotte, and Ermias, against the second group, consisting of Stephan's parents and his sisters. The game went on for one hour but neither of the teams won. Then they abandoned the game and Stephan and his father made a huge campfire whereas the rest sat on chairs in a circle around the campfire and talked casually, watching Stephan grilling marshmallows for Salem.

At nine in the evening Ermias decided to go. As he bade Liselotte goodbye, she asked him if he had time on Thursday evening. He said he had, whereupon she invited him to her birthday party. She was turning twenty-one, she said. He accepted her invitation and they exchanged telephone numbers and addresses. He was hoping to be with Seble for a minute, but Stephan proposed to bring him on his motorbike.

Once Ermias was alone inside his apartment, he sat on his study chair, closed his eyes, and listened to the tension that had built itself up inside his brain, which he now perceived, was physically painful. For some reasons, the day had been emotionally strenuous, even though he had barely been aware of it at the time.

The purpose of Seble's insistent invitation seemed obvious to him. Now that the people he had been doing an injustice were no longer unknown and faceless, it was impossible, as it were, to carry on in the same vein. What puzzled him was, however, that even before he had met Stephan and Salem, he had tried to disentangle himself, but encouragement was not forthcoming from her side.

And how was he to interpret the look of disapproval which she had given him today when she had spied him with Liselotte at the swings? Premeditated or not on her part, now one thing was clear for him beyond a shadow of doubt. He had to abandon his romantic pursuit and get over it.

Chapter 11

The three days leading up to Thursday's birthday party passed uneventfully and less painfully by. Ermias stayed away from Seble but greeted her twice when they met at the *Mensa*. Both times he was with his group and she was with the two elderly secretaries. On Thursday, he was in such a cheerful mood that Michel asked him what he was up to and Ermias told him.

He took the bus to Liselotte's at seven thirty in the evening. She lived on Werner-Sombart Strasse, in a pleasant looking, single-room student apartment, not very far from the Law Faculty. He was expecting the place to be crowded with young people, but to his surprise, there were only five people: her elder brother, who was completing his study at the department of mathematics in the same university, and his girlfriend; two of Liselotte's female friends, and a sickly-looking and taciturn theology student from the University of Wuppertal. After she had introduced him to the others, Liselotte offered him a bottle of beer, which he declined.

"Why not?"

"I don't drink beer."

"But you were drinking at Seble's birthday party, I saw you."

"Out of politeness. But here I don't need to be polite, do I?"

"So what shall I offer you?"

"You can offer me herbal tea, if you have some."

"I can offer you Rooibos."

"Thanks."

She offered him a chair and disappeared into her small kitchen to make tea. Except for the theology student, who said hardly a word throughout the evening, the others were cheerful and talkative. His reputation as a Cambridge experimental physicist had already gone out before him and all of them listened to him with palpable eagerness and admiration. Lotte, for that was how her friends addressed her, had so planned the evening that they would cook Shanghai dumplings together and play a game afterwards. She had written the recipe on a small blackboard which she hung on the wall in the kitchen. After thirty minutes of "warm-up" chatter, they all crowded into the small kitchen and divided the tasks amongst themselves: cutting the carrots, the eggplant, and the meat; chopping the onions, making and preparing the dough, and adding the filling and folding the dough carefully to form small parcels. Lotte herself plunged the dumplings into the boiling water and monitored the progress. The talk and laughter never flagged throughout the cooking process, which they completed around ten o'clock. This was the first experience of cooking homemade dumplings for all of them. For beginners, it was a successful endeavour.

After dinner, they played a game called *Phase 10*, eating lots of marzipan sweets and the three girls consuming large quantities of beer. But Lotte remained sober and drank only tea after dinner. The game lasted for more than two hours, because the girls were talking and laughing a lot. Ermias stayed until one o'clock in the morning and was the first to leave. As she saw him off, Lotte expressed her hope of seeing him again soon and suggested to undertake something together, such as going bowling. Ermias reciprocated by expressing his desire to see her again. He found bowling a good idea.

The next day he met Seble at the *Mensa* and she asked him to meet her in front of the guesthouse at four. She arrived on time and the two drove to the lake and sat on an elevated meadow next to an oak tree and talked. As if by prior agreement, they both avoided body contact. When he told her about his going to Lotte's birthday party, she was not surprised.

"There is a good chance that she may like you. I noticed her the other day how she paid attention to what you were saying and how she followed you everywhere with her eyes."

Ermias was not sure how much truth this statement contained. Was she testing him?

"She has a difficult personality, though. You should know."

"In what sense?"

"She tends to self-destruct. At times, she can be full of anger and rage."

"What's the reason behind it?"

"She has had a harsh upbringing and an eager mother who tries to decide everything for her."

"Same old story."

"Yeah, but Liselotte sometimes takes her rebelliousness dangerously too far."

"How about her father?"

"He's a withdrawn type, with a passive aggression of his own." Ermias, a little puzzled, recalled Lotte's brother, who had been composed and behaved gentlemanly the previous evening.

"Don't be deceived," Seble was quick to remark. "Men and women express their rebelliousness in different ways. I know this first hand from my own upbringing. Men tend to deteriorate first inward then outward whereas the deterioration of women is almost from the very outset outward."

"Do you think Liselotte is in danger?"

"Possibly. I know that the family worries a lot about her."

"Why?"

"Oh, for various reasons, I can't talk in detail now."

"Considering how you've portrayed the family, either their perception of her or the reality is inaccurate."

"But there are certain manifestations which cannot be mistaken."

"Does she know that she is in danger?"

"I suppose so. Look, I don't want to portray her as a problem girl or influence your opinion of her."

"I thought that was exactly your aim."

"If that much is what you've understood, you've a wrong perception of me."

"No, I don't mean in a bad way. I thought you wanted me to be informed. At any rate, my impression of her so far is positive. She was a great host yesterday, for instance."

"Maybe she conducts herself differently when she is in different company. That's quite possible."

"How about her education, does she take it seriously?"

"She seems to have full control on that front."

"So you see, maybe she'll manage to set her life in order, after all" he said, wishing to change the subject.

"If she falls in love with you and you're not sure, this may upset her and aggravate her situation."

He was hurt by her statement, but preferred not to contradict her.

"I'm just disclosing the possibilities as plainly as possible. I'm not trying to offend or hurt you."

"Why should I be responsible for her when I hardly know the girl?"

"All I'm saying is that she can be vulnerable. Don't give her hopes if you don't mean to fall in love with her."

"Were you vulnerable when you fell in love with me? Did I take advantage of you?"

Now it was he who hurt her. She drew both her legs towards her body, embraced them tightly with her arms and became thoughtful.

'Is this the beginning of our first quarrel?' he wondered anxiously.

"I'm sorry," he said aloud, but the words came out weightless.

"Yes, perhaps I was vulnerable," she observed without looking at him. "But, you too were vulnerable."

"Why should we torment ourselves over things we can hardly change?"

She kept silent.

"You bring up Lotte in order to prepare your heart for the passing of our love, which I understand," he said gloomily and lay down on the ground on his back and stared at the clear sky. The possibility of losing her shocked him. She too lay down on her back beside him. After five minutes or so, he heard a gentle snore and turned his face towards Seble. She was asleep, with her lovely lips gently parted.

She slept for more than twenty minutes. Ermias was anxious lest she would be late to get back home, but he did not wish to disturb her. Despite their disagreement, he felt close to her and the future seemed irrelevant to him when he thought of the closeness they had achieved to establish in such a short time. Seble woke up on her own and screwed up her eyes with her palms. Then she slowly turned on her side towards him, curled up her legs, and embraced him with her right arm.

"What's the time?"

He told her. They looked at each other in silence but with compassion.

"It's fine with me if you fall in love with a girl. But I want you to fall in love with a healthy and strong girl who loves, and is reconciled with, God. If she loves God, she'll find the strength to love life and to love you and to give herself unreservedly."

"But I don't want to fall in love with anyone when I'm in love with you. I know this should end, but all the same, I don't wish to fall in love with anyone right now. Speaking of God, who am I to ask and expect the love of God from someone when I myself am not sure if I have it?"

"You love God. You may not know it now, but you do."

"How can you be certain of that?"

"Believe me I know. You love life, you are unafraid of life. Whatever you do, you do it with passion and joy. All of these are confirmation of your agreement with God."

"The only thing I know right now is that I'm a sinner!" he said with sincerity.

"That, too, is a sign of your agreement with God."

"In Heidelberg there's a family which I consider as my second family. When I'm with them, I always find the strength to believe in God and to accept the significance of the world order he has put in place. I even find the strength to believe in the existence of a purpose for my own life, even though I'm yet to discover this purpose. But often I find myself away from them, in a defeated and cold world, where so many overwhelming questions and clouds of doubt gather around me. Then I feel like a patient who is etherised: my spirit is conscious and yet conscious of nothing in particular."

"I agree with you totally. We either reveal or conceal God in everything we do. There's no middle ground. And nothing conceals God worse than the fear of life."

"Do you love life?"

At this point her eyes were suddenly filled with tears.

"Yes, I love life. I've been tempted to reject it many times, but I chose to embrace it instead, because I love God."

"You have suffered, haven't you?"

"I can't say I've suffered more than the average person."

"Since you know what it means to suffer, you should be compassionate towards Liselotte."

"Believe me I'm compassionate towards her, but you won't help her by falling in love with her."

"Seble!" he bemoaned her inconsideration. "I've no plan to fall in love with her. Please, don't torment yourself."

"I want you to be happy. Only happy people can make others happy."

"Right now I'm happy and I'd give everything to keep this moment forever."

Chapter 12

Two weeks later Lotte phoned Ermias to ask him whether he was interested to accompany her to Baden-Baden on Saturday coming. She had received two tickets for a ballet performance at the Festspielhaus from her grandmother as a birthday present and guest dancers were coming from Hamburg to perform *Tatiana*, which was an adaptation of Pushkin's Eugene Onegin. She had already got a good offer, she said, for a room with a bunk bed at a youth hostel, but she had to confirm as soon as possible. Her invitation came as a nice surprise, for Ermias had been wanting to go to Baden-Baden since coming to Konstanz but the opportunity had not presented itself so far. Moreover, he had never been to a ballet performance.

It was an unusually sunny and warm afternoon when they left for Baden-Baden. Lotte was cheerful and chatty throughout the drive and sang aloud along to the various songs on the radio. Ermias too stretched his legs, leaned back, and relaxed, feeling fortunate to be with this young and intelligent girl. How much had he been willing four years ago to sacrifice everything—his time, his privacy, and his independence—in order to be with someone like her!

After a one-hour drive they made a stopover at a gas station to rest and drink coffee, and fifteen minutes later set off again to arrive at the ancient spa town shortly before five. They parked the car at a nearby car park, checked in at the hostel, and took a shower in turn. Then they strolled on the red carpets in the pedestrian zone, passed the congress centre by, and entered into a spacious meadow surrounded by various tall and spreading trees at the Lichtentaler Allee.

"I'd be very happy to run here tomorrow before we leave," Ermias remarked, scrutinising the spacious meadow with satisfaction.

"Do you really want to run?" Lotte asked him excitedly.

"Yes, very much."

"Then I'll show you a place. We have to get up early in the morning and run to the mountain over there," she indicated with her finger towards the high hills on the other side of the town, opposite to the meadow.

"There is an old, lonely castle in the middle of the forest. From there, we can enjoy a nice view of the town, the meadow, the valleys, and the mountains far beyond the town. It's a magnificent view."

"Have you been there before?"

"Many times."

They walked to the *Festspielhaus* and queued up. And the performance began at half past seven.

Watching the complexity, elegance, and agility of the dancers' movement and the subtle harmony in the ever changing and tantalising background scenes, Ermias' firmly believed that beauty is no random phenomenon and that it is rather a consequence of thoughtful and painstaking endeavour. He recalled Einstein who had once ruled out accident as the cause of Creation. The physicist had been compelled by the extreme care and precision with which the universe is arranged and by the higher level of mathematics and assiduity required to comprehend even a very small portion of it. He glanced at Lotte in the semi-darkness many times to see how she was responding. She had been transfixed the whole time. Indeed, he suspected that she was fighting off tears the whole time.

After the performance, Lotte became doleful. Ermias suggested eating something and they went to a nearby Argentinian restaurant. Twice she wanted to talk about something but both times she changed her mind. Instead, they talked about Pushkin, his Ethiopian origin, his contribution to classical Russian literature, and his own unfulfilled love life. After they had finished eating, he asked her if she was interested in visiting the casinos, but she declined. Midnight was fast approaching and she recommended instead returning to their hostel.

She woke him up the next morning at seven, fully dressed and ready for a run. Ermias quickly got up and got ready to go out. On the way, she was once again in a good mood and was running effortlessly. They run westward and crossed the town centre, passed by the ruins of the Roman baths, and entered into a clean, narrow footpath leading out of the town and towards the hills. Then they quickly came to a grassy hillside apparently strewn with many curved and criss-crossing sandy footpaths and from a distance they observed a huge bronze statue overlooking a tree-filled valley. Could it be of Dostoevsky? Ermias wondered. And, indeed, it was his likeness. They stopped briefly to appreciate the statue and to read the inscription.

Dostoevsky's statue was standing barefoot on a globe, wearing a cheap, rugged mantle and a pair of shabby and crumpled, undersized trousers. But his bearded face was solemn and thoughtful and his eyes were half-closed, either owing to regret or deep contemplation. The statue seemed to display the duality of the great writer: the clothes and his bare feet suggesting his despair and destitution on account of his reckless gambling and agonising loss at the roulette table, whilst his face, particularly the composition of his wide forehead, suggesting deep reflection.

After a short break, they resumed running up the hill for about twenty minutes and, at last, arrived at the old, lonesome castle. Lotte suggested running a little farther up and after five minutes or so, they arrived at a saddle point where they found a big rock at the edge of the hill and sat on it, gazing down at the forests, the valleys, the town below, and Mount Merkur in front of them.

When surveyed from such a height, the town seemed completely serene, almost as if it were asleep, as if its inhabitants were dreamless and had been reconciled amongst themselves the previous night. Or, perhaps, the night had possessed many troubled and guilt-ridden souls who now found no reason to get up from their beds.

"I used to come here with someone." Lotte remarked sadly.

He looked at her but she was resting her gaze on the mountain far ahead of her. He waited, wishing to give her time.

"You met him the other day, the theology student from Wuppertal. He was my boyfriend. He was such a positive person when I first came to know him, but gradually succumbed to depression. I was in love with him only briefly, and then, stayed with him for two years out of a sense of duty. But the relationship made me unhappy. Finally, I decided to terminate it. It was crushing for him and trying for me, because it felt like I was being unfaithful. He hasn't got over it to date. I understand Tatiana very well."

He remembered Seble. *Only happy people can make others happy.* He wanted to say something to comfort her, but afraid of sounding superficial, remained silent. Then he spoke at long last, also resting his gaze on the distant horizon.

"A relationship is supposed to build one up, but often times it tears one down."

"That's because the defect in one often magnifies and exacerbates the defect in the other."

"What was the reason for his depression?"

"There were several reasons, but at the centre of it all was a fear of failure."

"Has his situation changed since then?"

"He's still struggling. I doubt it will ever change."

"If he studies theology, he must believe in God."

Lotte reflected for a moment and, then, spoke: "When I was living in Africa—I lived in Uganda for a year, by the way—I met many Christians who were leading triumphant lives amid stark poverty and apparent absence of prospects. When I observe some of the Christians here, many of them struggle to be happy. Some, amid, material success, have given up altogether trying to be happy and are worse than the unbelievers in their misery and cynicism. I can't explain the difference. It's incomprehensible to me."

Ermias remembered Andrew who had once spoken of the problem of self-sufficiency and its tendency to disunite people. Andrew then maintained that striving to achieve self-sufficiency at all costs inevitably creates unwholesome gaps between individual members, the building blocks of a society, and tampers with the very foundation of social life.

Ermias himself remembered how in all his previous schools a strong emphasis had been placed on self-sufficiency. Weakness, whether of an academic or social nature, had been regarded by teachers as well as parents as a great social burden rather than as an opportunity for fellow pupils and teachers to discover in themselves their capacity for compassion and empathy. When something went wrong, one was pretty aware that the responsibility of making it right primarily rested upon one's own shoulders. One had to rely and count on one's own resources. Lotte waited for a reaction from Ermias but Ermias seemed to have no opinion to offer.

 "Come, we should run back to our hostel. I'm hungry."

Ermias obeyed.

Chapter 13

The following Saturday, around one o'clock in the morning, Ermias received a phone call from Liselotte. He was brushing his teeth and intending to go to bed when his phone rang.

"Do you have a driving licence?" Lotte asked him excitedly as soon as she heard his voice on the phone. He told her he had.

"Can you rescue me? I can't drive, I'm a little tipsy, I'm afraid!" she said, not in German, but in English.

"Where are you?"

"I can't say where I am other than saying I'm in a pub. Wait, let me ask."

There was a loud noise in the background, which he believed was a live jazz band playing. He waited for a long time but she did not get back to him. So, he hung up. She rang after twenty minutes and told him the street address. He looked it up in the

Internet to find that it was an Irish pub in the southern part of the city.

"I need about forty minutes to get there," he told her.

"I shall wait for you in front of the pub. Please don't be angry," she shouted, pleadingly.

"Wait for me there."

Ten minutes later Ermias was on the bus, but when he reached the final stop he had a hard time finding the pub and took ten minutes more than he had calculated to get there. When he finally found the pub, he saw Lotte standing outside, talking with two young men and apparently feeling chilly.

"There you are, finally!" she said with relief.

She was properly drunk. The young men greeted Ermias courteously and waited to take their leave. Lotte spent some time searching for her key inside her bag, and when she found it, gave it to Ermias.

"Good night gentlemen, I must go now. It was a pleasure. Can I lean on you gently?"

The young men took their leave and returned to the pub and Lotte and Ermias moved slowly away from the pub, taking the opposite direction to the one by which he had arrived.

"Where is your car?"

Lotte tried to remember where she parked her car but could not.

"I've no recollection where I parked the damn car," she said visibly embarrassed. "Wait, let me think. How did I get here, how did I get here? I came with the boys. They brought me here. Now I remember. Oh, dear, I've parked it in front of

Lexi, not very far from Petershausen, so far as I can tell. We must take a taxi there."

Lotte was talking with difficulty, not only because she was tipsy but also because her teeth were slightly chattering, since she was feeling cold. They took a taxi to Petershausen and, indeed, found her car parked alone, in front of another pub.

"Please drive carefully, the car cost me a fortune," she begged him.

"So much for being responsible," he mocked her without being sullen.

She ignored his mocking and leaned back on the passenger seat, closing her eyes and feeling her temples with her fingers. She seemed exhausted. Ermias found a reserve navigator inside the glove compartment and entered her address. It was not very far away.

"I'm really grateful. You are such a dependable friend!" she showered praises on him as he escorted her to her room. She looked very tired and pale.

"Shut up," he countered with a friendly tone.

"I'd feel so guilty if I sent you back at this time of the night. Do you want to stay here? I can let you have my bed and I'll sleep on the sofa."

She was still speaking in English even though the last three times they met, they had only conversed in German. Ermias too replied in English.

"I can't stay. I've lots of things to catch up on tomorrow."

"But it's Saturday."

"I know, but I've agreed with a friend to go to the lab with him in the morning."

"I'll give you a ride, I promise. I'll be fit by the morning. What time do you want to be there?"

"I know you'll be fit by the morning, Lotte, but I won't feel comfortable staying here. I need to rest properly in order to be able to concentrate on my work."

"But how can you get there at this hour?"

"I'll catch a night bus, don't worry."

"Well then, thanks. Good night."

From her sinking tone he sensed that she was disappointed. The truth was that he was thinking of Seble and somehow felt internally compelled not to spend the night with Lotte, knowing that Seble would disapprove of it. Lotte gave him a quick hug and Ermias left. It was already three o'clock.

As soon as he was inside the taxi, however, he felt bad for having been inflexible. Wishing to make up for his rigidity, he sent her a text message.

"How about the two of us have dinner together later today, at my place? I can cook Ethiopian food for us."

Her reply came at eleven in the morning.

"Accepted. What time?"

"At eight?" Ermias responded from the lab.

"I confirm." came her reply an hour later.

Lotte arrived ten minutes before eight, looking remarkably fresh in a pair of faded blue jeans and a black sailor's jacket. Underneath the jacket, she was wearing a plain and loosely fitting grey sweatshirt, which barely exposed the shape of her small breasts. Her wavy hair, on the other hand, was shining and seemed to have doubled in volume, making her face appear smaller than it really was.

She saw *The Idiot* lying on the table and picked it up, her face expressing curiosity and suspicion at the same time. After a cursory study of the image on the novel's front cover, she put it back.

"I've heard that he hates us Catholics," she remarked.

"I'm not sure about that."

"What does he say about life anyway? Many people are captivated by his ideas."

He deliberated for a second and told her what he thought was Dostoevsky's central idea.

"He believes that human freedom is the greatest miracle, God's greatest and daring experiment with Creation."

"Does he say that?"

"Yes, he does. And he believes that without human freedom love would've been impossible, and since love finds expression in a relationship, human freedom also enables human beings to have a loving relationship with God. Dostoevsky believed in a personal God and couldn't imagine the possibility of an egalitarian relationship without absolute freedom."

Lotte listened with interest.

"This place smells like sweat," she remarked when Ermias was done. He hurried to close the bathroom door.

"I was running half an hour ago. I didn't have the time to…"

"I didn't mean to embarrass you. I meant it rather as a compliment. I don't mind the smell of sweat."

"You pervert!" he joked.

"You can now safely add an additional label to those which already exist in your list. A pervert, who studies law to prey upon the unfortunate, a rebellious girl who is bent on destroying her life by heavy drinking and orgies."

"I see that you haven't forgiven me."

"I wouldn't have come here today had I not forgiven you."

He wished to ask her why she was talking to him in English the whole time yesterday, but he put it aside. She was in a good mood and he did not wish to spoil it. She went to his small shelf and browsed the book titles.

"When do you get the time to do reading, studying, and running, and pursuing other interests on top of that?"

"What other interests?" he asked her smiling, guessing what she was alluding to.

"I don't know, girls, for instance?"

"I don't know that many girls. I'm a poor hand when it comes to girls."

"Men! Always lying and never telling the truth."

He liked her nonchalance and her confidence to express her mind freely.

"Why do you drink?" he ventured to ask.

"I wouldn't normally answer a question like that, but I'll make an exception tonight because I owe you a favour. So, why do I drink? I don't have a monolithic answer to this question. Let's say I like it—though, not the hangover. Sometimes I drink because I like the company. Sometimes, it makes me feel free and talkative. Even your Dostoevsky testifies that there is nothing more precious than freedom or the illusion of it."

"I'm not sure if that is the sort of freedom Dostoevsky meant."

"Blast Dostoevsky, then," she retorted calmly, still browsing the titles.

Apparently, she found none of the books interesting. Then she opened the door leading to the balcony and stepped outside. It was dark outside, but they could see the weak ripples of the lake poorly reflecting the outdoor lights.

"You must have a magnificent view during the day," she said, folding her arms and gazing into the dark.

"What types of books do you like to read?" he asked her standing next to her and studying her profile which was partially obscured by her wildly abundant, curly hair.

"I don't have any preference. I read books mainly to relax. Of late, I've been reading *A Handful of Dust*, by Evelyn Waugh. He started off really brilliantly but spoilt the story towards the end. I like him because he's silly and sometimes even witty. I also like reading the Bronte sisters and Jane Austen, without taking any of them seriously."

They stood in silence for a minute or two, but both felt the cold breeze coming from the lake and decided to go in.

"It's getting late. Shouldn't you start cooking right away? I don't want to stay late another evening."

"I've already prepared everything. It'll take us about thirty minutes to cook and another thirty minutes to eat. By ten you'll be free as a bird."

"Let's begin then," she said cheerfully and accompanied him to the kitchen.

Ermias had planned to cook *Doro*. She cut the tomatoes, whilst he fried the onions and prepared the chicken. They talked and teased each other like old friends. He told her about his family and the Holms and she talked about her love of hiking and her travel to the Grand Canyon and to Colorado with two of her female friends the previous year. She also briefly talked about her ex-boyfriend.

"After the first three months into our relationship, we began to quarrel most of the time. He was a control-freak like my mother, and came up with an entirely new plan for my life. Some people are tempted to believe that they will attain security if they take away the security of others. What an irony!"

The *Doro* was ready in thirty minutes and Ermias served it with Turkish bread and natural yogurt.

"The food is delicious!" she remarked with genuine appreciation.

He was pleased with her accolade, but more pleased with her company and ease.

"I'm jealous of you. You do everything right and everything seems to be running smoothly for you. How do you manage things so well?"

"I've had difficulties of my own in the past and still struggle with some of them. You find me during a brief moment of repose. But I don't permit doubt and despair to take up permanent residence in me. Most of the things I do, I do with enjoyment."

"Doubt and despair seem to have taken a permanent residence in me. They've been living with me far too long. Your Dostoevsky is right; human freedom is the biggest risk God has taken."

"Nothing is permanent," he remarked sensing the lack of conviction in his own voice.

"Certain things are permanent, believe me."

"*Time takes over and puts an end to the good and the bad memory as well as the desire to live.*"

"Now that is a philosophical statement!" she told him.

"I was quoting from *Under a mantle of Stars*, a short play written by Manuel Puig, an Argentinian writer. I watched the play when I was in New York."

"Can you write it down for me?"

He wiped his fingers with a paper napkin, pulled a pen and a piece of paper and wrote the quotation down for her. She paused from eating and studied the verse carefully.

"Now that is a statement for real," she repeated, slowly oscillating her head up and down with deliberation.

"But pain seems to last forever."

Ermias stretched his hand involuntarily and took hers and looked at her kindly, his shyness disappearing for a moment.

"Forgive the past. Life is before you."

"I'm trying," she said smiling weakly.

He released her hand and they resumed eating.

"What's your highest aspiration in life?" she asked him after a while.

"I'm only twenty-three; I cannot say I've already found my highest aspiration, whatever that means. For the present, love and curiosity are propelling me through life. I feel very fortunate to have people around me whom I dearly love and care about. When I'm with them, my life is rich and colourful and I'm ready to regard every problem of life as a necessary challenge which I must overcome in order to discover my own strength. But when I'm lonely, this conviction tends to vanish and I incline to regard life as a great risk."

He recalled that this was the second time in about a month that he had spoken about the correlation and anti-correlation between love, loneliness, and the meaning of life. He had not really thought about these relations thoroughly nor had he committed them to paper. They had hitherto existed at the back of his mind as vague impressions. But after he had spoken about them twice, they seemed clearer to him and his conviction in their truthfulness became stronger.

After dinner they moved to the sofa and drank tea and talked about a variety of issues. She left shortly before midnight.

Chapter 14

Meanwhile Seble and Ermias continued seeing each other almost every Friday by Mindelsee. Seble's conscience did not allow her to make love to Ermias and yet it did not prevent her from arranging countless meetings with him in private, which Ermias found remarkable. Ermias was himself unable to make up his mind and preferred to submit himself to his current circumstances.

They would stay at the lake for about an hour on each occasion, during which they walked around the lake or through the forest, or, when the weather was windy or wet, they stayed in the car, talking. He was worried about her, for she seemed to have lost weight, but she reassured him that her weight was alright and that she had never felt better.

She would update him in detail about Salem and Ermias would update her about his work, Bordélique, or his grandmother. These were the safest subjects for both of them. Not only did they regard them emotionally harmless to one another, but also found genuine pleasure in talking about them. His grandmother had at the time decided to take up breeding goats as her preferred occupation and she had interesting events to relate over the phone almost every day. Bordélique, on the other hand, was experiencing the first test of being loved and admired, though she herself was not in love. Nevertheless, her great sense of respect for humanity prevented her from seeing this simple truth. Sometimes Seble would ask Ermias about Liselotte. If he had something to share, she would listen without interruption or reproach, but he knew she disapproved of his seeing her.

One Saturday evening in early December as Ermias was returning from running, he found Seble waiting for him at his door. At first he did not recognise her because it was partially dark in the corridor and she had tucked a scarf around her neck and had put on a woollen hat, which partly covered her forehead. Since he was not expecting anyone, he was surprised to find someone at his door. She removed her hat when she saw him and smiled.

"Is everything alright?" he asked her, in an alarmed tone, once he had recognised her.

"Open the door," she gestured. Her voice was gentle and she did not seem to be in a hurry.

"How did you get inside?"

"I waited until someone opened the front gate and that same person happened to know where you live."

"Did he recognise you?"

"I don't think so."

They entered the apartment. He was at once pleased and anxious to see her. She scanned the room without giving him any explanation whilst he watched her in suspense. She did not look troubled or agitated. In fact, her shoulders and arms were loosened and the muscles of her face were relaxed.

"I missed you." She stated as a matter of fact. "I'm staying with you tonight."

"What about Stephan and Salem?"

"Stephan is travelling and Salem is staying with her grandparents."

As much as he wished to be with her, he did not think this was a good idea.

"Seble, are you sure this is a good idea, won't you regret it later?"

"Why should I regret anything? I wish to be with you and I shall be with you. If you don't want me here, that is a different matter. Besides, we won't have sex—don't even think about it! No kisses either, nothing of that sort. As you know, I'm a Catholic—not that I deserve to be—and I take no protection. I only wish to sleep beside you. If anyone else has a problem with this, so be it."

From the look on her face, he knew that this was a time when she needed his unreserved reassurance. He went up to her and hugged her. At first she hesitated, but then she hugged him back.

"You smell of sweat! Go and take shower!"

She gently pushed him back with disgust. He kissed her on her cheek and forehead regardless and went to take shower.

"I've brought salmon sushi and salad for supper and croissants for breakfast," Ermias heard her saying.

Suddenly, he was flooded with joy prevailing over all of his concerns for Seble and for himself and began to sing softly in the shower. When he got back to her, she was making tea and preparing supper. He stood in front of the bathroom door for a moment and admired her beauty, the grace of her body, and her movements.

"I'm so happy that you are here," he told her and embraced her from behind.

She held his hands with hers but remained silent. Then he helped her with the preparation and they ate, talking about fitness.

"Thanks to you, I've now completely abandoned my Friday swimming. But to compensate for that, I'm taking Salem to swimming every Saturday afternoon. When Stephan comes along, I have some time for myself."

He remembered seeing a fully equipped fitness room in their house.

"Yes, but that is mainly for Stephan," Seble told him. "I work out there only occasionally. I don't know why, but I must go out of the house in order to enjoy sport."

He told her about his mother and her love of running.

"You should introduce me to her," she said eagerly.

"Do you mean it? I've already thought about it."

"Yes, I mean it. She'll certainly despise me if she knows I'm in love with her son. I'd be delighted to get to know her, nonetheless."

"My mom doesn't despise by nature."

"Every woman despises under the circumstances."

They talked about general matters until ten thirty, but when he saw her yawning several times, he finally stood up to clear the table and she went to the bathroom to shower. After he had finished, he picked up a book and tried to read, listening to the sound of water in the bathroom and to the lingering sound of her sweet voice in his head. She took what seemed an eternity in the bathroom but finally emerged wearing pink cotton pyjamas, her long black hair braided on one side and swept into a side bun.

"Man, don't you look like a goddess!" he confessed with genuine admiration.

"Shut up," she said smiling.

For the first time in their relationship he felt painfully envious of her husband. She came to him and sat on the edge of the bed.

"What are you reading?"

She took the book in order to see its title, but handed it back to him almost immediately.

"I'm sorry; I'm tired. But I can't sleep if the light is on."

He folded the book, put it on the side table, and turned off the light. She slipped into the bed and moved to the side of the bed closer to the window and lay down with her legs tucked up close to her body, turning her face towards the window. He put his left arm under her head and embraced her with his right. The calm she had exhibited the whole evening seemed to have waned, for now she began shaking.

"Your bed is cold!" she complained, even though the room was sufficiently warm.

"Everything is fine. Everything will be fine," he tried to reassure her.

"Tell me about your grandmother, what did you like most when you were with her, what do you remember most?"

He told her about his grandmother's orchard and how he used to set up his own fruit market and sell fruits to the neighbours, and his reckless passion for tree-climbing. She listened, still shivering, but her shivering ebbed gradually and was replaced by her gentle snoring.

He was unable to sleep for a long time, partly because his body was still excited from the running. His mind, on the other hand, was calm and contented like a child nestled in the protection and comfort of its mother's arms.

His left arm was still under her head but now he was lying on his back, his eyes open and peering into the dark. Then suddenly, without any conscious effort from his side, a scientific problem which had been frustrating him for many months, unravelled itself in his mind of its own accord.

In classical physics, corporal bodies, such as planets, are typically described by some well-defined properties, such as position, momentum, and velocity. If some of these properties are known, other properties can easily be determined by applying Newtonian laws. This is not the case with quantum particles. For example, one may measure the energy emitted by a quantum particle and yet may not be able to use this knowledge in order to determine the exact location of the self-same particle in all the three dimensions. One may only guess where the particle can be. Thus, the exact location of the particle it said to be a hidden state. In quantum physics, the hidden state and the measurement results are related by a quantity called observable or measurable. The observable is the experiment set up by which the experimental physicist conditions the outcomes of an experiment, so that from the experiment results, it is possible to get back to the hidden state. In quantum physics jargon the measurement values, as well as the hidden state, express a probabilistic reality as opposed to a deterministic reality. Hence, the three quantities can be statistically related by what one calls a Bayesian estimation technique, the main purpose of which is to enable the physicist update or revise their belief about the hidden state of the system whenever fresh measurement results become available.

For Ermias, this relationship resulted in a cumbersome equation which was difficult to evaluate. Now, however, if he represented the measurement values as the outcomes of many independent random variables, expressed his measurements in terms of the average of these random variables, and normalised the entire equation, a good portion of the denominator would be eliminated by a portion of the numerator and what would remain of the denominator would not only be integrable, but the result would also be a constant, leading to a simple expression.

Ermias went through the equations in his head again and again to make sure that the approach was plausible. Now he was both physically and mentally alert and became consciously restless. He cautiously removed his arms from under her head, but Seble was fast asleep. He raised himself from the bed cautiously, tiptoed to his study table, turned on the table lamp and set to work, his hands shaking slightly with excitement and his heart beating fast. He worked until five in the morning and finally proved that the equation was indeed integrable.

He knew that he had achieved an important milestone towards his dream of obtaining a PhD. He wanted to immediately inform his Cambridge supervisor by emailing him the results but wishing to exercise caution wrote to Anne instead, asking her to schedule a meeting for him next week with the group, so that he could officially present his results to them first. Satisfied with himself, yet still excited, he went to bed and lay down next to Seble. He was still unable to fall asleep, but was not bothered at all. Eager for the day to break, he thought of how to make additional experiments in order to validate his model. Towards seven o'clock he slumbered.

Seble woke him up at ten o'clock, having first prepared breakfast. It occurred to him that they had not discussed what time she intended to leave, so he jumped out of the bed immediately. He was half afraid that she would be guilt ridden when she realised the risk she had taken, but nothing could be further from the truth. She seemed to be in no hurry and was still in a good mood. She hugged and kissed him softly on his forehead and asked him how he slept.

"You've no idea how the night went by!" he told her eagerly, with a loud and singing voice and remembering his childhood eagerness with which he used to tell his grandmother his great discoveries.

"We've a reason to celebrate!"

"What's happened?" she questioned him, suddenly infected by his buoyancy and looking at him with curiosity.

He related enthusiastically how he spent the night.

"I'm happy for you. Your enthusiasm is infectious; do you know that? You've a healthy dose of a child's enthusiasm. It's my prayer that you keep it."

Throughout breakfast Seble remained cheerful and unhurried. Ermias stood up from his seat at frequent intervals and hugged and kissed her on her cheeks, her neck, her forehead, her shoulders, in short, everywhere except on her lips, the touch of which he was yearning for desperately. She finally scolded him and asked him to sit still. After breakfast, she got up and collected her things and looked at him with a mixture of sadness and thankfulness.

"It's been a great night; you've not let me down."

He was deeply moved by her approval and his eyes suddenly filled with tears.

"Good luck with your research. I'm confident you'll be successful. God bless you."

"Thanks. Your visit was the sweetest surprise I've ever had in my entire life and now its memory is deliciously mixed with my success at my research."

He spoke the truth. His heart was aching for her to be happy. Then he asked her where she parked her car.

"I came by bus," she answered. "You stay right here. There's a bus living in six minutes, I'll catch it. I hope I won't bump into someone from the institute. Since it's Sunday, hopefully everybody is still sleeping."

He let her go. Fifteen minutes later he was hurrying to the lab, impatient as the wind and eager like a child to validate his model.

That same day Ermias received an email from his mother informing him that his father and she were organising a big get together party in the upcoming summer to celebrate Bordélique's completion of her voluntary service in Nairobi and her acceptance by the University of Gottingen in the autumn to study medicine. The only problem was that Rhoda and Ermias too were planning a big surprise, namely, to take her for a one-month vacation to Honolulu. Rhoda had already secured a summer job in a surfing shop at Waikiki Beach and Ermias had been saving money for purchasing their tickets. Now the two planned events were in great conflict one with the other, because Aster and Dawit wanted the young people to stay in Addis for a whole month. When they became aware of the conflict, Aster tried to persuade Rhoda to shorten or postpone their trip to Honolulu, but Rhoda deferred her to Ermias, because he was the one with limited holidays.

Taking the opportunity, Ermias telephoned his mother to ask if she could invite Seble to Addis for Easter.

"Her family has been kind to me, and I want her to come and visit us in Addis."

"Why don't you invite her yourself?" she wanted to know.

This question was difficult to answer without giving himself away.

"It'll have more weight if the invitation comes from you."

"It's odd to invite someone I don't know."

"Seble is eager to make your acquaintance."

"Who'll pay for their ticket, or are you intending to invite her alone?"

"I'm not sure if her husband can make it. But she'll definitely not come without her daughter."

"And the tickets?"

"Perhaps she'll pay for their tickets."

"What do you mean perhaps?"

"I guess, she'll pay."

"You can't invite someone to Addis with perhaps and guesses." Aster recommended instead that he introduced Seble first to the Holms and then to think about the invitation to Addis. It was an ill-prepared proposal, so he accepted her recommendation. As regards the clash of schedules, they were unable to resolve it, since Rhoda's summer job would begin on the first day of July and end on the last day of September. Without her job, they could not afford to travel to Honolulu.

Chapter 15

Ermias presented his results to the team on Tuesday afternoon, after having worked on Sunday until midnight and on Monday from eight o'clock in the morning until ten o'clock in the evening, non-stop.

There was no strong objection to his results, but there was no evident enthusiasm either. Expressing stochastic processes in terms of ensemble averages was not something new in statistical mechanics. What was new to his approach was the experimental validation of two assertions he had made which could greatly simplify the fusion of data from a large number of nanosensors. The first assertion stated that the sensors reacted in the same way to one and the same input if one regarded the average energy they generated during a very short period of time, even though the instantaneous energy they emitted was random by nature. From the data he had gathered, he was able to determine the duration of this period. Likewise, the second assertion stated that compared to the variance in the magnitude of the energy they emitted, the variance of the energy they imparted to one another in the form of thermal energy or noise when the sensors were placed in close proximity to one another was significantly small. In other words, the sensors could be regarded, statistically speaking, as independent. These two assertions not only explained the extensive measurements he had gathered under different operation conditions, but also enabled him to mathematically relate the signals the nanosensors received from the celestial bodies with the energy they produced, the first step towards employing the sensors for practical purposes.

After the meeting was dismissed, Ermias sank into a heavy melancholic mood. Somehow he perceived the apparent lack of enthusiasm as a sign of their disapproval of his illicit relationship with Seble. He was conscious that he was bordering on paranoia, given the seriousness of the matter at hand. But he was equally aware that some of the brightest scientists he had met resembled in many respects the most ordinary people on the street and were often interested in and affected by ordinary affairs of life.

Even though Ermias was persuaded of the merits of his proposal, he now regretted his making too much of the whole thing. Had he been desperate to win the respect of his team undeservedly? Had he been deceived by his own folly and inexperience into rushing to the conclusion that the results he had produced in less than six months should have been afforded the audience of a highly regarded scientific team?

Had his colleagues been honest and critical and rejected his proposal after a genuine discussion, he would have taken the matter as a sign of their respect for his work, but now their indifference crushed him. Ridiculed by a harsh superego, he decided to leave the institute and go running.

After the run, he felt better but yearned for some company. He was desperate to ring Seble even though he convinced himself that she would not answer his phone call. Her cautiousness must have been inherited from her father who had undoubtedly mistrusted all forms of radio communications during the war.

Ermias phoned Lotte instead, but she was in Munich. Finally, he decided to go to the cinema alone, but as he was going by bus to Konstanz, Lotte phoned him back and asked if he could drive her home on Friday evening—she said she was invited to a Christmas party by the professor in whose research team she was working as a student assistant. Ermias volunteered and took the address of the restaurant, which was on the Island of Reichenau.

His dejected state lasted the remainder of the week, during which he checked and double checked the model he had developed, in case he had overlooked implausible or faulty components. Moreover, he took fresh measurements to make sure that the model was able to provide predictable outcomes. Perhaps he was biased towards his own approach, and therefore, was unable to find any error.

On Friday, he accompanied Seble to a sports outlet in Radolfzell to buy Christmas presents for Stephan and Salem. Armed with their purchases, they went to a café to have coffee. As they were waiting for their coffee to arrive, she asked him what was wrong.

"You've been dismal the whole time."

"My little model was met with a wave of indifference on Tuesday."

"I'm sorry to hear that, what did they say?"

"Nothing, really. Some asked me, out of politeness, to clarify some expressions I had used. But they managed to evade the central concept, which was the prime reason for the meeting."

"They may need some time to digest your ideas."

"I doubt it. I was too fast to serve a half-cooked meal."

"They should've given you an honest feedback, regardless."

"People find reservation the safest way to reject."

"Rejection. It's so commonplace in research institutions nowadays. Papers, proposals, job applications, all, are routinely rejected. Eventually, one learns to reject everything. You should get used to it."

"I know. Still, every rejection comes as a unique and unpleasant surprise, packed with an entirely different sort of pain."

After he had seen Seble off, Ermias returned to his apartment, ate cereal for supper and picked up *The Idiot*, which he had abandoned half-way through ten days ago, and resumed reading with interest, waiting at the same time for a phone call from Lotte. The phone call, however, tarried for a long time, until after midnight, and he resented her thoughtlessness and regretted his consent to pick her up.

"What is the point of this friendship anyway?" he inquired. "Don't I know that it's on the road to nowhere, in the same way my relationship with Seble has no destination?"

Her phone call came at quarter past twelve and he took a taxi at twenty to one. She was already waiting outside of the restaurant when he arrived. He had been brooding inside on the way, so that he forgot to smile when he greeted her.

"Is something bothering you?" she asked him anxiously.

He quickly checked himself.

"It's been a tiresome week."

"What happened?"

"Oh, nothing in particular. I presented some results to the team on Tuesday which were not received warmly."

"Warmth in winter?" she joked.

"True."

"Is it a bad sign?"

"I don't think so. I was a bit hasty, that's all."

"I'm sorry for being selfish. I didn't know you'd had a bad week."

"I rang you first when I was feeling bad. You did well in relying on me."

From her animated eyes, it was evident that she had been drinking, but she was not tipsy this time.

"How was your evening?" he asked her, as they were going towards her car.

"Boring. I drank more than I wanted to in order to occupy myself."

"Odd. No one was interested to engage a smart and intelligent girl like you?"

"I'm bad at small talk, particularly, when I'm in a new environment and sober. Most of the participants were former and present PhD students, none of whom I knew very well. Besides, most of them were rather stiff."

She yawned and rubbed her eyes.

"I knew it'd be a long evening, but I also knew that there was a show, which I hoped would be a good diversion."

"It wasn't?"

"There were many intermissions, each lasting an aeon."

"Why did you accept the invitation in the first place if you knew it would be boring?"

"Out of courtesy and a sense of duty. Never heard of them before?"

Once they were inside the car, Ermias waited for her to give him directions, but instead she suggested driving somewhere, where they could take a short walk.

"I feel a little suffocated, a walk in the cold will refresh me, what do you think? Tomorrow is Saturday, you can sleep longer."

"You haven't dressed for a cold night," he remarked.

"It isn't that cold, I should be fine."

"Besides, it's really late..."

"Oh, dear, how cautious you are! You've reminded me of a verse in the Bible..."

She closed her eyes and thought for a moment and, then, recited:

When it was evening, the disciples came to him and said, "This is a deserted place, and the hour is now late; send the crowds away so that they may go into the villages and buy food for themselves."[j]

"Do you remember this verse?"

"Did you not say that you regard religion and God as your enemies?"

"Not in the ordinary sense, you Heathen! But you didn't answer my question."

He told her the place from where she picked the verse.

"You see, this verse is about relying on objective evidence, such as the measurements you take in your lab. There's nothing to eat, the time is too late, and the place is a wilderness. There is a perfect spacetime problem for you. Which human problem, however monstrous, doesn't permit itself to be described by these words?"

"Existence, for example."

"Do you consider existence as a problem?"

"Sometimes, yes. There are many who regard existence as a great burden."

"Man, you are depressed! All right, even if we assume existence to be a burden, we can describe it in those three terms. We suffer because we feel that our needs aren't taken care of, or our dream is far from being attainable, or it's too late to mend anything."

"You're philosophical today!" he teased her.

"It's the wine; otherwise, I'm timid when I'm temperate. Are we going for a walk or not?"

"Where shall we go?"

"How about to the old city, for a start?"

"To the old city we shall go, then."

He drove towards the city centre, taking directions from her. In less than fifteen minutes they arrived and parked the car at Konzilstrasse and walked slowly towards the park. The place was completely deserted, except for the few taxis which could be seen crisscrossing the streets every now and then, like flies. The night was cold and moderately windy, but Lotte did not seem to mind. They walked into the park and after a while Ermias noticed from her unsteady voice that she was feeling cold. He stopped. She took a step ahead and stopped and turned her face towards him.

"You're feeling chilly," he remarked.

"A little," she replied timidly.

"Let me give you a hug."

Without waiting for her consent, he pulled her gently towards him and embraced her tightly. Then, pushing back her notoriously wild hair and holding her chin with both hands, he kissed her on her lips and tasted and smelled the wine she had drunk at the Christmas party. She looked at him with wide and terrified eyes.

"Are you sure that is what you wanted?" she asked him.

He caught her terror instantly and started to apologise.

"There's nothing to apologise for," she hurried to reassure him. "I liked your kiss, you were sweet. But your whole body betrays your ambivalence, which is why I asked."

"How about you?"

"I've conveyed my desire with many hints and clues which you failed to capture. Everything depends on you."

"Oh, dear, aren't you being unkind?"

"What are you afraid of?" she asked him with a serious tone, looking at him fixedly.

He sighed deeply and unfurled his arms in the air.

"Perhaps you're in love with someone else? Be honest." she inquired inarticulately, her teeth chattering.

"No." he lied.

"Perhaps I'm not your type?"

"Lotte, what are you talking about?"

"Be honest."

To lie to her, he thought, was a sin. But to tell the truth was impossible, or so it seemed to him, for it would put someone else and himself in danger.

"If I fall in love with you," he fumbled, instantly making up an excuse, "I want it to last forever. But my tenure at RIEP is temporary and will come to an end in less than five months. Then we shall be separated, each finding comfort in our old way of life and reluctant to give it up."

He talked so slowly and thoughtfully that he nearly believed his own lie.

"Perhaps, it was a lie containing a grain of truth, after all," he thought.

"So you make a careful calculation before you decide to fall in love?" She gestured with her hand, pointing her index fingers, and making a movement with her body like a dancer.

"There's a built-in self-protection mechanism in all of us, over which we have little influence."

"Why don't you simply admit that you're being selfish?"

He suddenly felt exhausted and looked at her in silence, conscious of a frozen sheepish grin on his lips. Noticing the change in his mood, Lotte softened her tone.

"I'm sorry, that was a bit blunt."

"It's all right."

"We should take time to think clearly. But I must tell you one thing. I may be rebellious, but I'm a good and honest girl."

"And you are, perhaps more than you are aware."

They hugged and walked forward in silence, with the memory of the awkward moment lingering in their conscience.

"Shall we return? I'm rather feeling cold," she said presently.

They returned in silence and drove off. It was a mere ten minutes' drive to her place. Ermias stepped out of her car, but she remained seated, her face downcast.

"Would you care to have tea with me?" she asked without looking at him.

"It's late now. Perhaps, tomorrow. Besides, you don't owe me any apology."

During the drive, she had expressed regret for having spoilt the occasion.

"You haven't been honest with me," she said, still seated and her face downcast.

"In what sense?"

"As far as your feelings towards me are concerned."

"It was unthoughtful of me to make an advance so early in our relationship. I thought you had accepted my apology."

"I don't mean the kiss."

"Rather?"

"What do you think of me?"

"You're an intelligent and honest person who respects and values straight talk."

"Well then, be honest and tell me the truth, do you like me?"

"I suppose I do, but you were right in saying I was undecided. I should've waited with the kiss until the clouds had cleared in my head."

"Why the fuss about the damn kiss? If you regret the kiss, it's got nothing to do with me."

She got up.

"But how are you going to get back now?" she asked with a different tone, after she had closed the door.

"I'll take a taxi."

"Let me at least pay your taxi."

"Save the money to buy me lunch."

"Since there will be a lunch date, that means you're not offended, right?"

"What do you mean by offended? You've raised a legitimate question."

"I wish to know what your real feelings are; it's important to me. I value your feelings."

"This is a heavy responsibility," he moaned.

"All I ask is honesty. I'll also be honest with you."

She came to him unhurriedly, put her arms around his neck, and looked at him irresolutely, as if uncertain of her next move. Then, she stood on her tiptoes and kissed him softly on his lips and walked to her apartment languidly. Upon reaching at the entrance door of the building, she turned her face towards him and waved a goodbye, and, then, disappeared into the building. He stood and waited to see the light of her room turned on. Then, he left.

Chapter 16

It was the longest and loneliest weekend Ermias had endured ever since coming to Konstanz. He had lost the motivation to undertake anything, including running and reading, the two occupations he was reluctant to sacrifice even when he was under intense stress and uncertainty, such as when he was awaiting the decision from Cambridge during his undergraduate studies. He avoided going to see José or Michel or even venturing outside to collect his mail, instead spending the weekend inside his apartment, actually doing nothing except for consuming tons of cereal and bananas.

On Monday evening, Michel and Ermias went by bus as usual to Konstanz to play football with the university students. This was the first time the two of them had been alone since Ermias had presented his results to the team last week. Ermias was hoping that Michel would talk about the results and even drop a couple of encouraging words, but neither was forthcoming. Indeed, Michel appeared to be a little embarrassed for some reason, so that Ermias, too, became self-conscious and avoided looking at him. This was their last training of the year, after which there would be a break for a month. At the end of the week, Ermias would travel to Addis and stay there for two weeks.

There were not many players present that day, so they ended up playing four against four, which was exhausting, but not a bad thing for Ermias given his desire to be occupied. After football, Michel excused himself and left in a hurry. Ermias was surprised by his sudden departure, since Michel had not mentioned on the bus that he had planned to leave early. The rest of them went to a pub to socialise, as this was the last time they would see each other that year.

On Thursday afternoon Frank and Martha came to RIEP unannounced. Frank had been attending a conference in Lausanne for the past three days and Martha had accompanied him. On their way back to Heidelberg, they decided to visit RIEP and take Ermias with them on Friday afternoon. But later Ermias suspected that his mother, made curious by his untimely request to invite Seble to Addis, must have induced them to meet her in person. After securing clearance from the technical department, he showed them around the labs which were accessible to guests and exhibited some of the most interesting inventions of the institute. They were impressed by what they saw and proud that one of their own was a part of the institute.

After the tour, Frank revealed that Aster had told them about an Eritrean secretary working at the institute. Ermias was already intending to introduce them to Seble. So, he took them to her, but she received them with the same aloofness with which she had received him on his first visit, and he was dismayed by her coldness. But she put his apprehension to rest when she invited them to sit down for tea. Frank and Martha were in no hurry and accepted her impromptu invitation. They all sat down on the sofa.

Hardly ten minutes had passed when Professor Steinbrecher himself suddenly came in and studied the guests tentatively, assuming that they were there to see him. Seble stepped in quickly and told him that they were her guests.

"The young man here with a shy smile, Mr. Ermias Dawit, is a guest researcher from Cambridge."

He remembered the two bottles of wine Ermias had brought him last May, for which he now thanked him and asked how he was doing. Before Ermias could give a reply, Martha interposed with enthusiasm to express her admiration of the achievements of the institute. Professor Steinbrecher, who was very sensitive to any form of accolade or criticism, obliged by sitting down to tea with them and, mostly addressing Frank, shared his most ambitious plan for RIEP.

"In five years, it should be amongst the most prestigious labs in the world. Perhaps, amongst the top five, certainly amongst the top ten."

He would have loved to have chatted longer, he said, but he had some pressing assignments to which he must now return. He excused himself and left. Then Martha asked if Seble and her family had time to have dinner with them that evening, but Seble invited them, instead, to come to her house and have dinner with her family.

"I'll ask my husband to join us, but even if he can't, we can eat without him, whatever is available at home, if that's fine with you."

That was all right with the Holms. They took her address and left with Ermias. Once outside, Frank and Martha commented on her beauty and modesty and her flawless speech. Then Martha interrogated Ermias about where she had grown up, what and where she had studied, and how he had come to know her and all. It was at that moment that Ermias grew suspicious of his mother. She must have shared with them the substance of their latest conversation over the phone and commissioned them to investigate closely the nature of their relationship.

After they had left for their hotel to shower and rest, it occurred to Ermias that, if somehow they had gotten word of what he had shared with Rhoda and Bordélique during his last visit, they would associate it with his request to invite Seble to Addis and easily figure out what was going on between Seble and him. But he was also confident that the girls would not betray him this way.

When Ermias and the Holms arrived at their hosts' that evening, Stephan, carrying Salem in his arms, opened the front door for them. After the greetings and introductions, he admitted them into the living room and announced that Seble was in the kitchen. He looked tired and reserved. When she heard the voices in the living room, Seble herself came in and greeted them nervously. Then she invited them to sit down on the sofas and asked them what they wished to drink. Martha and Ermias, in unison, requested a cup of tea whereas Frank preferred to drink a bottle of beer. Then, Seble excused herself and returned to the kitchen.

Stephan and Frank talked much of the time, about cars and navigation systems, but Martha went to the kitchen to help Seble. Ermias too wished to follow Martha, but decided against the idea. Salem had been looking at him surreptitiously since they had arrived, undecided whether or not she should come and speak to him. Curious to know what she would finally decide to do, Ermias pretended to be interested in the conversation. Inch by inch she approached him and stood by his side. Then she gently touched his arm.

"Little Salem, how have you been doing lately?" he asked her smiling broadly. He took her on his lap and inquired about her Lego project.

"Do you want to come to my room and see my new Castle?" She asked eagerly but shyly.

"Yes, I'd be delighted." She jumped from his lap and took the lead and Ermias followed her.

"But the meal will be ready soon," they heard Stephan saying.

Salem proudly exhibited a magnificent pink castle she had recently received from her aunt in Florida. Listening to her explanation about the purpose of the rooms, the figures, and the utensils, and watching her smile, reflex, and facial expressions, he felt closer to Seble. After some time, Seble herself knocked at the door and came in.

"What are the two of you doing there?" she jokingly asked in German, for Salem and Ermias could communicate in German only. For a fleeting moment Seble and Ermias looked at each other with inexpressible desire, but she turned her eyes first, towards Salem and announced that dinner was ready. As they left the room, Salem in front of them and Seble and Ermias side by side, their hands barely touched at the door and he pressed her fingers gently. She pressed his in return, without turning her face towards him, and released them quickly.

The table was covered with a variety of traditional cuisines, displaying Seble's unmistakable cooking skills.

"I love Ethiopian food," Frank declared with passion, as he put down *injera* on his plate, ready to enjoy his meal.

"Seble is Eritrean," Martha corrected him.

"Never mind the politics," interjected Seble. "The two countries have a lot in common, more than our politicians are willing to admit."

The food was delicious and all of them ate with appetite. After the meal, Stephan persuaded Marta and Frank to try some wine from his collection and went down to the basement only to return with two bottles of wine, one of them red and the other white. Before the group could settle on the sofa, Seble announced that it was time for Salem to go to bed. Salem kissed her father and said good night to the rest and left with her mother. The others cleared the table and put the dishes and cutlery in the dishwasher and the leftover in the refrigerator, and moved to the sofa. Stephan lit the fire and they talked about climate change.

Ermias had been uplifted throughout the day by Frank and Martha's arrival, but now he felt his peace being eroded by ambivalence. Watching Stephan's handsome face and his muscular upper body and listening to his calm and measured voice, he could not help feeling that it was wrong to fall in love with his wife. His sadness was amplified when he thought about how much more Seble, whose sense of right and wrong was sharper than his, must have been suffering.

"I must interrupt my visit and return to Cambridge as soon as possible," he decided for the hundredth time. "I shall write my supervisor tomorrow."

Chapter 17

On Friday morning Ermias received unexpected phone call from the secretary of his supervising professor to tell him that the professor wished to see him in his office.

"When?"

"Right now."

"This is not a good sign," he thought, putting down the telephone handle on its cradle.

So far, he had never been to the professor's office and the two of them never had the opportunity to talk to one another in private. What could be the purpose of this private interview? Ermias wondered anxiously but being fully persuaded that it had something to do with his latest presentation.

When ten minutes later he entered into the professor's office, he saw Anne sitting at a circular table in the middle of the room, tentatively studying a paper which was placed in front of her. She glanced at him, smiled shyly, and returned back to her studying. Knowing Anne and her kind nature, Ermias could not imagine that she would be negatively disposed towards him. But he also remembered how oddly Michel had behaved on Monday evening and was at once anxious and impatient to learn the purpose of this meeting. The professor himself was talking on the phone.

"This is not a good sign," he thought repeatedly. "Is it possible that they have taken my latest blunder seriously?"

The professor signalled with his hand for Ermias to take a seat and Ermias sat in front of Anne. To make matters worse, the conversation on the phone seemed to last an eternity, during which time Ermias imagined all sorts of difficulties and how they would affect his life. He even imagined the sudden termination of his studentship and the advent of a regrettable end of his pursuit of a PhD at Cambridge. But that would be improbable, he knew.

After a solid twenty minutes the professor ended his conversation and joined Ermias and Anne at the circular table.

"Thank you for coming, and I'm sorry that the telephone conversation lasted longer than expected."

The professor stretched his big hand towards Ermias for a handshake, smiling good naturedly. Now that he was addressing Ermias in English, he knew for certain that something was amiss, for they all knew that he could speak German fluently.

"I wasn't able to attend your presentation last week," the professor began, pulling up a chair in front of them and his small and alert eyes studying Ermias keenly, but still smiling. Ermias struggled to return a steady gaze. His shyness resurfaced whenever he was afraid, mistrusting, or dishonest, or when he felt inadequate or inferior. Now he awkwardly shifted his focus between the professor's forehead and his right chest pocket. The professor was wearing a white t-shirt with two small chest pockets upon which there were inclined blue stripes.

Some of his employees maintained that he had never read a single research paper to the end after the defence of his dissertation, having been firmly persuaded that every quantum reality could be expressed by Schrödinger's Wave Equation, Taylor Series, and Fourier Transform. What interested him as a scientist and a researcher was not so much the mathematical formulation of problems, rather the identification of the problems themselves.

"You maintained that the energies of the nanosensors can have identical statistics if one chooses the appropriate observation period and that the sensors can be regarded as independent from the influence of one another if one chooses the appropriate boundary between them. Is that correct?"

"It's correct."

"We can discuss the first assertion shortly. As to the second assertion, if one defines or chooses the boundaries between the nanosensors such that they can be spatially considered independent, shouldn't one at the same time violate the assertion that the signals extracted from them are spatially correlated? There appears to be a contradiction in your approach."

"By taking the wavelengths of the signals we receive from the target planets into consideration, I've determined the minimum distance separating the neighbour sensors, so that my assumption pertaining to spatial correlation can still be preserved. If we manage to identify a substrate with the suitable heat conduction and electromagnetic propagation properties upon which we can develop the array, then the assumptions pertaining to the spatial correlation and statistical independence can be valid at the same time. I've discussed the issue with our Swiss partners and have received their assurance that such materials can be fabricated."

Ermias pulled sheets of paper from the middle of the round table and mathematically explained for about twenty-five minutes the essence of his assertions. The professor and Anne listened without interruption.

"I see your point, but I also see some difficulties," the professor remarked when Ermias was done, if one was to tell from his voice, softening his stance.

"If there were any bad news, he wouldn't begin with this," Ermias thought fleetingly.

The professor contested the assertion that the properties of the signals coming from the target planets could be known in advance, since they would be corrupted by noise and by other signals originating from nearby planets. He was partly right. Nonetheless, Ermias was persuaded that the undesirable signals mainly modify the amplitudes of the desired signals and not so much their wavelengths and phases. Hence, the distance he had determined should still be regarded as valid, even though its precise value should be subject to refinement and calibration during fabrication, for the fabrication process itself would introduce its own imprecision.

"This is something we should investigate more closely. Now as to your first assertion, there is some indication of its plausibility. We've sent some of your measurements to the University of Konstanz in order to independently verify your claims. Initial results suggest that your claims have some foundation."

Ermias could not see why the professor should not send the datasets to the University of Konstanz, and yet, he was dismayed by the fact that he had not been informed of it.

"Now this may appear uncongenial, since this hasn't first been communicated to you. But independent verification is something we routinely do. Claims made in our institute should pass the severest tests of reproducibility before we publish our results to the public."

One would expect that the arrows of transparency and integrity should indicate in both directions. Ermias suspected that had the verification at the University of Konstanz contradicted his claims, the professor would have ignored the results without the need for contradicting Ermias and let Ermias complete his research visit as planned, but Ermias would have lost his respect and this would have not escaped the notice of his supervisors at the University of Cambridge. Ermias had studied and worked long enough to realise that the communication of the most powerful people at higher institutions were tongued with subtle hints and clues.

"Now I have a proposal," the professor went on. "If I remember correctly, the remaining time you have left with us is less than, uh, four months, however, the interesting task has just begun. By now you've acquainted yourself with the work ethics and culture of our institute and, I presume, feel confident with our experiment infrastructure. It'd be a great waste of time and energy to have learnt all this and not use the knowledge effectively to your own as well as our advantage. So, my proposal is to extend your stay by one extra year or even by two. To compensate for this, we shall pay you the salary of a full-time researcher in addition to your studentship at Cambridge. You can also make as many short term visits to Cambridge as you deem important and we shall cover all your travel expenses. You can stay at the guest house as long as you please, but if you prefer to live in Konstanz or elsewhere in a private apartment, we can also support you in that. I hope you'll agree that this is a generous offer. I've discussed this with our Cambridge colleagues and they've accepted my proposal, provided that you are happy with it."

Ermias was speechless. Doubtless, he was hurt and disappointed, yet this proposal was not only a confirmation of the significance of what he had been doing but also an honour he should not undermine. He thought of his family, particularly, his grandmother, and how they would all feel proud of him upon hearing these glad tidings. He could not suppress a smile.

"I can understand if this comes as a surprise. It may have some conflict with some of your future plans, I don't know," the professor continued on presently. "Think about it, and let us know of your decision after the New Year."

Ermias accepted the proposal, expressed his appreciation of the professor's generosity, and left.

Chapter 18

Seble was the first person with whom Ermias wished to share the news. Though he had already been intending to go to her office to deliver her Christmas present in person and to say goodbye to her before Frank and Martha arrived to pick him up, the news presented him with an extra reason to harness the courage to go to her office. But when he went to his office to collect the Christmas present, he found Stephan sitting on a chair next to his table and waiting for him. Michel was already at his place, staring at the computer screen in front of him with an earnest and very pale countenance. Stephan stood up but was not inclined to shake hands.

"I was at the institute and decided to pay you a visit," he said calmly.

He was wearing that same reserved look from the previous evening and still looked tired.

"Something is definitely wrong," Ermias thought, swiftly reminding himself to be prepared for every conceivable eventuality.

"Please sit down," he invited Stephan.

"Do you mind taking a walk with me along the shore?"

"Not at all."

Ermias was relieved by this implicit expression of interest for privacy. Whatever was going to happen, it would be better if it happened in private, he thought. They left the office and walked side by side in silence. Since Stephan made no pretence at being sociable, Ermias also chose to maintain a sober silence. The awkward silence endured until the two of them had left the building.

"I've been worrying lately about Seble," Stephan started as soon as they were outside and after he had made sure that no one was around.

"Is something the matter with her?"

"That's what I'm intending to find out. Seble doesn't sleep well these days. I mean, she's been suffering from insomnia for a long time, since she was thirteen, really, sleeping on average three or four hours a day only, but of late, it's gotten worse."

Seble had never shared this piece of information with Ermias.

"I'm sorry, I didn't know."

"I've heard that you two see each other regularly?"

Stephan gave Ermias a quick side glance and turned his face away. He was holding his right thumb in a closed fist, which Ermias took for a sign of alertness or stress.

"Didn't I tell you the other day that we see each other about once a week?"

"You two have been spotted by Mindelsee on several occasions," Stephan observed without emotion.

"We see each other about once a week, but she's never told me about her sleep problem."

"You're just evading the real issue in question, as if your meetings at Mindelsee have no bearing on our present conversation."

"What's there to evade?"

"Perhaps she's shared other concerns with you?"

"Not that I can recall. She's a little melancholic by nature, but I never suspected that something serious was troubling her."

Meanwhile, they left the compound. Stephan walked in silence for a few metres and then stopped.

"Let me get straight to the point," Stephan spoke, now turning his face towards Ermias and looking at him fixedly. "I know you've been seeing my wife outside of office hours. Would you mind telling me exactly what's going on?"

"Nothing, really. We're friends, that's all. We talk about common interests, our upbringing. Seble often talks about her life in Addis as a child."

"Once again, allow me to be straightforward. Do you think she's developed an attachment to you?"

"What do you mean?" Ermias asked, startled.

His instinct to protect himself and Seble took charge of his reflex actions, his tone and his facial expressions, so that Ermias showed genuine surprise at this question.

"I don't mean to insult you," Stephan looked at Ermias with an air of confusion. "Something is bothering my wife and I suspect that it has something to do with you."

"How can I be her problem when you yourself said that she's been suffering from insomnia since her childhood?"

"Even though she suffers from lack of sleep, she's grown accustomed to living with it, often spending much of the night reading or doing things which interest her. The few hours she sleeps are normally sufficient for her. But of late, it's gotten much worse and I have reason to suspect that something fresh is troubling her."

It occurred to Ermias that the night she had stayed with him, she had slept peacefully throughout the night, without any interruption. But this was not a piece of evidence he was ready to pass to Stephan.

"Have you talked to her about your concerns?"

"Yes, I have, many times. But each time she tried to reassure me that everything was fine."

"Perhaps everything is fine and you are imagining difficulties on your own?"

"It's obvious that she isn't fine!" Stephan retorted with a tone of irritation and impatience. "Yesterday, for instance, she was unable to sleep until four in the morning. I could tell that she was very excited and restless long after you had left."

Stephan used the second-person plural pronoun "ihr" instead of "du".

"How serious do you think her condition is?"

"Very. It may even put her life in danger. With a very short sleep time at night, she could slumber in the daytime while driving and have a terrible car accident. Or she may suffer a heart attack."

This revelation shocked and distressed Ermias and his inability to help Seble distressed him even more. By holding back the truth from her husband, he was no doubt making her situation more grievous. At the same time, however, who gave him the right to disclose anything about Seble without her consent? If her husband had to experience the truth, must he not do so from Seble first-hand?

Besides, Ermias was afraid, both for Seble and for himself, afraid of the monumental consequences of the revelation for Seble's marriage and family, but also afraid of being judged, by Stephan and his family, by his own colleagues at RIEP, by Liselotte and all, that their case would be judged not as the case of two individual people, but rather as the case of two ungrateful foreigners who had kicked up their heels against the people who had been gracious to them.

He was unable to determine what to do or say, so much so that he was unable to walk forward, unable to hide his indecision. Was it not because of the question of honesty that his datasets had been sent to the University of Konstanz without his knowledge or consent? Was he not proving them right by holding the truth from Stephan when the happiness of his family, and, perhaps, the life of his wife too, were in great danger?

"Let's say you're right in suspecting that Seble has feelings for me. I, too, have feelings for her. But it's not what you think."

Upon hearing this confession, Stephan's face turned first crimson and then pale, and the light was extinguished from his eyes, so that he looked for a brief moment like a terrible ghost. In that fleeting instant Ermias was certain that the look would be engraved upon his memory for the rest of his life.

"It's just feelings, an idea, if you like, but we haven't gone any further, if that means anything," he added foolishly, his own voice sounding strange and unconvincing to him.

After a brief hesitation, Stephan resumed moving forward with long strides. Ermias also walked as fast as he could in order to keep up with him, expecting that Stephan would suddenly turn back and shout at him or seize and shake him violently. But Stephan did none of these. They continued to walk in this fashion southward, Stephan in front and Ermias trailing a step or two behind. Then Stephan stopped suddenly and regarded Ermias with eerily ghostly eyes.

"You... took advantage of her vulnerability! This is not only immoral but also mean and cruel. Why, there are so many singles around you with whom you can make out. You seem to have grown up in a loving and caring family. Whatever induced you to cross a sacred line?"

These words pierced into Ermias painfully. He had frequently asked himself similar questions in the past but hearing them emerge from another man's mouth, from the mouth of the very same person to whom he had done a great injustice, was awful. He wanted to leave Stephan on the spot and run back to his office, but he could not.

"Can we work together to help Seble?" he asked naively instead.

Stephan unfurled his arms in the air to diffuse his anger and looked at Ermias with the same wounded pride, but remained silent.

"Though Seble and I are attracted to one another, we've strived to keep our relationship honourable. I ask you to trust your wife."

"I trust my wife. It's you whom I don't trust! You are like an imbecile vermin which is trying to destroy the happiness of my family."

Ermias ignored his insult and now looked at him with unconcealed contempt.

"Stop seeing my wife privately or else I'll ruin your life!"

"I shall be going to Heidelberg today and will not be back to RIEP before the New Year. As soon as we are done here, I'll return to my office and write an email to my supervisor in Cambridge, to let him know of my decision to return to Cambridge as soon as possible."

"But you are here for a year, so I'm told."

"I was already thinking of cutting my stay short. I've partially achieved my purpose, so my host professor should accept my wish to return to Cambridge."

"If, indeed, you are not vermin and are serious about your proposal, I might ask someone I trust to intervene on your behalf."

It was obvious whom he was referring to.

"That shouldn't be necessary. I want to do this by myself, without anybody's intervention."

"I don't trust you. If word reaches my ear ever again that you've been seen with my wife, consider yourself as good as dead. The reason you are still standing intact is because I care for my family."

Stephan was speaking so calmly, calculating his words, devoid of emotion, that Ermias was very disturbed.

"Now, if you excuse me, I must return to my office."

Without waiting for Stephan's reaction, Ermias turned back and walked towards the institute, the first few steps calmly, but thereafter in a hurry. But he had barely covered a fifty metre distance when he heard the hurried footsteps of Stephan closing in on him.

"Wait, I'm not done yet!" Stephan was saying.

Ermias knew instinctively that Stephan was up to something ominous, but he regarded running away both unwise and cowardly. At that moment, he also saw Seble approaching the wooden gate leading out of the institute's compound. For a fraction of a second he felt at once relieved and distressed. Wishing not to alarm her and half-hoping that this would force Stephan to check himself, he stopped and turned to Stephan. Perhaps Ermias was right. Stephan stopped at a few metres distance from Ermias and put both hands on his hips, looking irresolute.

"Can I ask you a question?"

"Sure."

"What is it that you could give her that I was unable to give her?"

"I don't know."

"You can be honest with me."

"I think, deep down, Seble loves me as a brother and not as a lover."

Stephan reflected for a moment.

"You may go now."

Ermias was grateful that the minutes of Armageddon were delayed by some miracle in his favour. He left Stephan, his legs barely trembling. Suddenly, a verse from T.S. Elliot's *The Wasteland* crossed in his mind:

> *My feet are at Moorgate, and my heart*
> *Under my feet.*[k]

He recalled that the poet had written this verse at a time of great emotional distress. Was Ermias, too, trampling upon his own heart? He wondered.

Seble must have checked in his office and learnt from Michel that Ermias had gone out for a walk with Stephan. As she came nearer, Ermias could see the panic in her face.

"Stephan dropped in unexpectedly and invited me to take a walk with him. But then it occurred to me that Martha and Frank will be coming to pick me up soon, so I decided to interrupt the walk," he said trying to appear calm.

"You're not telling the truth. You were not walking as someone who was coming back from a walk," she whispered in a hurry, her eyes anxiously looking behind him, towards her husband.

"No, I wasn't telling the truth. Stephan knows about us."

"You told him?"

"He already suspected it, but yes, I told him the truth."

She released a sigh of despair.

"I'm glad the lying is over, though. I feel free now. Was he mad at you? Did he try to hurt you?"

"He wasn't mad at me and he didn't try to hurt me."

Meanwhile, Stephan joined them and stood a little farther away, as one who was a stranger, an outcast. The three of them looked at each other in silence and in painful confusion.

"So what are you going to do now?" Seble asked Stephan anxiously.

"I'm not going to do anything. None of us needs to do anything. We've to talk about this calmly," he tried to reassure her, but his voice was trembling.

"I shall move out as soon as possible," she said tears gushing from her eyes.

"Have you lost your mind? It's your house as much as it's mine. None of us need to move out anywhere. Pull yourself together. I'm willing to go through this with you."

"But how can this be? I've been unfaithful to you."

"We shall work this out together," he emphasised, his tone revealing his agony.

He turned to Ermias and asked him to leave them alone.

"No, not now," Seble begged him with a faint voice.

Her husband's face went crimson once again and he gave Seble a mortal look.

"Please forgive me!" she mumbled almost inaudibly, avoiding his eyes.

"Then, I shall leave you alone."

Stephan left them deeply offended and hurt. She was trembling like a leaf blown about by the cold wind. Ermias shuddered at the realisation that they had crossed a frightful line, but he was ready to accept the consequences, whatever they were. He deeply regretted underestimating Seble's attachment to him.

"I can never be yours, do you understand? Perhaps, I'll join a convent after all, provided that I can find one which is willing to take me."

Her voice, like her entire body, was shaking.

"Calm down for now," he forced himself to say. "Everything will be all right."

"What is to become of Salem? I'm terrified for her," she whispered.

"Salem will be all right. Everything is going to be all right. Stephan understands your situation and is willing to help you through."

She did not seem to have heard him.

"Why do you torment yourself so mercilessly? Since you believe in a loving God, do you really think he'll abandon you when you're in need of his help?"

"Say anything, but please don't mention the name of God," she beseeched him.

Ermias saw a wooden bench nearby and gently guided Seble to it. They sat close to one another. She was leaning forward, burying her face deeply in her hands and resting her elbows on her lower limbs, whilst he sat erect, gazing blankly at the lake, feeling the gentle pressure of her left arm. Even though he was shocked and terrified, he had no desire to be anywhere else, meet anyone else, or undertake anything else.

Then they heard a familiar voice addressing them from behind. It was Martha.

"There you are!"

Ermias got up from his seat but Seble stayed put, as if she had not heard Martha or did not care. Upon noticing the state Seble was in, Martha stood still and studied the young people alternately with concern.

"What's the matter?" she asked as she approached them cautiously.

Ermias was unable to give her an answer, but made a desperate gesture with his hands and head.

"Seble dear, what's upsetting you?" Martha asked, as if she had known Seble for a long time, sitting down next to her.

But no answer was forthcoming from Seble. Instead, her shoulders began to shake terribly and they heard her stifled sobs.

"Calm down, my dear, calm down," Martha was saying, putting her arms around Seble tightly.

Ermias stood and watched them helplessly, now completely bereft of the brief peace of mind he had experienced a moment ago, and feeling awfully guilty.

"Have you two quarrelled?"

Martha looked at Ermias questioningly, but he turned his face away from her.

"No." he forced himself to say with a thick voice.

"Seble, stop it. It's not healthy to cry like this."

But Seble's shoulders continued shaking violently as she buried her face deeper into her hands. Martha tried to forcefully pull Seble up and free her face from her hands, but Seble refused to cooperate.

"Come and help me," Martha shouted at Ermias at last.

He obeyed. Together they managed to free her face.

"Now, stop it."

Martha gently leaned Seble against her chest and stroked her hair.

"Whatever is the reason for being so distraught?" she enquired, looking at them alternately once again, but neither of them could give her an answer.

"You don't seem to be of much help here, Ermias. Why don't you leave us alone and go to your office? You'll find Frank sitting in your office."

It was more of an order than a suggestion. Ermias waited to see how Seble would react. Either she had not heard properly or did not mind his going, for she was unresponsive. Her eyes were closed but her sobs were subsiding. Ermias left reluctantly.

Epilogue

Ermias returned to the institute feeling like a convict who had managed to break out from his prison for a fleeting moment but had now been caught and was being taken back to his solitary confinement. He searched for an obscure place behind his office building and sat on a wooden bench next to a stone-built tennis table.

"What now?" he asked himself in despair.

The same anxiety which had haunted him in Dresden during his loneliest days now spread its oppressive and vicious wings over him. Only this time it felt like sorrow and was physically painful. He closed his eyes and tried to think, but in vain. He opened his eyes, still trying to think what he should do next. Frank must have spotted him through the office window, for he came to him and sat beside him. Now concentration and thinking became even more difficult and Ermias felt uneasy and self-conscious. They sat side by side for a long time without exchanging a single word, Ermias being conscious of Frank leaning forward, resting his arms on his thighs, interlocking his fingers, and staring at the ground through the opening of his arms. In spite of his desire to be left alone, Ermias felt the shadow of anxiety slowly receding, and he was glad that Frank was there.

"He must love her," a terrible thought flashed in his mind. "He understands what it means to suffer."

He recollected a time when they were living in New York…

He came home from school one day to the sight of his mother and Frank standing in the middle of the living room. There was some distance between them, Frank with his arms hanging loosely, and his mother with hers folded. Both of them appeared to be staring straight at the front door. His mother was wearing a golden jumper, which fully covered her neck, and a pair of blue jeans. Her flowing, long hair was neatly combed and hung smoothly against either side of her face, tumbling gracefully over her shoulders. There seemed to be nothing unusual, nothing unnatural about their poses. Besides, Ermias had already known that Frank was coming to New York and that he was coming to visit them. Why he should have recalled that scene so vividly, he could not tell…

At long last, Martha persuaded Seble to see a doctor. In a city where Ermias could turn to virtually no one, Martha's coming was simply a miracle. The doctor diagnosed Seble with acute nervous exhaustion and recommended that she be admitted to the University Hospital where she indeed stayed for eighteen days. It turned out that she had been exhausting her last reserves of energy.

Martha and Frank visited her at the weekends, but Ermias was not permitted to visit her. Nor was he able to communicate with her, for they had removed all forms of communication media from her surroundings. After she had completed the treatment, she was sent to Italy for recuperation. Ermias stayed in Konstanz until the end of March, each day hoping, against all odds, that he might somehow meet Seble in the institute, in the corridor of their building or at the *Mensa* or at the wooden bench where they had first held hands. But she never came back to the institute. Then, in the first week of April, he returned to Cambridge.

Exactly one year after he had last seen her, Ermias received a brief email from Liselotte:

> Dear Ermias,
> I'm writing to you because, in spite of everything, I cannot forget our last and inconclusive conversation. I want to give you the chance to finish it when you feel ready.
> Love,
> LL

He read the email over and over that day and the following days, moved by and feeling undeserving, of her consideration.

He tried to compose a reply several times, but each time he stalled his plan, because he was not sure of the sincerity of his words. Yet he knew that he had to give her a reply. It was just a matter of time.

End Notes

[a] Bordélique means messy (French).

[b] "Wie läuft's". — How's it going?

[c] "Es läuft gut." — It's going well.

[d] *"And we all go with them, into the silence funeral..."* — T.S. Elliot: *Four Quartets, East Coker.* This and the subsequent verses reflect Ermias' state of mind and his difficulty in assigning a specific cause to his pain.

[e] *"On Margate Sands..."* — T.S. Eliot: The *Wasteland, The Burial of the Dead.*

[f] ibid.

[g] This lecture is based on an actual guest lecture entitled *Death and the Ancient Philosophers* which was given by Professor Jonathan Barnes (University of Oxford) at the University of California, Berkley, as a part of the Howison Lectures in Philosophy series. I moved the setting to the University of Gottingen for literary convenience but tried my best to deliver the substance of the lecture unaltered.

[h] *Esat wey Abeba* — translated: *Fire or Flower* (Amharic).

[i] *Fikir eske Mekabir* — direct translated: *Love up to the Grave,* is a popular tragic romance written in Amharic by the late Hadis Alemayehu.

[j] *"When it was evening, the disciples came to him...* —This verse is taken from The Gospel According to Matthew, Chapter 14, verse 15.

[k] *"My feet are at Moorgate..."* — Once again a verse taken from T.S. Eliot's *The Wasteland, The Fire Sermon.*